WALKING ON GLASS

WALKING
ON GLASS

IAIN BANKS

LITTLE, BROWN & COMPANY

A *Little, Brown* Book

First published in Great Britain by
Macmillan London Limited 1985
First published in paperback by Futura Publications 1986
Published by Abacus in 1990
This edition published by
Little, Brown and Company in 2001

A CIP catalogue record for this book
is available from the British Library.

ISBN 0 316 85853 6

Typeset in Stemple Garamond
by Palimpsest Book Production Limited,
Polmont, Stirlingshire
Printed and bound in Great Britain by
Clays Ltd, St Ives plc

Little, Brown and Company (UK)
Brettenham House
Lancaster Place
London WC2E 7EN

www.littlebrown.co.uk

For my mother and father

Contents

PART ONE
Theobald's Road 3
Mr Smith 16
One-Dimensional Chess 35

PART TWO
Rosebery Avenue 59
Clerk Starke 92
Open-Plan Go 106

PART THREE
Amwell Street 129
Mrs Short 146
Spotless Dominoes 162

PART FOUR
Penton Street 205
Mr Sharpe 221
Chinese Scrabble 235

PART FIVE
Half Moon Crescent 263
Dr Shawcross 300
Tunnel 310

PART SIX
Truth and Consequences 337

ONE

Theobald's Road

He walked through the white corridors, past the notice-boards with their offers of small rooms and old cars, past the coffee bar where people sat at tables, past a hole in the white floor where an old chair stood sentry over an opened conduit in which a torch shone and a man crawled, and as he left he looked at his watch:

TU 28
pm
3:33

He stood on the steps for a second, smiling at the figures on the face of the watch. Three three three. A good omen. Today was a day things would come together, a day events would coalesce.

It was bright outside, even after the painted lightness of the marble-flaked corridor. The air was warm, slightly humid but not sultry. The walk would be a pleasure today. That was good too, because he didn't want to arrive at her place hot and flustered; not today, not with her at the end of the walk, not with that subtle but unequivocal promise there, waiting, ready.

Graham Park stepped out on to the broad grey pavement outside the School and during a break in the traffic jogged across Theobald's Road to its north side. He relaxed to a walk on the pavement outside the White Hart pub, his large black portfolio held easily at his side by its single handle. Drawings of her.

He looked up at the sky, above the blocks and squat towers of the medium-rise office blocks, and smiled at its blue, city-grimed segmentings.

Everything seemed fresher, brighter, more real today, as though all his quite normal, perfectly standard surroundings had until this point been actors fumbling behind some thin stage curtain, struggling to get out, but now stood, triumphant expression frozen on face, hands spread, going 'Ta-Raah!' on the boards at last. He found this young-love rapture almost embarrassing in its intensity; it was something he was delighted to have, determined to hide, and wary of examining. It was enough to know it was there, and the very commonness of it was reassuring in a way. Let others have felt this way, let them feel it now; it would never be exactly like this, never be identical. *Revel in it*, he thought, *why not*?

A worn and grubby old man stood with his back

against the wall of another tall grey-and-brickred building. He wore a heavy grey-green coat, even in that heat,
and one of his shoes was open at the toe, baring skin
inside. He held two huge boxes of mushrooms. It was
the sort of sight – the poor, the strange – which usually
alarmed Graham.

So many strange people in London. So many of the
poor and the decrepit, the still spinning shrapnel, walking wounded of society. Usually they oppressed and
threatened him, these people with little threat to offer,
and much to fear. But not today; today the old man, hot
in his thick coat, blinking from his grey face, clammy
hands round his two two-pound boxes of mushrooms
was merely interesting, just a possible subject for a drawing. He passed the Post Office, where a young black man,
tall and well dressed, stood talking quietly to himself.
Again no fear. He realised that maybe he really was after
all, just a little, the country hick he had tried so hard to
avoid being. He had been so determined to be ungullible,
city-wise that perhaps he had gone too far in the other
direction, and so read a threat in everything the big city
had to offer. Only now, with the promise of the strength
she might give him, could he afford the luxury of thinking so closely about himself (you had to have armour in
the city, you had to know where you stood).

He had opted for the cynical, guarded approach, and
now he could see that for all the safety it had brought
him – here he was, in his second year, still solvent, heart
intact, unmugged and even succeeding in his studies,
despite all his mother's fears – every defence had its price,

5

and he had paid in a separating distance, incomprehension. Perhaps the young black man was not mad; people did talk to themselves. Perhaps the old man with the torn shoe was not some desperate down-and-out with fists full of stolen mushrooms; maybe he was just an ordinary person whose shoes had split that lunchtime, while shopping. He looked at the traffic roaring by, and over it through railings at the leafy greenness of Gray's Inn, edging into view on his right. He would remember this day, this walk. Even if she did not . . . even if *all* his dreams, his hopes did not . . . ah, but they would. He could feel it.

'Put that fantasy down, Park, you don't know where it's been.'

He turned quickly to the voice and there was Slater, bounding down the steps of Holborn Library, wearing a pair of one-and-a-half-legged jeans, with a shiny black shoe on one foot and a knee-length boot on the other; the jeans were cut to suit, so that one leg ended normally, in a stitched hem over the shoe, while the other leg came to a frayed stop just above the top of the boot. Above, Slater sported a well-worn hacking jacket over a black shirt and a black bow tie which appeared to have lots of small, dull red stones set in it. On his head sat a tartan cap, predominantly red. Graham looked at his friend and laughed. Slater responded with a look of pretended chilliness. 'I see nothing to cause such hilarity.'

'You look like—' Graham shook his head and waved one hand at Slater's jeans and footwear, and spared a glance for his cap.

'What I look like,' Slater said, coming forward and taking Graham by the elbow to continue walking, 'is somebody who has discovered an old pair of RAF pilot's boots at a market stall in Camden.'

'And taken a knife to them,' Graham said, looking down at Slater's legs and shrugging his arm free of the light grip which held it.

Slater smiled, put his hands in the pockets of his mutilated jeans. 'There you show your ignorance, young man. If you had looked carefully, or if you knew enough, you would appreciate that these are, in fact, specially designed pilot's boots which, with the aid of a couple of zips, convert into what was doubtless, in the forties, a pretty neat-looking pair of shoes. The whole point is that if the intrepid aviator got shot down while blasting Gerry out of the skies above enemy territory, he could simply unzip his boot-legs and have a pair of civilian-looking shoes on his feet, and thus pass for a native and so escape those dreadful SS men in their tight little black uniforms. I have merely adapted—'

'You look silly,' Graham interrupted.

'Why you straight old straight,' Slater said. They were walking slowly now; Slater never liked to rush. Graham was only a little impatient, and he knew better than to try to hurry Slater up. He had left in plenty of time, there was no hurry. More time to savour. 'I just don't know *why* you turn me on at all,' Slater said, then peered closely at the other young man's face and said pointedly, 'Are you *listening* to me, Park?'

Graham shook his head, grinning slightly, but said,

'Yes, I'm listening. You don't have to camp it up with me.'

'Oh my God, pardon *me*,' Slater said melodramatically, one hand fanned over his upper chest, 'I'm offending the poor hetero boy. Under twenty-one as well; oh *say* it ain't so!'

'You're a fraud, Richard,' Graham said, turning to look at his friend. 'I sometimes think you aren't even gay at all. Anyway,' he went on, attempting to increase their pace a little, 'what have you been up to? I haven't seen you around for a couple of days.'

'Ah, the change-of-subject,' Slater laughed, staring ahead. He grimaced and scratched his short, curly black hair where it stuck out from under his tartan cap. His thin, pale face contorted as he said, 'Well, I shan't go into the seamy details . . . the more basic facets of life, but on a cleaner if more frustrating theme, I have been trying to seduce that lovely Dickson boy over the last week. You know: the one with the shoulders.'

'What,' Graham said contemptuously, annoyed, 'that tall bloke with the bleached hair in first year? He's thick.'

'Hmm, well,' Slater said, bobbing his head in an arc – a gesture somewhere between a nod and a shake – 'thick set, certainly, and not *awfully* bright, but *God* those shoulders. That waist, those hips! I don't care about his head; from the neck down he's a genius.'

'Idiot,' said Graham.

'Trouble is,' Slater mused, 'he either doesn't realise what I'm up to, or he doesn't care. And he has this awful friend, called Claude . . . I keep telling *him* how earthy

I think he is, but he hasn't got it yet. Now he really *is* thick. I asked him what he thought of Magritte the other day, and he thought I was talking about some girl in first year. And I *can't* get him away from Roger. I shall *die* if he's gay. I mean if he got there first. I'm sure Roger isn't really stupid, it's just his friend who's infectious.'

'Ha ha,' Graham said. He always felt slightly uncomfortable when Slater talked about being gay, though his friend was rarely specific, and Graham was hardly ever directly involved – he had, for example, only ever met one of Slater's (supposedly many) lovers, at least as far as he knew.

'Do you know,' Slater said, suddenly brightening, as they crossed John Street, 'I've had this really good *idea*.'

Graham gritted his teeth: 'Well, what is it this time? Another new religion, or just a way of making lots of money? Or both?'

'This is a literary idea.'

'If it's *The Sands of Love*, I've already heard it.'

'That was a great plot. No, it isn't romantic fiction this time.' They stopped at the corner of Gray's Inn Road, waiting for the lights to change. A couple of punks on the far side, also waiting to cross, were pointing at the oblivious Slater and laughing. Graham looked up at the skies and sighed.

'Imagine, if you will,' Slater said dramatically, sweeping his arms out wide, 'a—'

'Keep it short,' Graham told him.

Slater looked hurt. 'It's a sort of Byzantine future, a degenerate technocratic empire with—'

'Oh, not science fiction again.'

'Well, no, it's not really, smart-ass,' Slater said. 'It's a . . . fable. I could make it a fairy-tale instead, if I wanted to. Anyway. It's the capital of the empire; a courtier starts a liaison with one of the princesses; the demands she and the Emperor make on his time get to be too much, so he secretly has an android made to impersonate him at the endless court rituals and boring receptions; nobody notices. Later he has the android's brain upgraded so it can cope with hunting expeditions and personal meetings, even Cabinet discussions with the Emperor present, all so that he can spend more time dallying with the princess. But he gets killed in some over-energetic love-play. The android continues to fulfil all its courtly duties and even becomes a trusted confidant of the Emperor, and the princess discovers it actually makes a better lover than the original. The android can fit in all its commitments because it never has to sleep. But it develops a conscience, and has to tell the Emperor the truth. The Emperor smiles, opens up an inspection panel in his chest and says, "Well, by a funny coincidence . . ." End of story. Pretty good, eh? What do you think?'

Graham took a deep breath, thought, then said, 'These pilots: so they could disguise their boots. What about their uniforms?' He frowned seriously.

Slater stopped, a look of horror and confusion on his face. '*What*?' he said, aghast.

Suddenly Graham realised – with a small, disquieting feeling in his stomach – that they were standing right outside a place which always made him feel apprehensive.

It was only a small picture-framing shop which sold prints and posters and more-tasteful-than-average lampshades, but it was the name which held unpleasant associations for Graham: Stocks. That name chilled him.

Stock was his rival, the great threat, the cloud hanging over him and Sara. Stock the biker, the macho black-leathered never-properly-seen image of Nemesis. (He had looked up the name in the London telephone directory; there were one-and-a-half columns of them; enough for quite a few coincidences, even in a city of six-and-a-half million people.)

Slater was saying, '—to do with it?'

'It just occurred to me,' Graham said defensively. He wished now he hadn't decided to tease Slater.

'You haven't listened to a word I've said,' Slater gasped. Graham nodded to indicate they should keep on walking.

'Of course I have,' he said. They passed Terry's fruit-stall next, with its smell of fresh strawberries, then a chemist's. They were at the junction of Clerkenwell Road and Rosebery Avenue. By the side of Gray's Inn Buildings, which led on up the Avenue, some tall green wooden hoardings jutted out over part of the street and pavement, shielding some roadworks. Graham and Slater walked down the narrow alley formed by the seedy, decaying stonework and the painted wood; Graham saw the grimy glass of cracked windows; fading political posters flapped in a slight breeze.

'But don't you think it's a laugh?' Slater said, trying to edge round Graham to peer into his face. Graham avoided his friend's eyes. He wondered if Slater intended

to walk the whole way with him, or whether he was only
going as far as the Air Gallery, now only just across the
street, where he sometimes went in the afternoons.
Graham didn't mind Slater knowing about Sara – he had
introduced them to each other, after all – but he wanted
to keep this day private. Besides, he got embarrassed at
the stares people gave Slater, even if Slater himself didn't
seem to notice. The least he could do, Graham thought,
was take off that ridiculous tartan cap.

'It's . . . all right,' he conceded as they came out from
between the decaying buildings and the green hoardings,
'but . . .' he smiled and looked at Slater, 'don't give up
your day job.'

'And don't you quote my own lines back at me, you
young pup!'

'Okay,' Graham said, looking at Slater again. 'Stick to
ceramics.'

'You make me sound like a glaze.'

'That's your expression.'

'Oh-ho,' Slater said, 'well, touché, or toushe, anyway.'
He stopped by the pedestrian crossing which led over
Rosebery Avenue to the square, red-brick building of the
Air Gallery. Graham turned to face him. 'But don't you
like the latest scenario?'

'Well,' Graham said slowly, deciding he had better say
something nice, 'it's good, but perhaps it needs a little
work.'

'Huh,' Slater said, stepping back and rolling his eyes.
He came forward again, eyes narrowed, pushing his face
close to Graham's so that the younger man shrank back

just a little. '"A little work", eh? Well, bang goes *your* commission from the National Portrait Gallery when I'm famous.'

'Are you going over there?' Graham indicated the far side of the road.

Slater slouched a little and nodded, looking over the road to the gallery.

'I suppose so. You're trying to get rid of me, aren't you?'

'No I'm not.'

'Yes you are. You've been hurrying me all the way.'

'No, I wasn't.' Graham protested. 'It's just that you walk slowly.'

'I was talking to you.'

'Well, I can walk and listen at the same time.'

'Oh, wow, the Gerry Ford of the Art School. Anyway, not to worry; I bet I know where you're off to, hmm?'

'Oh?' Graham said, trying to look innocent.

'Yes, I can tell,' Slater said. 'Stop trying to look so damn nonchalant.' A smile appeared on his face like oil surfacing on still water. 'You've got the hots for our Sara, haven't you?'

'Oh, intensely,' Graham said, trying to over-play it; but he could see Slater wasn't taken in. But it wasn't like that; it wasn't that crude, or even if it was it shouldn't be talked of in such a way; not now, not yet.

'They aren't worth it, kid,' Slater said, shaking his head sadly and wisely. 'She'll let you down. Later if not now. They always do.'

Graham felt happier with this direct assault; this was

just gay misogyny, not even genuine at that, but another of Slater's roles. He laughed and shook his head.

Slater shrugged and said, 'Well, when it does go wrong, at least you know you *can* come running to me.' He patted his right shoulder with his other hand. 'I have very good shoulders for crying on.'

'Not,' Graham laughed, 'while you're wearing that cap, chum.' Slater narrowed his eyes and straightened the tartan cap on his head. 'Well,' Graham went on hurriedly, 'I really have to go now,' and took a couple of steps backwards.

'All right, then,' Slater sighed wistfully. 'Do all the things I wouldn't dream of doing, but don't forget what your Uncle Richard told you.' He grinned, blew Graham a kiss, waved one hand, then stepped on to the crossing during a lull in the traffic. Graham waved back, then walked away. 'Graham!' Slater called suddenly from the other side of the road. He turned to look, sighing.

Slater stood outside the gallery, in front of one of its large windows. He put one hand in his jacket pocket, and as he did so his bow tie lit up; the small red stones were really lights. They flicked on and off. Slater started laughing as Graham shook his head and walked away up Rosebery Avenue. 'A quick flash!' Slater bellowed in the distance.

Graham laughed to himself, then had to break his stride as a long-haired biker in dirty denims bumped a large Moto Guzzi across the pavement in front of him and into the courtyard entrance of the buildings called Rosebery Square. Graham looked darkly at the man pushing the bike, then shook his head, telling himself not to be so stupid. The man looked nothing like Stock, the bike was quite different from the big black BMW Stock rode, and anyway omens were nonsense. Stock's time was over; he could tell that from what Sara had said over the phone that morning.

He breathed deeply and put his shoulders back, shifted the large black portfolio from one hand to the other. What a blue sky! What a great day! He thrilled to everything around him, no matter what; the brightness of the June day, the smell of cheap cooking and exhaust fumes; birds singing, people talking. Nothing would, nothing *could* go wrong today; he ought to find a betting shop and put some money on a horse, he felt so lucky, so good, so in tune.

Mr Smith

Sacked!

Lips tight, fists clenched, eyes narrow, breath held, back straight, stomach in, chest out, shoulders back, Steven Grout stamped away from the depot he had just been fired from, away from their stupid job and those awful people. He came to a car parked by the kerb, stopped, took a deep breath, then walked on. Never mind the name of the road, he thought; they would only change it. He watched the cars and buses and vans and trucks pass by him, and calculated how far he had to go to get to the next parked car which would shield him from them.

The pavement had been much repaired, and it was difficult to synchronise his steps so that the middle of each foot fell exactly on the cracks between the paving stones, but with some concentration and a few judicious half-steps he managed it; then he came to a long blue-grey line of asphalt where a pipe had obviously been repaired, and walked along that instead, free from the worry of the paving stones between the cracks.

He still felt hot and sticky from the attack by the Microwave Gun. He thought back, again, to the confrontation in Mr Smith's office.

Of course, he had known they would use the Microwave Gun on him; they always did when he was up in front of somebody, whenever he was at a disadvantage anyway and needed all the help he could get, whenever he was going for an interview for a job, or being asked things by the Social Security people or even clerks in the Post Office. That was when they used it on him. Sometimes they used it on him when he was waiting to be served by a barman, or even when he was just standing waiting to cross a busy street, but mostly it was when he was talking to somebody official.

He had recognised the symptoms as he was standing in Mr Smith's office.

His palms were sweating, his forehead was wet and itching, he felt shivery, his voice was shaky and his heart was beating fast; they were cooking him with the Microwave Gun, bathing him in its evil radiations, heating him up so that he broke out in a lathering sweat and looked like a nervous kid.

Bastards! He'd never found the Gun, of course; they

were very clever, very clever and cunning indeed. He had given up dashing through to adjoining rooms, running to look downstairs or above, craning his head out of windows to look for hovering helicopters, but he knew they were there somewhere all right, he knew what they were up to.

So he had to stand there, in the office of the Roadworking Operatives Supervisor in the Islington Council Seven Sisters Road Highways Department Depot, sweating like a pig and wondering why they didn't just get on with it and sack him as he listened to Mr Smith and his eyes hurt and he could smell his own body odour again.

'. . . were all hoping that this would not be a continuing situation, Steve,' Mr Smith said, droning nasally from behind the chip-board desk in his low-ceilinged office on the depot's first floor, 'and that you would be able to consolidate your position here by forming a positive working relationship with the remainder of the road gang, who, in all fairness, I'm sure you'd be the first to agree, have done their very best to, well . . .'

Mr Smith, a man of about forty with large soft bags under his eyes, leant over his paper-strewn desk and looked down at the No-Nonsense pen he was fiddling with. Steven watched the pen, mesmerised for a second.

'I really do think . . . ah . . . Steve – oh, and please don't hesitate to interject if you feel you have anything you wish to articulate; this isn't a star chamber here. I want you to play a full and meaningful part in this discussion if you feel that thereby we can ah, resolve . . .'

What was that? He wasn't sure he'd heard that right. Something about a Star Chamber? What was that? What did it mean? It didn't sound like it fitted in with this period, this setting, this age or whatever you wanted to call it. Could Mr Smith be another Warrior, or even further up the hierarchy of Tormentors than he'd thought?

God! Those bastards and that Gun! He could feel sweat start to gather in the lines of his forehead and in his eyebrows. Soon it would roll down his nose, and then what? They might think he was crying! It was unbearable! Why didn't they just throw him out? He knew it was what they wanted to do, what they had planned to do, so why didn't they just *do* it then?

'. . . resolve this apparent impasse in some viable way conducive with the efficient operation of the department. I don't think I'm running a particularly tight ship here, Steve; we like to think that people will appreciate . . .'

Steven stood smartly to attention in the middle of the office, his hard hat held tightly under his right arm, close to his side. Out of the corner of his eye he could just see Dan Ashton, the road-gang foreman and union representative. Ashton was leaning, thick bronzed arms folded, against the edge of the doorway. He was about fifty, but the fittest as well as the oldest man in the gang; he stood there grinning unpleasantly, his cap pushed back on his head, a damp, unlit roll-up hanging from his mouth. Grout could detect its soggy odour even over the smell of Mr Smith's *Aramis*.

Ashton had never liked him either. None of them did,

even the one or two who didn't continually make fun of him and tease him and play jokes on him.

'. . . over backwards to accommodate you, but it really does look, I'm afraid, as though this incident with the canal and the cat has to be just about the last straw . . . ah . . . Steve. I understand from Mr Ashton here—' Smith nodded at the older man, who pursed his lips and nodded back, '—that Mr ah . . .' Mr Smith looked at some of the papers on his desk for a moment, '. . . ah yes, Mr Partridge had to go to hospital for a tetanus injection and stitches after you struck him with a shovel. Now, we don't think he's going to press charges, but you must realise that if he did you would in fact be facing a charge of assault, and coming as this does on top of your other verbal and written warnings – all within, I'm afraid to say, Steve,' Mr Smith sat back in his seat with a sigh and flicked through a few more of the papers on his desk, shaking his head at them, 'a very short interval of time considering the length of your employment with us, and all regarding previous lapses in . . .'

Partridge! He wished he'd knocked his head right off. Calling him those names! Bastard, was he? Mad, was he? Simple, eh? That fat Cockney with his stupid tattoos and his jocular manner and his dirty jokes; he should have dumped *him* in the canal!

The sweat was gathering in his brows, getting ready to slide down his nose and make a dewdrop at the end which would either stay there wobbling about very obviously and making him want to sneeze, or force him to draw attention to it by wiping it away. To wipe his brow

would be a sign of weakness, too, though; he *wouldn't*
do it! Let them see his proud contempt! They wouldn't
break him, oh no! He wouldn't give them the satisfaction.

'. . . appreciated what you have said about not really
meaning to offend anybody, I just can't square this version
of accounts with that of your workmates, Steve, who
insist, I'm afraid, that you seemed quite serious about
back-filling the canal with the tarmac allocated for laying
on Colebrook . . . ah . . . Colebrook Row, in fact. As for
Mrs Morgan's cat, all we can do is—'

They were talking about cats, to him! One of the
mightiest warlords in the history of existence, and they
were talking about bloody cats! Oh, how the mighty were
fallen, right enough!

The sweat left his right eyebrow. It didn't roll down
his nose; it went straight into his eye instead. A terrible,
furious, impotent anger filled him, making him want to
strike out, to shout and scream. He couldn't do that,
though; he had to keep cool, despite the Microwave Gun,
and only answer back, if even that. *Discipline*; that was
important.

'. . . but I take it you have nothing else to say?' Mr
Smith said, and stopped talking. Grout sucked in his
breath; was he supposed to say something? Why didn't
people make things *clear*? What was the point, though?
Might as well get the whole thing over with as fast as
possible.

'I was only kidding!' he heard himself say.

It had just leaped out! But it was true; it was only a

sign of their stupidity – or their fear? – that they were taking him so seriously. Of course he hadn't been going to fill the bloody canal in! It would have taken him all day even if they'd *had* enough tarmac in the back of the pickup! It was all just a sort of angry joke because the rest of the gang, and Ashton in particular, wouldn't agree with him about the best way to fill holes in. But they would see; those holes they'd patched in Upper Street at the start of the morning shift would soon show who was right!

Of course, he knew speaking out would do no good, but he couldn't help it sometimes. He *had* to tell people when they were doing things the wrong way.

It was more than he could bear to see the stupidity around him and just suffer it in silence. That would drive him to madness, to the place they most wanted him, the place in which it would be even more difficult to find the Key; an institution, a hospital where they filled you up with all sorts of disgusting drugs and deliberately kept you as stupid as the rest. That was part of their game, of course; leave him to search for the way to escape, but alone. If he started trying to find any others like him, other Warriors, they would have an excuse for locking him away. It was fiendishly clever.

'. . . really excuse your actions Steve. Let's be fair, now; I don't expect it makes much difference to Mrs Morgan, or her cat,' Mr Smith said, and a small smile played over his lips as he glanced at Dan Ashton, who grunted and looked down at his feet while Smith continued, 'whether you were joking or in deadly seriousness.'

The other eyebrow discharged its sweat, rolling it down into Grout's other eye. He blinked furiously, almost blinded, eyes red and stinging. Intolerable!

'. . . typing your final written warning now, but really, Steve, without wishing to sound patronising in any way or form, I really do think you're going to have to mend your ways very considerably indeed if you're to—'

'Right!' Steven shouted hoarsely, shaking his head, sniffing hard and blinking all at the same time. 'My contempt for all . . . all of you is just *it*! I resign! I won't give you the satisfaction! I quit; I resign; I throw in the towel! There, I've said it before you did! Don't tell me I couldn't; I'm stronger than you know!' He could feel his lips trembling; he fought to control them. Mr Smith sighed and leaned forward over his desk.

'Now, Steve—' he began tiredly.

'Don't you "Now Steve" me!' Grout shouted, standing there and quivering. 'It's *"Mr Grout"* to you. I'm resigning; give me my papers! I demand my papers; where are my papers?' He stepped forward towards Mr Smith's desk. Smith sat back, surprised. Grout saw him exchange looks with Dan Ashton, and thought he could see the older man nod, or give some sort of sign or signal to Mr Smith. Certainly the foreman was no longer leaning against the door-jamb; he was standing properly now, arms unfolded. Maybe he thought Steven was going to offer some violence to Mr Smith; well, let them fear! He'd show them! He wasn't frightened of any of them.

'I really do think you're being a little rash in this—' Mr Smith began, but Steven interrupted,

'I believe I asked for my papers, *please*! I shan't leave without my papers. *And* my money! Where are they? I know my rights!'

'Steve, I think you're allowing your understandable—' Mr Smith began, pushing his chair back from his desk slightly. The sunlight glinted on his discreet SDP lapel-badge.

'Enough!' Steven shouted. He took another step forward, and with his right hand made as though to hit Mr Smith's desk. His hard hat, held in the crook of his right arm, fell out from between his arm and his side and hit the floor, rolling briefly. Steven stooped quickly and retrieved it, banging his head sharply on the front edge of Mr Smith's desk as he straightened. He rubbed his head rapidly, feeling his face turning red. Damn that Gun!

Mr Smith was on his feet now. Dan Ashton had come forward, and was leaning over from the side of Smith's desk, whispering something into his boss's ear. Grout glared at them both as he rubbed his smarting head. Oh, it was easy to see what they were both up to!

'Well,' Mr Smith began, a pained expression on his face as he turned to look at Grout again, 'if that's the way you really feel, Steve . . .'

Dan Ashton had smiled thinly.

So he'd won in the end. He hadn't given them the satisfaction of firing him there and then; he'd shown them the contempt he felt for them . . . let them suffer!

A strange fierce joy had filled him after that, and he hadn't really heard anything Ashton or Smith had said to him. They'd given him some papers, and somebody had gone to the cashier for his money (it made a nice fat bulge in his hip pocket; he patted it now and again as he walked, just to make sure it was still there) and eventually he'd signed some papers. He hadn't wanted to sign anything, but they had said they wouldn't give him any money unless he did, so he'd pretended to read the papers carefully, and then signed them.

Ashton had tried to see him out after that, and even wanted to shake hands with him, but Steven had spat at his feet and made a rude sign at him.

'You bad little fucker,' Ashton had said, which was typical of him. Steven had told him he was a foul-mouthed ignoramus, and stuffed his various papers and forms quickly into his trouser pockets and walked off. 'Here!' Ashton had shouted after him as he strode down Seven Sisters Road, head held high, 'Your P45. You dropped it!' At least that was what Steven thought he had shouted; it might have been a different number, but it was something like that. He had glanced back, to see Ashton standing at the depot gates, waving a piece of paper at him. Grout turned away, straightened his back and brought his head up, ignoring Ashton pointedly as he walked proudly away.

Ashton had started after him; Steven heard his trotting steps behind him; so he ran, ignoring the older man's shouts until eventually he outdistanced him. Ashton had shouted one last thing at him, but Steven had been too far away, breathing deeply, an expression of triumph on his face. He'd got away from them. It was a small escape, a little rehearsal, but it was something.

So now he walked, still angry with them, but glad to be away, glad to have salvaged something from yet another of their attempts to grind him down, make him feel small, drive him into despair.

They wouldn't succeed that easily! They had surrounded him with horror and stupidity, with all the paraphernalia of this so-called-human excess, and they expected it to bring him down, to reduce him still further from the once proud state he had fallen from, but they would not succeed. They were trying to wear him down, but they would fail; he would find the Key, he would find the Way Out and escape from this . . . joke, this awful solitary confinement for Heroes; he would leave them all behind and take his rightful place in the greater reality again.

He had Fallen, but he would Rise.

There was a war somewhere. He didn't know where. Not a place you could necessarily get to by travelling anywhere from here, late Twentieth Century London, Earth, but somewhere, sometime. It was the ultimate war, the final confrontation between Good and Evil, and he had played a major part in the war. But something had gone wrong, he had been betrayed, lost a battle with the forces of chaos and been ejected from the real battle-ground to languish here, in this cesspit they called 'life'.

It was part punishment, part test. He could fail entirely, of course, and be demoted still further, with no hope of escape. That was what *they* wanted, the ones who controlled the whole seedy show; the Tormentors.

They seemed to want him to try and call their bluff,

to stand up and say: 'Right, I know what it's all about, you can drop the pretence. Come out wherever you are and let's get it over with', but he knew better than that. He had learned that lesson as a child, when the others had laughed at him, and they sent him to see the school shrink. He wasn't going to try that again.

He wondered how many people in all the mental hospitals in the country – or the world, come to that – were really fallen Warriors who had either cracked up from the strain of trying to live in this hell-hole, or simply made the wrong choice and thought that the test was just seeing through the whole thing and then having the courage to stand out and make that challenge.

Well, he wasn't going to end up like one of those poor bastards. He would see it through, he would find the Way Out. And he might not even stop at simply escaping; he might just smash up the whole foul contraption of their testing and imprisonment apparatus – this 'life' – while he was about it.

He was starting to feel faint. He had about another ten paces to go to the next parked car, within the wheelbase of which he would be safe from the laser-axles of the passing traffic.

All the traffic, every single vehicle which passed him was equipped with lasers in its axles; they could register a hit on his legs unless he was above them, or shielded by a wall, or between the wheels of a parked car, or holding his breath. Of course, he knew that the lasers didn't hurt; you couldn't see them and they did no harm by themselves, but he knew that they were another of the ways that they – the Tormentors – took points off him. He knew all this from dreams, and from having worked it out. As a child he had done the same thing, as a game; something to make life more interesting, give it some purpose . . . then he had begun to have dreams about it, to come to realise that it was *real*, that he had had an insight when he started to play the game. He *had* to do it now; it felt horrible and uncomfortable when he tried to stop, even just to see what it was like walking down a street breathing 'normally'. It was like the feeling he used to get when he played another game from his childhood; that of closing his eyes and walking for a certain number of steps along, say, a wide path in a park. No matter how certain he might be immediately before he closed his eyes that there was plenty of space in front of him, no matter how positive he was as he walked with eyes closed that he wasn't veering off to one side and there was tarmac under his feet rather than grass, he still found it very hard, almost impossible, to walk more than about twenty paces with his eyes closed. He would be certain, *positive*, that he was about to walk into a tree, or a post or sign he hadn't noticed; even that somebody had been watching from behind a tree and was about to leap out and punch him hard on the nose.

Better to keep your eyes open; better to trust your instincts and take deep breaths between the parked cars. You couldn't be too careful.

He got to the car and stopped opposite it, breathing deeply. He took off his hard hat and wiped his brow, after

checking for scaffolding. The safety helmet was another
of his discoveries, his good ideas. He knew how vulnerable people's heads were, and how important his own
was. He knew *they* would just love to arrange a little
'accident' with some spanner or brick falling from a building, or, more plausibly still, from some scaffolding. So he
had worn that hard hat, since even before he left the home.
No matter what the job was, or what else he might be
doing, he wore the hat when he was outside. They had
laughed at him in the road gang; who did he think he
was? they said. Poncy engineers wore hard hats every-
where, not your labourers. Or was he frightened of
pigeons then? Going a bit thin on top as well as inside,
eh? Ha ha. Let them laugh. They wouldn't get the hat off
him. He had two spare hats in his room just in case he
ever lost his usual one, or somebody stole it. People had
done that before now, too.

He started walking again, treading carefully on the
cracks between the paving stones. A careful, steady stride
was very important, anyway. Good for the breathing and
the heart rate. People stared at him sometimes, jumping
from one paving stone border to another, then taking
some mincing little half-steps over others, his face going
strange colours as he ran out of stored air in his lungs,
sweating under a hard hat with no construction sites
anywhere in evidence, but he didn't care. They'd be sorry,
one day.

As he walked, he wondered what he would do today
with his new-found freedom. He had lots of money;
perhaps he would get drunk . . . the pubs would be open

soon. He supposed he ought to go and sign on; let the
unemployment people know he was out of a job again.
He wished he could remember what you were supposed
to do when you wanted to register as unemployed, but
he always forgot. Obviously the whole unemploy-
ment/Social Security system had been set up to confuse,
anger and demoralise him. He kept meaning to take notes,
write down all the separate moves you were meant to
make, forms fill out, offices visit, people see, but he always
forgot. Anyway, he always told himself that this would
be the last time; this time he would find some really good
job in which he would get on really well and his talents
would be appreciated and people would like him and he
would surprise all his Tormentors, so there would be no
reason to go through the whole fraught and sapping business of signing on again. He wondered vaguely about
going back to Mrs Short's boarding house and getting a
pen and paper.

He would go back to his room. He always felt better
there, and he still felt like a good wash; he needed to get
rid of all this sweat and clamminess, wash all the dust and
the lead off his face and hands. He could do that back at
Mrs Short's. He would gain strength from being back
with his books, his bed and his little bits and pieces. He
could have a look at the Evidence, again; that would be
good. He could start re-reading a book.

He had a lot of books. Most of them were Science
Fiction or Fantasy. He had long ago realised that if he
was going to find any clues to the whereabouts of the
Way Out, the location or identity of the Key, there was

a good chance he might get some ideas from that type of writing. He knew this from the way he felt attracted to it.

It was a contemptuous sop of a clue, something they thought they could afford, but it might be useful. Obviously they thought that by letting this sort of thing out they would have an excuse for putting him away if he ever attempted to call their bluff. 'Ha!' they would be able to say, 'Crazy; read too much SF. Bonkers; let us put him away and keep him under sedation and have done with him.' That was the way their minds worked.

That realisation was supposed to put him off, but he was too clever for them. He bought all the most fantastic 'unrealistic' fiction he could find and afford; by the rules they must have hidden a clue away in it somewhere. One day he would open up a book – some new sword-and-sorcery trilogy, probably – and something he would read there would trigger what he knew was locked away in his own brain somewhere. It might be the name of a character (there was one already he was sure sounded familiar; it was one of his bits of Evidence), it might be the description of a place or a sequence of events . . . all he needed was that Key.

Escapism, they called it. Oh, they were clever all right!

His room was full of books; thick, dog-eared, broken-spined gaudy-covered paperbacks. They lay on the floor, stacked on their sides because he didn't have any proper shelves. The floor of his room was like a maze, with tower-blocks of books, whole walls of them set out on the thin carpet and holed linoleum so that only small corridors for him to walk in remained between them. He could go from bed to window and table, to cupboard and door and fire and wash-handbasin, but only by certain routes. Making the bed was difficult. Pulling the drawers in the cupboard out properly needed great care. Coming back to the place drunk, especially when he couldn't find the light switch, was horrendous; he would wake to a sight like Manhattan after a severe earthquake. In paperback.

But it was worth it. He needed both those avenues of escape; drink because it felt like escape, a way out of their fetid reality for a while . . . and the books because they soothed, they offered hope. He might lose himself in the books sometimes, but he might find the Key there, too.

A car he was heading for to draw his next breath suddenly drove off. Steven cursed inwardly and had to step up on to a low wall above the height of the laser-axles to empty and fill his lungs again. He got down from the wall and walked on.

He'd show them all, one day. All the people who had taunted him and hurt him and confused him and denied him. Even the ones whose names he had forgotten. When he found the Key he'd get them. People like Mr Smith, Dan Ashton and Partridge. He'd find that Way Out, but he wouldn't leave until he'd found them again and sorted them out. They'd pay all right.

Couldn't even take a joke. Throw a shovelful of tarmac into the canal and they went to pieces. It hadn't been his fault he'd tripped over the cat. He knew he shouldn't have hit the animal, but he'd been angry. Then Partridge had tried to wrestle with him, claiming later that he was only trying to 'restrain' him. Partridge had got all angry and upset soon too, because as he was struggling with Steven a magazine fell out of his trousers on to the towpath of the canal and the other men had picked it up and it had been a spanking magazine so all the other men who weren't laughing and shouting already started teasing Partridge; Partridge started trying to wrestle Steven to the ground but Steven had got free and clouted the other man with the shovel, which was still bloody from hacking the cat to bits, and after that, with the magazine coming apart as the other men grabbed at it and Partridge rolling about dazed on the towpath in the cat's blood and almost falling into the canal, Dan Ashton had said soberly that enough was enough and they'd better go and see Mr Smith the supervisor because they just couldn't go on like this. They weren't getting the work done.

It was all horribly sordid, but the more he thought about it, the more he became certain that, far from being a disaster, leaving the Highways Department was in fact a real step forward. It hadn't been much of a job after all; he had thought at first from the sound of it that it might mean travel, but it didn't.

He would definitely go to the pub later, he decided. It was a day to celebrate. For two reasons, he reminded himself. Not that it meant very much, because when you thought about it it wasn't something really to celebrate, but today, June 28th, was his birthday.

He stopped, opposite a car, of course, and looked at his reflection in a shop window. He was tall and thin. He had longish, lank dark hair he didn't wash often enough. It stuck out from under his red hard hat in scrappy curls. His trousers were slightly too short, and showed off his purple nylon socks and his tar-stained desert boots. His Paisley pattern shirt didn't go too well with the greying Marks & Spencer pullover he wore instead of a jacket, and he knew his fingernails were dirty. But it was a good disguise, he told himself. Great Warriors didn't want to attract too much attention to themselves when they were trying to think their way out of their penalty period in the ultimate war.

A young woman who was dressing the female dummies in the lingerie department window Steven was looking at frowned at him and gave him a suspicious, disapproving look which he noticed her just in time to see. He saw the half-dressed models then, and quickly walked away, only just taking a deep breath in time as he walked out from the cover of the parked car.

'Many happy returns,' he said to himself, then suddenly gulped as he put his hand to his mouth and looked around. What was he *saying*?

One-Dimensional Chess

Quiss paused near the topmost window in the winding-stair. His old body, for all its girth, thick size and seeming weight of muscle, was less than fit, and not so warm either. The cold air of the castle fumed from his mouth as he rested, gathering breath. It was dark in the turret stair, the only light coming from a small open window just round the twist in the rising steps. The steamy clouds of his breath were first caught in the light from above, then pulled slowly away in a draught from the same source. He wondered if Ajayi had finished the game yet.

Probably not. Prevaricating woman. He sighed and set off up the stairs again, pulling himself up by his hands on the thick, frozen rope fixed to the outside of the staircase, the castle's concession to their earlier request for a handhold on the often ice-slicked steps.

Ajayi was in the games room still, hunkered over the small table in her furs, huge as a bear, perched on a small stool all but hidden beneath the furs and cloths which smothered her old frame. She didn't look up as Quiss – panting heavily – appeared at the top of the stairs and made his way down the length of the dimly lit room. She seemed to notice him only as he came closer, up to his chair, facing her across the small, four-legged table with the dully glowing red jewel in its centre. Ajayi smiled and nodded, perhaps at the man, perhaps at the thin, wavering line of squares which seemed to hang in the air over the small circular table.

The thin line of squares – alternately black and white, like tiny isolated tiles of shadow and mist – stretched over the table, through the air on either side of it, and disappeared into the distant side walls of the broad games room, over fallen slates and past rusting columns of wrought iron. The flat string of squares flickered slightly, just sufficiently to show it was a projection, nothing real; but although it was apparent the line of squares itself was merely an image, on its surface sat seemingly real and solid wooden chess pieces made from black and white wood, and set on that strange line like tiny isolated guard towers on a chequered frontier wall.

Ajayi looked slowly up at her companion, her old lined face gradually contorting into a smile. Quiss looked down at her. Maybe there's something of the reptile in her, he thought. Maybe she slows down in the cold. As though I didn't have enough problems.

'Well?' the old woman said.

'Well what?' Quiss said, still breathing hard from his walk up the stairs from the castle's lower levels. What was she asking *him* questions for? He was the one who should be doing the asking. Why hadn't she finished the game yet? Why was she still just sitting looking at it?

'What did they say?' Ajayi asked patiently, smiling a little.

'Oh,' Quiss said, shaking his great bearded head quickly as though the whole subject was of too little consequence to be worth discussing, 'they said they'd see what they could do. I told them if we didn't get more light and heat up here soon I'd tear a few more of them apart, but after that they only started acting all stupid, and anyway they'll soon forget; they always do.'

'You didn't see the seneschal himself then?' Ajayi said. She sounded disappointed, and a small frown creased her forehead.

'No. He was busy, they said. Just saw the little bastards.' Quiss sat down heavily on his small chair, wrapping some more furs around himself to keep warm. He stared mournfully at the bright strip which appeared to float in the cold air over the small table. In the centre of the table's delicately carved surface the jewel, which was the colour of blood, shone like something warm.

Ajayi pointed at one of the wooden chess pieces – a black queen – and said, 'Well, I think you're too hard on them. That's not the way to get results. By the way, I think that's checkmate.'

'You don't know—' Quiss began, then gave a start as the last part of what his adversary had said sank in. He frowned deeply and peered at the narrow line of black and white spaces hanging in the air in front of him. 'What?' he said.

'Checkmate,' Ajayi said, her old voice slightly cracked and uneven. 'I think.'

'Where?' Quiss said indignantly, sitting back with a smile somewhere between annoyance and relief. 'That's only check; I can get out of it. There.' He leaned forward quickly and took hold of a white bishop, placing it one black square further forward, in front of his king. Ajayi smiled and shook her head; she put her hand just to one side of the glittering, projected line of squares and seemed to fumble with something invisible in the air. A black knight appeared, as though out of profound shadow, on the surface of the ultimately narrow board. Quiss took in his breath to say something, then held it.

'Sorry,' Ajayi said, '*that*'s mate.' She said it quietly, but then wished she hadn't spoken at all. She frowned to herself, but Quiss was too absorbed glaring at the board – looking desperately up and down its length for useful pieces that were not there – to notice what she'd said.

Ajayi sat back in her little stool and stretched. She put her arms out from her sides and back, arching her spine and wondering vaguely as she did so why it had been thought necessary or relevant to give them such old bodies. Perhaps to keep the idea of the passing of time, simple mortality, to the forefront of their minds. If so, it was a redundant measure, even in this strange and singular place, even given their odd, frozen state (as the castle was frozen, so were they; as the castle was slowly crumbling but they stayed in their stasis, so their hopes, their chances decayed). She got up stiffly from the table, with one last look at the scowling form of the man trying to work a way out of his hopeless situation, then walked slowly, limping a little, over the scratched glass floor of the room to the bright chill of the balcony.

She leaned slackly against the square pillar in the middle of the row of columns which divided room from terrace, and looked into the snowy distance.

An unbroken plain of white stretched to the far horizon, only the faintest shadings of light indicating any variation in the almost dead flat land. To the right, Ajayi knew, if she leaned out from the balcony (which she did not like to do as she was a little afraid of heights), she would be able to see the quarries, and the start of the thin, also snow-covered and treeless line of stunted hills. She didn't bother to lean out. She had no particular desire to see either the hills or the quarries.

'Aaah!' Quiss roared behind her, and she turned in time to see him sweep his arm over the surface of the thin, artificial board in a gesture of fury and frustration. Chess pieces scattered from the board, but blinked out the instant they dropped below the level it was on, as though falling beneath some invisible beam. All except a couple of knights, which vanished as soon as they left the board itself. The board flickered for a second or two, then

39

slowly faded until it was gone, and Quiss was left sitting looking angrily at the small wooden table. The faint glow from the jewel in the middle of its filigreed surface dimmed, went out.

Ajayi raised her eyebrows, waiting for the man to look at her, but he did not; he simply sat, torso perched forward, one elbow on his knee, hairy chin in one hand. 'Fucking stupid knights,' he said at last. He scowled at the table.

'Well,' Ajayi said, leaving the open entrance to the balcony as a light wind picked up and blew a small flurry of snow around her booted feet, 'at least the game's over.'

'I thought we had a stalemate.' Quiss seemed to be addressing the table, not his opponent. 'We had an agreement.'

'It was quicker this way.' Ajayi sat down on the small stool on the other side of the table. Light from the ceiling moved uncertainly over the carved wood Quiss was still staring at. Ajayi looked at her companion's face in the dimness. Quiss had a broad, dark grey face, covered with mottled black and white hair. His eyes looked small and yellow, set in a tracery of deepening lines which seemed to radiate from his eyes like waves in a small still pool. He still did not look at her, so she shook her head slowly, resignedly, and looked about the room.

It was long and wide and very dark, with many pillars. Most of the light came from the openings onto the balcony. There should have been light from above and below, but in fact there was almost none, and it was partly because of that, and because it was also rather colder than it had to be, that Quiss had set off something like an hour before to find some of the castle's attendants. He was supposed to have asked politely for more heat up on their level, but from what he'd said Ajayi suspected he had been his usual brusque and threatening self. She would have gone herself, but her leg was stiff and sore again and she wasn't sure she would have been able to manage the stairs.

She looked up at the ceiling, where one of the room's many odd columns flared into the flat, thick, pale green glass. A single sinuous shape, shedding milky light, moved in the cold, murky water overhead.

It was one of the castle's many peculiarities that the interior lighting was produced by several species of luminescent fish.

'Where's the bell?' Quiss said suddenly, sitting upright and looking about the room. He got up from his seat as quickly as his thick furs and old muscles would allow, kicked some slates and books out of his way across the glass floor and started inspecting a pillar a few metres away. 'They've moved it again,' he muttered. He started looking at some of the nearby pillars and columns, his boots scraping on the glass slabs of the floor as he moved. 'Ah,' he said, when almost out of sight, back in the depths of the room, not far from the small winding-stair he had entered the room by a few minutes earlier. Ajayi heard a distant scraping noise as Quiss pulled on the bell-chain.

Ajayi picked up a small, thin slate from the floor at the base of the pillar behind her. She turned the slate this way and that, trying to understand the curious markings scratched on its black-green surface, wondering idly which part of the walls the slate had fallen from. She rubbed her back at the same time; bending to the floor had hurt her.

Quiss came back to the table by way of another small, though taller, table over on the far side of the room, where a few dirty cups and cracked glasses stood in a small tin basin under a dripping tap. The tap was joined to a slightly bent length of pipe which appeared from a wall seemingly composed of tightly compressed paper. Quiss poured himself a glass of water, drank it.

Back at the games table he sat down in his straight-backed chair and stared across at Ajayi, who put down the slate she was studying. 'Of course the damn thing's probably not working.' Quiss said gruffly. Ajayi shrugged. She pulled the furs more closely around her. The wind moaned through the balcony window.

The castle had two names, as befitted its dual owner-ship. The side Quiss belonged to called it Castle Doors, Ajayi's side named it the Castle of Bequest. Neither name seemed to mean anything. As far as they could tell, it was the only thing which existed here, wherever 'here' was. Everything else was snow; the white plain.

They had been there . . . they did not know how long. Quiss had found himself there first, and after a little while, when he realised that there was no night and day, just the one flat, monotone light always there beyond the windows, he had started to keep a tally of the number of times he slept. The record was scratched on the floor of a small cell in a corridor off the games room; his bedroom. There were nearly five hundred scratches on the glass floor now.

Ajayi arrived, seemingly deposited on one of the castle's high, flat, rubble-strewn roofs one night, when Quiss had made eighty-three scratches. They had bumped into each other that 'day', and were delighted to find each other. Quiss had been lonely with only the castle's shy and dwarfish attendants for company, and Ajayi was pleased to find somebody who already knew their way round the cold, forbidding stump of rock, iron, glass, slate and paper which was the castle.

It had taken them only a short time to realise they were from opposite sides in the Therapeutic Wars, but it had caused little friction. They had both heard of this place, they both knew why they were here. They both knew what they had to do, and how hard it was going to be to escape; they knew they needed each other.

They had been Promotionaries, on their respective sides of the Wars (which were not, of course, between Good and Evil at all, as non-combatants of every species always assumed, but between Banality and Interest), with great things expected of them once their training and indoctrination was completed; but they had each done something silly, something which called into question their very suitability for exalted rank, and now they were here, in the castle, with a problem to solve and games to play, being given one last chance; a long shot, an unlikely appeal procedure.

And an unlikely setting.

What strange architect had designed this place? Ajayi

found herself wondering every so often. The castle, rising on a single outcrop of rock from the plain, was built very largely of books. The walls were mostly slate, apparently quite normal, grained rock produced by a perfectly standard physical process of alluvial deposition. But when you loosened one of the slate blocks from the castle walls – an easy job, as the castle was slowly crumbling away – and split it open, on every surface so exposed a series of cut or engraved figures was revealed, arranged in lines and columns, complete with word and line breaks and what looked like punctuation. Quiss had demolished a significant part of the castle when he first discovered this, unwilling to believe that the stones, every one of them, all the tens of thousands of cubic metres the castle must be composed of, all those kilotonnes of rock really were saturated, filled full of hidden, indecipherable lettering. The castle's stunted squad of masons and builders were still working to repair the damage the old man had done by tearing down walls in his attempt to prove these hidden glyphs were isolated aberrations, not – as they indeed were – ubiquitous. This caused much grumbling and complaining, as the masons considered they were anyway fighting a losing battle against the castle's accelerating decay without its guests adding to their workload.

'You called?' a small, cracked voice said. Ajayi looked up at the door to the winding-stair expecting to see an attendant, but the voice had come from behind her, and she could see Quiss's face starting to turn red, his eyes widening, the lines around them spreading out further.

'Fuck off!' he shouted over Ajayi's shoulder towards

the balcony. The woman turned round and saw that the red crow was perched on the balustrade, flapping its wings like a man trying to keep warm and looking in at them, its head cocked to one side. An eye like a small black button glittered, fastening on them.

'Given up on the game then?' the red crow croaked. 'Could have told you the Silesian Defence wouldn't work in One-Dimensional Chess. Where'd you learn to—?'

Quiss stumbled out of his seat, almost falling, scooped a flat piece of slate from the floor and threw it at the red crow, which screamed and jumped out of the way, spreading its wings and dropping away, flying into the cold clear space below the balcony, its final call echoing briefly, like laughter. The slate Quiss had thrown sailed out through the balcony doorway after the bird, a stony imitation of its flight. 'Pest!' Quiss spat, and sat down again.

The rooks and crows which lived in the decaying stumps of the castle's high towers could talk; they had been given the voices of Quiss and Ajayi's respective rivals, unfaithful lovers and hated superiors. They would appear from time to time and taunt the old couple, reminding them of their past lives and the failures or mistakes which had brought them to the castle (though never detailing them – neither Quiss nor Ajayi knew what the other had done to justify sending them here. Ajayi had suggested they swap stories, but Quiss demurred). The red crow was the most malicious and cutting, and was equally proficient at taunting either of the elderly pair. Quiss was the more easily riled, so he tended to suffer more than his fair share of the bird's abuse. He shook with fury sometimes, as much as cold.

It was cold because something had gone wrong down in the castle's boiler room. The heating system was breaking down, needing repair. Hot water was supposed to circulate beneath and above every floor. In the games room, supported by slate and iron pillars, a tracery of iron girders held the low glass ceiling. Inside the glass was water, about a half-metre or so of slightly cloudy and salty water the boilers were supposed to keep warm. The same went for the glass underfoot; another half-metre of water lay underneath the transparent slabs which made up the floor, gurgling under the scratched surface and around the slaty pedestals supporting the columns above. Long gelatinous-looking bubbles of air moved like pale amoebae under the false ice of the glass.

Luminous fish lived in the salt water. They swam like long rubbery strip-lights through the water's gentle currents, and kept the rooms, corridors and towers of the castle bathed in a silky, pervasive light which sometimes made distances hard to measure and gave the air a thick sort of look. When Ajayi had first arrived the games room had been just right, held at a pleasant temperature by the warm fluid circulating above and below, and enjoyably light as well, thanks to the fish. The odd system had seemed to work.

But now there was something wrong, and most of the fish had retreated to the castle's still warm lower levels. The castle's black-cloaked seneschal had scowled darkly on the previous occasions when Quiss had tracked him down in the kitchens and asked him what was going on and what he intended to do about it; he made dour excuses and talked of the corrosive effects of salt water and what a mess it made of his pipes and anyway materials were very hard to come by these days – *What days?* Quiss had exploded. There was only one day, wasn't there, or did they have days here but they were just very long? The seneschal had gone quiet at that and sunk his thin grey face back into his hooded cape, while the huge human stood glaring at him, quivering with impotent rage.

Time was another problem in the Castle Doors. It went quicker the closer you were to a clock. The further away from a time-piece you were, the more it not only seemed to but did drag. The clocks in the castle were immovable, and erratic too, going sometimes faster, sometimes slower. There was one great clock mechanism buried deep in the warmer depths of the place, some vast assemblage of gears and creaking cogs which powered all the clock faces in the ramshackle shell of the castle. Rotating shafts buried in the walls transmitted the energy from the central machinery to the faces, and rumbled in some places, squeaked in others, and leaked oil ubiquitously.

The oil mingled with the warm salty water which leaked from places in the ceilings, and that was one of the reasons they had asked for some sort of banister rail to hold on to in the narrow winding-stair. The smell of oil and brine permeated the castle, making Ajayi think of old harbours, and ships.

Why time should go faster the closer you were to a clock, they didn't know, and none of the castle's waiters and attendants had any explanation either. Quiss and Ajayi had carried out experiments, using identical candles, lit at the same time, one hard by the face of a clock, the other in the middle of the room with them; the candle by the clock burned nearly twice as fast. They had formulated some vague ideas which would let them use this effect to shorten the perceived time it took to play the games they had to play, but the castle clocks, or perhaps the castle itself, seemed unwilling to cooperate. Taken near a clock, the table stopped working; the red jewel in the middle stopped glowing, the projection of the board and the pieces disappeared. Added to this was the fact that the clocks themselves were so erratic; every so often they slowed down, so that time went more slowly the closer you were to them.

Whatever was affecting the rate time passed at seemed to obey the inverse square law, the phenomenon apparently radiating from each clock face, while at the same time there was a more generalised sort of effect emanating from the huge central mechanism buried somewhere in the castle's many lower levels, making everything down there happen more quickly.

The chaotic kitchens, where the seneschal had his office and where vast quantities of food were continually being prepared in conditions of the utmost confusion, noise and heat, seemed to be the worst affected place of all. Ajayi could smell the cooking odours from Quiss's ragged furs as they sat, waiting.

'Ah, here you are then,' said a small voice. Ajayi looked, Quiss turned, and there at the head of the winding-stair stood an attendant. The attendant was short, about half the height of either of the two humans. It was dressed in a sort of grubby grey cassock knotted with red string at the waist. The cassock had a thin hood, held in place over the attendant's head and face by what looked like the brim from an old and worn red hat; it was squeezed down over the attendant's head, the top of the hood showing through where the hat's crown should have been. The attendant's face was hidden by a *papier mâché* mask, as worn by all the attendants and waiters. The mask was set in an expression of abject sadness.

'Well, better late than never,' Quiss snarled.

'Dreadful sorry,' the attendant squeaked, shuffling closer. Little red boots, quite shiny, flickered under the hem of its cassock as it moved. It stopped near the table and bowed, putting its small gloved hands into the opposing cuffs of its robe. 'You've finished the game then, oh, good. Who won?'

'Never mind who won,' Quiss barked. 'You know why we've sent for you, do you?'

'Yes, yes, I think so.' The attendant nodded, its high voice not altogether as certain as the words. 'You've got an answer, no?' It lifted its shoulders slightly, or dropped its head a little, as though frightened of being struck if its supposition was wrong.

'We've got an answer, yes,' Quiss said sarcastically. He glanced at Ajayi, who smiled back and motioned towards the small attendant. Quiss cleared his throat and leaned forward towards the small figure, which shrank away without actually stepping back. 'Right,' Quiss said, 'the

49

answer to the question is: You can't have both in the same universe. Got it?'

'Yes,' nodded the attendant, 'yes, I think I've got it: "You can't have both in the same universe." Very good. Very logical. That sounds like it to me. *I* thought that. That sounds—'

'We don't *care* what you thought,' Quiss interrupted, baring his teeth and leaning closer towards the small attendant – who shrunk back so much further Ajayi felt sure it was about to overbalance and fall backwards – 'Just do whatever you have to do and let's see if we can get out of this filthy place.'

'As you say, right, yes, will do, will do,' the small figure said, backing off, half-nodding, half-bowing as it made its way backwards to the winding-stair. It tripped on a book and almost went flying, but it just succeeded in remaining upright. It turned and hurried away into the darkness. They heard its steps clattering and fading in the distance.

'Hmm,' Ajayi said. 'I wonder what it does, where it goes.'

'Who cares as long as it's the right answer,' Quiss said, shaking his head and then scratching his chin. He turned to look back at where the doorway to the stairs stood in the gloom. 'I bet the little idiot forgets.'

'Oh, I shouldn't think so,' Ajayi said.

'Well, I do. Maybe we ought to follow it. Find out where it goes. We might be able to short-circuit this whole ridiculous process.' He turned and looked speculatively at Ajayi, who frowned at him and said,

'I *don't* think that would be a good idea.'

'It'll probably turn out to be something really simple.'

'Would you care to bet on that?' Ajayi said. Quiss opened his mouth to speak, but then thought the better of it. He cleared his throat instead, and traced some of the pattern on the top of the small wooden table between them with one stubby, yellow-grey finger. Ajayi said, 'Perhaps we could just ask one of them. Ask that one when it comes back; see what it says. It might tell us.'

'We shouldn't need to ask it anything, not if that's the right answer,' Quiss said, looking at the old woman. 'This was your answer, remember.'

'I remember,' Ajayi said. 'The next one can be yours, if this one isn't right, but we did agree to do it this way; it was just luck it's my answer first. We agreed to do it this way, do you remember?'

'*That* was your idea, too,' Quiss said, not looking at her, but lowering his eyes to watch his finger moving over the table's cut patterns.

'Just don't start any recriminations, that's all,' Ajayi said.

'I won't.' Quiss widened his eyes, held his hands up and out, his voice suddenly high in protest, so that he reminded Ajayi of a very large young child. 'It's going to be a long time before we get another chance though, isn't it though?'

'That's just the way things have been set up,' Ajayi said, 'that isn't my fault.'

'I didn't say it was your fault, did I?' Quiss said.

Ajayi sat back, putting her gloves back on. She looked

51

doubtfully at the man on the far side of the table. 'All right then,' she said.

It had taken them almost two hundred and fifty of Quiss's 'days' to discover what the way out was. They had to answer a single question. But first they had to play a series of odd games, working out the rules for each one in turn, playing each one to a conclusion, without cheating or colluding. At the end of each game they had one chance and one chance only to answer the riddle they had been set. This was their first game, their first attempt to answer the question. One-Dimensional Chess hadn't been all that difficult once they worked out the rules, and now their first answer was being carried or transmitted or processed – whatever – by the small attendant with the little red boots.

The question they had to answer was quite simple, and they had been told by the seneschal that *he* had been told that it was an empirical question, not a purely theoretical one, though he had also said he found this difficult to believe, as even the mysterious powers and forces which moved the Wars themselves could not control such absolutes . . . The question was: What happens when an unstoppable force meets an immovable object?

Simple as that. Nothing more complicated or obtuse; just that. Ajayi thought it was a joke, but so far all the castle's inhabitants, all the attendants and waiters, one or two other subsidiary characters they had discovered, the seneschal himself, and even the ever-facetious rooks and crows which infested the decaying upper storeys had treated the question with extreme seriousness. That really was the riddle, and if they got the answer right they would escape from the castle, be taken from this limbo and resume their duties and positions in the Therapeutic Wars again, debt paid.

Or they could kill themselves. That was the unspoken alternative (or at least unspoken by all except the red crow, who cheerily brought the subject up on every third or fourth visit), that was the easy way out. It was a long drop from the balcony of the games room; the castle apothecary carried a line of lethal poisons and draughts; there were ways out of the castle, a postern or two, and a narrow winding path through the fractured rocks and fallen masonry all tumbled round the castle's plinthed base like scree, then a long cold walk into the snowy silence . . .

There were times when Ajayi considered that way out; not as attractive then and there, but for when – if – there ever seemed to be no hope, at some time in the future. Even so, she found it hard to imagine ever becoming so desperate. Time would have to drag on a lot longer than it had, she would have to get a lot more fed up and tired with this old, time-frozen body before suicide became a serious alternative. Besides, if she went, Quiss would be abandoned. The self-destruction of one partner meant that the games could not go on. The other one could not play on alone or find somebody else to play, and if the games could not be played and ended, the riddle could not be answered.

'Ah . . . excuse me . . .' They both turned to look at the winding-stair door, where the small attendant was peeking round the side, most of its body hidden in the twisted darkness beyond.

'What?' Quiss said.

'Ah . . . sorry . . .' the attendant said, in a small voice.

'Eh?' Quiss shouted, his voice altering in pitch. Ajayi took a deep breath and sat back on the stool. She'd heard. She thought Quiss had too, but he didn't want to admit it to himself. 'Speak up, you wretch!' Quiss roared.

'That wasn't it,' the attendant said, staying in the doorway. Its voice was still small; Ajayi found herself straining to catch its hesitant words; 'that wasn't the right answer. I really am—'

'Liar!' Quiss rose off his seat, shaking with rage. The attendant yelped and disappeared. Ajayi sighed. She looked up at Quiss, who stood, fists clenched, glaring at the distant, empty doorway. He turned, whirled round to look down at her, the scraps of fur around him flying out. 'Your answer, lady,' he shouted at her, '*your* answer; remember that!'

'Quiss—' she began quietly. He shook his head, kicked the small chair he had been sitting on, and marched off across the squeaking, grating glass floor, heading for his own apartments. Before he left the games room for the short corridor which led to his rooms, he stopped by the side wall of the room, where more conventional paper and cardboard books lined the slate fabric of the castle – the mason's lame attempt at insulation. Quiss clawed at the wall, tearing the faded, yellowing books away from it, throwing them behind him like a dog digging a hole in the sand, bellowing incoherently and tearing and swiping at the wall, baring the green-black slate beneath as the torn, ripped pages fluttered away behind him, falling to the grimy glass floor like some flat, grubby snow.

Quiss stormed off, slamming a door somewhere, and Ajayi was left alone. She walked over to where the just-savaged books lay strewn across the floor, and stirred them with the toe of her boot. Some of the languages she knew, she thought (it was hard to tell in the uncertain light, and she was too stiff to be bothered bending down), and some she did not recognise.

She left the pages where they lay, one-dimensional flakes littering the murky floor, and she went to stand by the balcony window again.

Against the unending, unaltering whiteness of the plain, a flight of dark birds flew. The same sky looked down, blank and forgettable and grey, itself unchanging.

'And what next?' she asked herself in a low voice. She shivered and hugged herself tighter. Her short hair refused to grow any longer, and her furs had no hood. Her ears were cold. What was next, they knew already from the castle seneschal, was something called Open-Plan Go. Goodness knew how long *that* would take them to work out and play, assuming Quiss came back from his sulk. The seneschal had muttered something about this next game being the closest analogue of the Wars themselves, which worried Ajayi for a start. That sounded awfully complex, and long.

She had asked the seneschal where the ideas for these odd games came from. He said from a place which was the castle's chosen Subject, and had hinted, she thought, that there was another way to get to this place, but refused to be more specific. Ajayi was trying to cultivate the seneschal's acquaintance (when her sore leg and stiff back let her get down to the basement levels where he was usually to be found) whereas Quiss had started out trying to intimidate him. When the man had first arrived he had tried to torture information on how to escape from one of the waiters. It hadn't worked, of course, just made the others frightened.

Ajayi's belly rumbled. It must be mealtime soon. Waiters would appear shortly, if they weren't too frightened of Quiss being in a bad mood. Damn the man.

Open-Plan Go, she thought, and shivered again.

'You'll be saw-ree!' croaked a passing rook, cruising past on black wings and using the voice of an old, bitterly remembered lover.

'Oh, shut up,' she muttered, and went back inside.

TWO

Rosebery Avenue

On the bridge which carried Rosebery Avenue over
Warner Street, there was a smell of paint. Black dust lay
on the pavement, collecting in the spaces of the bridge's
primed balustrade. Graham hoped they would paint the
bridge tastefully. He looked into the cradle the painters
were using to paint the outside of the balustrade from,
and saw an old radio so spotted with paint it could have
been an art exhibit. The man in the cradle was whistling
to himself and coiling a length of rope.

Graham felt oddly satisfied at seeing life go on around
him like this; he felt almost smug at walking past people
and them not giving him a second glance, at least not now
he'd got rid of Slater. He was like some vital cell in the

bloodstream of the city; tiny but important; a message bearer, a point of growth and change.

She would be waiting for him now, getting ready, perhaps only now getting dressed, or still in the bath or shower. Now at last it was coming out right, the bad times were over, Stock deposed. It was his time, his turn.

He wondered what she thought of him now. When they had first met she thought he was funny, he guessed, though kind too. Now she had had time to get to know him better, see other sides of him as well. Perhaps she loved him. He thought he loved her. He could imagine them living together, even marrying. He would make a living as an artist – probably just a commercial artist at first, until his name became known – and she could do . . . whatever she wanted.

On his left were more buildings; light industrial and office premises topped by flats. Outside an open door of something called the Wells Workshop, at the kerb, stood a large American sports car. It was a Trans Am. Graham frowned as he passed it, partly at its loud white-lettered tyres and obtrusive styling, but partly because it reminded him of something; something to do with Slater, with Sara even.

Then he remembered; appropriately enough it had been at the party when Slater had first introduced Graham and Sara to each other. The coincidence amused Graham.

A smell of new shoes from another workshop wafted around him as he looked up at the old, stopped clock jutting out, two-faced, over the pavement from the first floor of the workshop, hands frozen at twenty-past-two (he glanced at his watch; it was actually 3:49). Graham smiled to himself, and recalled that night, another of Slater's never-to-be-written plots.

'Right. It's Science Fiction. There's this—'

'Oh *no*,' Graham said. They were standing by the mantelpiece in the front room of Martin Hunter's large house in Gospel Oak. Mr Hunter – Martin, to his students – was one of the lecturers at the Art School, and was giving his customary late Christmas party, in January. Slater had been invited, and had persuaded Graham he would not be gate-crashing if he came along too. They took along a box of wine they bought between them, and were drinking the red *vin de table* from plastic half-pint glasses. Apart from some salty garlic bread, neither of them had had anything to eat for some hours beforehand so, despite the fact that the party was hardly properly underway yet, they were both feeling the effects of the drink.

Music played loudly from the dining-room next door, where the carpets had been rolled back so that people could dance. Most of the people in the front room were sitting on couches or beanbags. Martin Hunter's own paintings, large gaudy canvases which looked like close-ups of minestrone soup seen under the effects of a powerful hallucinatory drug, adorned the walls.

'Just listen. There's this lot of weird aliens called the Sproati and they decide to invade Earth—'

61

'I think this has been done before,' Graham said, taking a drink. Slater looked exasperated.

'You won't let me finish,' he said. He wore a pair of grey shoes, baggy white trousers and what appeared to be a red tuxedo. He took a drink and went on, 'Okay, so they're invading Earth, but they're doing it as a tax dodge so that—'

'A *tax* dodge?' Graham said, leaning forward and looking Slater in the eye. Slater giggled.

'Yeah, they have to spend so much of the galactic year out of the Milky Way or the galactic tax federation hammers them for gigacredits, but instead of paying for expensive inter-galactic travel they camp out on some backwater planet still *in* the galaxy and just hide, see? But: something goes wrong. They're coming in on a starship disguised as a Boeing 747 so that the locals won't suspect until it's too late, but when they land at London Heathrow their baggage gets lost; all their heavy weaponry ends up in Miami and gets mixed up with the luggage of some psychiatrists attending an international symposium on anal-fixation after death, and: Freudians take over the world with the captured high-tech. arms. The Sproati all get interned by the British immigration authorities; thanks to a false reading on a spectograph when they were planning the operation they've all taken too many tannin pills and they're almost black. Usually they're light blue. One—'

'What do they look like?' Graham interrupted. Slater looked confused, then waved his free hand dismissively.

'I don't know. Vaguely humanoid, I suppose. Anyway,

one of them escapes and sets up home in an abandoned but working carwash in Hayes, Middlesex, while the rest die of starvation in the internment cells.'

'Doesn't sound like there's all that many of them, for an entire species . . .' Graham grumbled into his glass.

'They're very *shy*,' Slater hissed. 'Now will you be *quiet*? This one Sproati – we'll call him Gloppo—'

A couple of girls entered the room from the hall. Graham recognised them from the Art School; they were talking and laughing. He watched to see if they would look over at him and Slater, but they didn't. He had on his new black cords for the first time (they were a Christmas present from his mother. He'd told her what to get; she'd been going to get him *flared jeans*!), and he thought he looked pretty good in his snow-white shirt, black jacket, white trainers and lightly blonded dark hair.

'Look, stop looking at those females and pay attention; you *are following* all this, aren't you?' Slater put his face towards Graham's, leaning forward along the mantelpiece.

Graham shrugged, looked at the red wine in his glass, and said, 'I don't know about following, feels more like I'm being pursued.'

'Oh, très droll.' Slater smiled artificially. 'Anyway, Gloppo installs a brain in the car-wash so he can have sex with it – all those brushes and rollers and foam and stuff, you know? – while in Florida the Freudians are tightening their grip; they ban all phallic symbols including gear sticks, Jumbo jets, submarines and rockets and missiles. All motorbikes have to be ridden side-saddle and bondage is *right out*: rolled umbrellas, stretch jeans and fishnet stockings are banned, on pain of having a Sony Walkman taped permanently to your skull playing a looped tape of Barry Manilow's Greatest Hits . . . except for Barry Manilow fans, who get John Cage instead.'

'What about,' Graham said, pointing one finger at Slater, who pursed his lips and tapped his foot impatiently on the fire-surround, 'those people who like Barry Manilow *and* John Cage?'

Slater rolled his eyes. 'This is Science Fiction, Graham, not Monty Python. Anyway, Gloppo discovers the car-wash has been unfaithful in his absence with a metallic-blue Trans Am—'

'I thought that was an airline.'

'It's a car. Now be quiet. Gloppo finds the Trans Am has been screwing the car-wash—'

'And the car-wash's been riding the car,' Graham sniggered.

'Shut *up*. Gloppo disconnects the low-fidelity car-wash. Now then . . .'

There were more people in the room now; groups of men and women; most of them young, about his age, stood and talked and drank and laughed. The two girls he had noticed earlier were standing talking to some other girls. Graham hoped they all realised that just because he was standing talking to Slater, that didn't mean he was gay too. He looked back, nodding appreciatively, as Slater, talking quickly, waving his arms about, eyes glittering, seemed to approach the end of the story.

'. . . shit-scared because he's about to be blasted into

particles even smaller and more radioactive than Ronald
Reagan's brain, goes to the loo; by sheer coincidence the
crap he does solidifies in the intense cold of outer space
and the pursuing spaceship runs into it at about half the
speed of light and is totally destroyed.

'Gloppo and his pal discover the joys of oral sex, the
Freudians blow up the world, but that was going to
happen anyway, and our two heroes live comparatively
happily ever after.' Slater grinned widely, took a deep,
panting breath, then a drink. 'What do you think? Good,
isn't it?'

'Well . . .' Graham said, looking at the ceiling.

'Don't tease, you young blaggard. It's terrific; admit
it.'

'You've been reading that book,' Graham said. 'You
know; that book by that guy . . .'

'Specific as ever, Graham. What an incisive mind;
straight for the capillary. I stand in awe.'

'You know the one I mean,' Graham said, looking
down at the blocked-off fireplace and snapping his
fingers. 'That one that was on the telly . . .'

'Well, we're narrowing it down,' Slater said with a
thoughtful nod. He took another drink.

'Earth got blown up in that one too . . . ah . . .' Graham
kept snapping his fingers. Slater was silent for a second,
gazing disdainfully at Graham's snapping fingers, then he
said tiredly,

'Graham, either concentrate on searching for the title
of the book you're talking about or devote your full ener-
gies to practising calling for a waiter; I'm not convinced

you possess the RAM for doing both at the same time.'

'The Hitch-Hiker's Guide To The Universe!' Graham exclaimed.

'Galaxy,' Slater corrected dourly.

'Well, it sounds like it.'

'Nothing like it. You just don't recognise real talent when you meet it.'

'Oh, I don't know . . .' Graham grinned, looking over at the two Art School girls, who were now sitting on the floor on the other side of the room, talking to each other. Slater slapped his forehead.

'Thinking with your gonads again! It's pathetic. Here I am, yours for the asking; talented, handsome, lovable and affectionate, and all you can do is gawk at a couple of brainless broads.'

'Not so loud, you idiot,' Graham – feeling somewhat drunk – scolded Slater. 'They'll hear you.' He took a drink and looked at the other young man. 'And stop going on about how wonderful you are. You can be very boring, you know. I keep telling you I'm not gay.'

'My God,' Slater breathed, shaking his head, 'have you *no* ambition?'

Now, on this June day, Graham smiled at the memory. It would have been a good party anyway, even if he hadn't met Sara, he thought. The people were friendly, there was plenty to eat if they'd wanted it, and from what he'd seen there were quite a few unattached girls around. He'd been thinking of asking one of the two who had entered the front room during Slater's monologue – the more attractive of them – for a dance even as Slater was telling him how desirable Richard Slater was.

It was funny, Graham thought; the party seemed so long ago, but the memory was more fresh and real for him than things that had happened even just last week. He breathed deeply as he thought about it, passing postal workers from the Mount Pleasant sorting office standing talking just outside a small café. A big red Italian car was parked at the kerb. Slater would have liked it. Graham smiled and crossed the road to the sorting office, smelling its new coat of paint.

Slater saw Sara standing at the door of the room. His face lit up, he put his plastic tumbler down on the mantelpiece. 'Sara darling!' he called, and went over to her, through a couple of groups of other people, and put his arms round her. She didn't respond, but when Slater drew back her face held a slight smile. Graham was staring, and saw the woman's eyes flicker his way for a moment. Slater led her past the other people, over towards the mantelpiece and him. Graham felt frozen. People were still talking, chattering away. Hadn't anybody else in the room *seen* her?

She was slim, quite tall. Her hair was black and thick and looked tangled, as though she had just got out of bed and not brushed it. Her face, all her exposed skin, was white. She wore a black dress, an old thing with slightly tattered lace which filmed about her like some black froth. On top of the thin dress she wore a brightly coloured, predominantly red, Chinese padded jacket; it seemed to sparkle in the room's dim lights. Black tights, black low heels.

She was taking off her gloves as she approached. Her upper chest, exposed for the breadth of a hand by the black dress, showed a strange white mark, like a sort of ragged and wide necklace settled loosely over her shoulders. As she came closer he saw it was a scar, the scar tissue even more white than the skin around it. Her eyes were black, wide as though with some sustained surprise, the skin from their outer corners to her small ears taut. Her lips were pale, and nearly too full for her small mouth, like something bled but bruised. He had never seen anyone or anything quite so beautiful in his life; instantly, in less than the time it took her to walk from one side of the room to the other, he knew he loved her.

'This is the little *ingénu* I keep trying to seduce, Sara,' Slater said, presenting Graham with one delicate roll of the hand. 'Mr Graham Park, this is Mrs Sara ffitch. Quite the most gorgeous and elegant thing to come out of Shropshire since . . . well, me.'

She stopped in front of him, her head lowered just a little. His heart was beating too hard. He must be shaking. She was looking at Slater through the black web of her hair; now her head tilted, she turned to face him, put her small hand out. A Mrs! She was married! He couldn't believe it. For the merest instant, some final, irreducible unit of desire, he had glimpsed a feeling, an urge within himself he had not imagined himself capable of, but now this tiny, standard piece of information, these few letters, had switched his hopes off like some cheap lightbulb.

(Two summers ago, on holiday in Greece with a school pal he had since lost touch with, he'd been on a small, crowded, ramshackle train heading out of Athens over a scrubby plain in blistering heat. Parched ochre land and scrappy shrubs moved monotonously by. The rattling carriage was full of rucksacks and hikers, and black-dressed Greek ladies with chickens. Then his friend Dave shouted 'Look!' and when he turned, for a few moments only he glimpsed the Corinth canal; a sudden gulf sliced in the landscape, blue space sparking, a ship in the deep distance; fathomless light and air. Then the barren plain resumed.)

'Hello,' she said, and from his own eyes, hers flickered down to where her hand was held out to him. He was aware of Slater drawing in a breath and putting his head back the way he always did when he was rolling his eyes, but before Slater could say anything, Graham quickly nodded, switched his glass to the other hand, and took the woman's small hand in his, shaking it formally.

'Ah . . . hello.' Her hand was cold. How old was she? Mid-twenties? He let her hand go. She was still looking at him. Her figure even looked good; he wanted to weep, or throw her over his shoulder and just run. What was she? How could she do this to him? She was still looking at him. Such calm, steady eyes, the iris and the pupil almost one. Arches of deep dark brows like some perfect mathematical line. He could smell her; a cold sharp distant sort of musk, like a window on to a forest of winter pine.

'You mustn't worry,' she was saying, smiling at him, 'Richard hasn't said very much about you.' She looked at the other young man, who had retrieved his glass and was watching Sara and Graham with a smile on his face, almost a smirk. He shrugged.

'He's never even—' Graham swallowed, tried to stop himself sounding too amazed, '– *mentioned* you.' She smiled at that, first at him, then Slater. She stuffed her black gloves into a pocket in the padded jacket.

'Well,' she said, looking at them in turn again, lifting her face to gaze directly at Graham, 'if I may make so bold, chaps, how about a drink? I was bringing my own but I put it in the wrong pocket of my coat and it fell through the lining and smashed.' Her eyebrows arched suddenly. Slater laughed.

'What a wonderful story, Sara. I'm sure none of us would mind if you just didn't bring any at all.' He turned to Graham. 'Mind you, Sara does dress in the early Oxfam style, so she might be telling the truth.' He looked at the woman, patting her shoulder and putting his glass on the mantelpiece again, 'Allow me ma'm.' He walked off through the press of people now all but blocking the way to the door. Graham suddenly noticed the room was crowded, and getting hot. He was alone with her, though, Slater gone. She stooped, brought one foot up, fiddling with a strap on her shoe, then started to over-balance, tipping towards him! He put one hand out; she put out hers and gripped his forearm, looked up briefly and made a noise which might have been 'thanks', and went on working at the strap of her shoe.

He could not believe this was happening to him. He actually tingled where she touched him. His heart seemed to be beating in some huge dry place, an echoing cavern. His mouth had gone dry. She let go of his arm, lifting the shoe she had taken off, showing it to him and smiling. She laughed, 'Look,' she said. 'See? Wine.'

He gave a small dry laugh of his own – all he could manage – and looked at the small black shoe. The hour-glass shape of white leather inside it, raked from toes to low heel, was stained pale red, and still looked damp. She pushed it closer, laughing again and lowering her head as though shy, 'Here, smell, if you can stand it.' Her voice was deep, slightly hoarse.

He did his best to laugh, said heartily, nodding his head, bobbing it from side to side, achingly conscious of how stupid he must look, 'Yup, looks like wine to me.'

A terror seized him. He couldn't think what to say to her. He found himself looking round for Slater as she put one hand on the mantelpiece and slipped her shoe back on, fastening the strap again. A wine box appeared above the crowd of heads by the door. He watched it come closer, relieved.

'Ah . . . here comes your drink, I think,' he said, nodding to where Slater was pushing through the crowd, lowering the wine box and a glass he was carrying; smiling at them when he saw Sara and Graham.

'I've been proving to Graham I really did have some wine and it smashed,' Sara said as Slater, turning briefly to greet somebody he had just passed, came over to them. He set the wine box on the white mantelpiece, held the fresh glass beneath the little tap, and filled the container almost to the brim.

'Indeed. I trust he was suitably impressed.'

'Bowled over,' Graham said nervously, then wished he could gulp the words back somehow. Neither of the others seemed to think anything of it though. But he felt bowled over, and could hardly believe it wasn't obvious to every single person in the room. He took his plastic tumbler up again and sipped at the wine, watching Sara over the lip of the tumbler.

'Well then, Sara,' Slater said, leaning one-elbowed on the shoulder-high wood of the mantelpiece, smiling at the pale-skinned woman, 'how are we, then? How's the old home town?' Slater meant Shrewsbury, if Graham recalled correctly. Slater glanced at Graham, 'Sara and I were next-door neighbours for a while. I do believe our parents may even have intended us for each other at one time, without actually saying anything about it, of course.' Slater sighed, looked Sara up and down. Graham's heart, or his guts, something deep inside him, ached, as Slater went on, 'Not for me, of course, though looking at Sara I almost wish I was a lesbian, sometimes.'

Graham laughed, biting the sound off the instant he thought he was laughing too long. He hid behind the wine glass again, putting his lips to the liquid but not drinking despite his dry throat; he would get too drunk. He *couldn't* disgrace himself in front of this woman. Was she as old as he'd thought? Was Slater serious about them being some sort of childhood sweethearts, or even just close enough in age for their parents to think . . . ? He shook his head for a second, trying to clear it. The room seemed suddenly stuffy and close. He felt claustrophobic.

There was a scream from somewhere in the house; the chatter of voices quietened briefly and he could sense heads turning to the open door leading from the room.

'That, I suspect, is Hunter,' Slater said unconcernedly, waving one hand. 'His idea of a party trick is to tickle his wife until she wets her knickers. Sorry, Sara, I interrupted you . . .'

'Nothing,' she said, 'I was just going to say it's dull and horrible. I hate the winter there.'

'So you're here,' Slater said. The woman nodded.

'I'm . . . staying in Veronica's place for now, while she's in the States.' He heard something strange in her voice.

'Oh God, that awful place in Islington,' Slater looked sympathetic. 'You poor thing.'

'It's better than where I was,' she said quietly. She was mostly turned away from him; he could just see the curve of her cheek, the line of her nose, and as he watched she put her head down very slightly, and her voice altered again. Slater tut-tutted to himself, looking into his glass.

'Finally left him, then?' Slater said, and Graham felt his eyes widening, that pulling back of the skin towards the ears he thought he had seen frozen on her face. Left? Separated? He stared at her anxiously, then at Slater, and tried hard not to look as interested as he felt. She was looking down, into her glass. She hadn't drunk very much.

'Finally,' she said, bringing her head up, shaking her head not in negation but a sort of defiance, so that the tangled black hair bobbed once.

'And the other one?' Slater said. His voice was cold

now, expression deliberately blank. Something about his eyes was hooded, making his eyes, briefly, resemble hers. Graham felt himself leaning forward, wanting to catch her reply. Had she started talking? Both their voices were low; they didn't really mean to include him in the conversation, and it was noisy in the room; people laughed and shouted, the music next door had been turned up.

'I don't want to talk about it, okay, Richard?' she said, and to Graham her voice sounded hurt. She turned fractionally away from Slater and drank deeply from her glass. She looked at Graham, not smiling, then her lips trembled and a small smile did appear.

Park, you idiot, Graham told himself, you're looking at this woman as if she was ET. Get a grip of yourself. He smiled back. Slater giggled briefly, then said to Graham, 'Poor Sara married a cad who had the ill taste to become manager of a sewage works. As I've told her, now that she's left him and his personal life's in such a mess, perhaps he'll do what these managerial types usually do in such circumstances, and throw himself into his work.'

Graham started to smile, though he thought the joke itself might be in rather poor taste, but then he was aware of Sara turning quickly, putting her glass on the mantelpiece and looking straight at him, coming closer, her face set in strange hard lines, eyes bright, taking him by the elbow and turning her head as if to emphasise that she was talking to Graham, ignoring Slater, saying,

'You do dance, don't you?'

'Oopsie-doopsie, me and my big mouth,' Slater said quietly to himself as Sara took Graham's plastic tumbler and put it on the mantelpiece beside her own glass, then led him, stunned, unprotesting, through the crowd towards the room where the music was.

And so they danced. He couldn't remember a single record, track or tape played. Her body was warm through the layers of clothing they wore, when they danced slow dances. They talked, but he couldn't remember what about. They danced and danced. He was hot, sweating, his feet hurt after a while and his muscles ached, as though they were not dancing but running, pounding through a strange, noisy jostling forest of soft, moving trees in darkness; just the two of them.

She kept looking at him, and he kept trying to hide what he felt, but when they danced together, holding each other, he kept wanting to stop and just stand there, mouth hanging open; express through sheer immobility something he possessed no dynamic for. To touch her, hold her, smell her.

They went back to the other room eventually. Slater had gone, so had the wine box and Sara's glass. They shared Graham's glass, taking turns. He tried not to stare at her. Her skin was still white, though a sort of heat seemed to radiate from her now, something which he caught and felt, became infected by. The room seemed darker now, and smaller than it had. People moved and pushed and laughed and shouted; he was vaguely aware of them. Around her neck, the white-on-white semi-circle of scar tissue seemed to glow in the dim light, like something itself luminous.

'You dance well,' she said.

'I don't—' he began, cleared his throat, 'I don't usually dance all that much. I mean . . .' his voice trailed off. She smiled.

'You said you draw. You're at the School?'

'Yeah. Second year,' he said, then bit his lip. Was he trying to prove how old he was? People sometimes said he had a baby face. He'd been questioned about his age in pubs several times. What age was she? What age did she think he was?

'What sort of things do you draw?' she said. He shrugged, relaxing a little; he had dealt with this sort of question before.

'What they tell me to. They give us exercises. What I really—'

'Graham, who is this lovely young thing?'

Graham looked round in despair at the sound of Mr Hunter's voice. Their host was a huge, lugubrious man, who reminded Graham of Demis Roussos. He was wearing some sort of brown caftan. Graham closed his eyes. Mr Hunter was what he resembled: a refugee from the sixties. His fat hand squeezed Graham's shoulder. 'You are a dark horse, young man.' He swept forward towards Sara, almost hiding her from Graham. 'Graham's obviously so speechless with you he won't introduce you to me. I'm Marty Hunter—' (*Marty*? thought Graham) '– and I just wondered if you'd ever thought of doing any mod—'

At that point the lights went out, the music groaned in a deepening bassy slide, and people made appreciative animal noises.

'Oh *fucking* hell,' Graham heard Mr Hunter say, and then something huge squeezed past him in the darkness saying, 'that's Woodall; he always finds the mains switch at parties . . .'

Matches flared, lighters grazed sparks, just as, with a hiss, Sara came forward, hugged him. The lights flickered on before Graham could do more than put his arms round her. She pushed herself away again as soon as the lights came on, shook her head, looking down, her perfume still spiralling away between them. The music started again, people went 'Aww . . .'

'Sorry,' he heard her say, 'I'm silly. I get frightened at thunder . . . too.' She looked around, distracted, for the glass, but he was holding it, and handed it to her. 'Thanks,' she said, and drank.

'Don't be sorry,' he said, 'I quite enjoyed it.' She looked up briefly then, smiling uncertainly, as though she didn't believe him. He licked his lips, moved forward, put one hand out and touched hers where it gripped the glass. She kept looking at the empty glass, avoiding his face. 'Sara, I—'

'Can we . . .?' she began, then looked quickly at him, put the glass on the mantelpiece, shook her head, saying, 'I don't feel all that well . . .'

'What?' he said concernedly, taking her by one hand and a shoulder.

'I'm sorry, can I . . .' she motioned towards the door,

and he helped her through the packed people, using his elbow to get them out of the way. In the hall they found Mr Hunter again, holding a slack, bored-looking black cat. He frowned when he saw them.

'You look rather pale,' he said to Sara, then, to Graham, 'Your friend isn't going to throw up, is she?'

'No, I'm *not*,' Sara said loudly, raising her face. 'Don't mind me; I'll just go and lie down in the snow or something . . .' She started as though to make for the front door, but Mr Hunter held up a hand to stop her.

'Not at all. I do beg your pardon. I'll find you . . . here, come with me.' He put the cat on top of an old sofa which had been shoved against the hallway wall, and led Graham and Sara towards the stairs.

On the far side of Farringdon Road, Graham passed Easton Street, where another painter's or window-cleaner's cradle lay on the pavement, up-ended for some reason, neat coils of rope around it. Summer; the season for painting and scaffolding. Getting things done after the winter cover-up. He found himself smiling, recalling yet again that first meeting, that strange, almost hallucinogenic evening. He stepped past an old lady, standing still in the middle of the pavement, seemingly looking across the road at a man in elbow-crutches waiting to cross the street. Graham, almost automatically, tried to imagine drawing the scene.

'I saw Slater heading out the door with some rug-chested young Romeo,' Mr Hunter said as they got to the second-floor landing in the big house. 'I hope you weren't depending on him for a lift, were you?' he asked Graham. Graham shook his head. Slater didn't even drive, as far as Graham knew.

Mr Hunter unlocked a door and opened it, switching the room light on. 'This is our little girl's room; you lie down, young lady. And take good care of her, Graham; I'll send my wife up to make sure you're all right.' He smiled at Sara, then Graham, then closed the door behind them.

'Well,' Graham said awkwardly as Sara sat down on the small bed, 'that's us told.' He bit his lip, wondered what he was supposed to do now. Sara put her head in her hands. He stared at the sooty-looking ball of black chaos that was her hair, wanting her, terrified of her. She looked up at him. He said, 'Are you all right? What's wrong? I mean, do you . . . are you hurting?'

'I'll be okay,' she said. 'I'm sorry, Graham; you go back to the party if you want. I'll be fine.'

He felt himself tense. He went forward, sat on the end of the bed with her. 'I'll go if you want . . . but I don't mind just sitting. I don't want you . . . sitting here by yourself, all alone. Unless you want to be. I wouldn't enjoy myself anyway, I expect, I'd be thinking of you. I—'

He had been going to touch her shoulders with his arm, but she came towards him anyway, her head on his shoulders so that the perfume of her hair enveloped him, made his head feel light. She seemed to slump; it was not an embrace and her arms seemed heavy and slack. Her

79

hands stayed in her lap, limp as puppet limbs. He held her, felt her shiver. He swallowed hard, looked round the room, at Snoopy posters, posters of horses in sunlit meadows, posters of Adam Ant and Duran Duran. A small white dressing table in one corner looked like something from a doll's house, gleaming and bright with tidy arrangements of bottles and jars. She shook again in his arms, and he realised she might be crying. He lowered his head to her hair instinctively.

She brought her head up, and her eyes were dry. She put her hands on the bedspread, looked into his eyes, an anxious searching as her gaze shifted about his face, first focusing on his right eye, then his left, then slipping to his mouth. He felt inspected, plumbed, and like a moth in front of some anti-lighthouse, casting a shadow-beam, making him want to pull back, fly away from the intensity of those black, searching eyes.

'I'm sorry, Graham, I don't want to be a tease,' she said, lowering her head again, 'I just need somebody to hold right now, that's all. I'm going through . . . oh,' she shook her head, dismissing whatever she had been about to explain. He put his hand on hers.

'Hold me,' he told her. 'I know what you mean. I don't mind.'

Without looking at him, she slowly came closer again, then leant against him. Finally her arms went gently round his waist, and for a long time they sat there, while he listened to the sounds of the party, and felt – against his side, and within the perimeter his arm made around her – the gentle ebb and flow of her breath. Please, *please*, don't come now, Mrs Hunter. Not now, not in this perfect, fragile moment.

Steps thudded on the stairs, and his heart seemed to try to echo them, but the steps and some laughing voices went away. He held her, wrapped in her smell, warmed by her nearness. He felt drugged, by her perfume and her presence; he felt . . . like he had never felt in his life before.

This is absurd, he told himself. What is going on here? What is happening to me? Right now I feel more happy, more satisfied than in any post-coital daze. Those Somerset nights, in friends' cars, other people's houses, once in a moonlit field; my carefully scored and compared encounters to date; they all mean nothing. Only this matters.

God, you fool.

In a rambling old house in Gospel Oak, in London in January I lose my heart. What are the chances she'll ever love me? Christ, to be like this for ever, to live, to be together, to hold her like this in bed some night when she's afraid of the thunder, when I'm there to hold her, to be held by her.

She stirred against him, and he mistook it for something like the small movements of a child asleep, and smiled down at her through the slow current of perfume rising from her black, turmoiled hair; but she was awake and brought her head up, drawing away from him a little, looking at him, so that he had to hide his smile quickly, because it wasn't something he had meant her to see.

'What are you thinking?' she asked him. He took a deep breath. 'I was thinking,' he said slowly, conscious of her arms still round his waist (no; one hand went to her brow, smoothed her hair away from her eyes; there, though, it went back again, clasped lightly behind him!), 'about . . . whether you could tell from the wine on the inside of a shoe what type it was. The wine, I mean; the vineyard and vintage . . . um . . . whether it was south slope or the soil had been especially acidic that year.'

A broad smile, slackening her tensed-up, vulnerable face, filled the white space in the dark mass of hair. His heart seemed to leap inside him, at the sheer beauty of her now, and the realisation he had produced this change. He felt his mouth open involuntarily, and closed it again, speechless.

'Or you could have champagne-tasting competitions from ladies' slippers,' she said, laughing. He grinned, nodded. She sighed, her expression changed again, and she took her arms away from him, bent over as though hugging herself round the middle. 'I think I'd better go to the loo,' she said, then looked at him. 'Will you wait?'

'I'll wait,' he said, too solemnly, he thought. He smiled, touched her hand again, 'You sure you're okay?'

'Just nerves.' She shook her head, looking down at his hand. 'Thanks for . . . well, thanks. I'll be back.' She got up quickly, went to the door and out. He collapsed back on the bed, eyes wide and staring at the white ceiling.

All his life he had not believed anything could be like this. You stopped believing in Father Christmas, tooth fairies, paternal omniscience . . . and in the sort of over-the-top crazy heart-thudding happy-ever-after love they told you was the ideal. Life was sex, infidelity, divorces. Infatuation, yes, but love at first sight, smell, touch? For him? Where was that carefully nurtured fine cynicism now?

He lay on the bed like that, waiting for her. He got up after a while and paced round the high-ceilinged room, looking at the layered posters and the soft toys, the two old wardrobes, the small ring-tree on the window ledge, hung with little cheap, colourful rings. He touched the long, dark green curtains, looked out into the garden and over it at the house beyond, tall and dark. A dim sodium-yellow glow filled the sky; patchy snow blemished the garden. The door opened. He smiled and turned.

A tall, drunk-looking woman in a red jump-suit swayed in the doorway, holding on to the outside of the jamb. Her face was thin, hair yellow. 'You all right, dear?' she asked Graham, looking round the room. Graham made a small smile.

'I'm fine, Mrs Hunter. Mrs ffitch is ah . . . in the loo.'

'Oh,' the woman said. He didn't think she remembered him; he had seen her, he recalled, at the end-of-term dance. 'Right, then. Well . . . don't mess up the bed.' She withdrew, closing the door. Graham was left frowning at the door, wondering exactly what she meant. It opened again and Mrs Hunter re-appeared 'You haven't seen my husband, have you? I'm Mrs Hunter, Marty's wife.'

He shook his head. He felt unfairly urbane; almost contemptuous of the drunk woman. 'No, Mrs Hunter,' he said, 'not for a while.'

'Hmm,' she said, and was gone. He watched the door

for a bit, but nothing more happened. The party sounded loud behind it. He thought he could smell dope; grass or resin fumes. He went back to looking out the window, sometimes watching the reflection of the room in it. He looked at his watch, wondering how long she'd been away. It seemed like ages. Should he go and check? Would she want him to? What if something had happened; she'd fainted?

He didn't even know where the toilet was up here. He'd been once to the one on the ground floor, that was all. Should he go looking for her? It might look like nosiness, he might open the wrong door, embarrass people. He paced the room, then lay down for a while, hands clasped behind his head. He got up and went back to the window, willing the door's reflection to move.

It moved; he turned, just in time to see it start to close as a male face disappeared after a brief inspection. 'Oh, sorry,' a voice said. A girl giggled outside, steps sounded. He faced the window once more.

Finally, a sick feeling in his belly, as though something there was twisted, pulsing pain, he left the room. He found the toilet a floor down. He thought: I'll try the handle; the door will be open and the room will be empty. She's gone. I mean nothing to her.

He tested the handle. The door was locked.

It'll be a man's voice, he told himself. It was a woman's. 'Won't be long; sorry.'

'Sara?' he said, uncertain, his voice shaking. There was silence, and his eyes smarted. *It isn't her*. It wouldn't be her. It wouldn't be her at all.

'Graham? Look, I'm really sorry. I'll be out soon. God I'm sorry.'

'No, no,' he said, almost shouting; he had to lower his voice, 'That's okay. That's fine. I'll wait . . . in . . . the room, all right?'

'Yes. Yes please. Five minutes.'

She was there! He went bounding up the stairs, three or four at a time, praying to himself the room hadn't been taken over by some amorous couple while he'd been away, cursing himself for doubting her. Now she'd think he didn't trust her.

The room was empty, as he'd left it. He sat down on the bed, his hands in his lap, his heart thumping in his chest. He stared at the bottom of the door. I go into ecstasies because a woman is in the loo, he thought. This is enough to make me feel like I own the world. Can I tell anybody about this? Can I tell Slater? Can I tell mum? Did she and dad ever feel like this?

She came back. She looked whiter than ever. Her breath was ragged and faint, pulsing. She lay down on the bed, not speaking to him. She made him feel frightened, but as she lay down, eyes closed, on her side and facing him, something else in her, some frail, scavenging eroticism made him shake with desire. Oh my God, I feel like a rapist. She's *ill*.

'Are you—' he choked on the dry words, began again. 'Are you really poorly? Should we get an ambulance?'

'"Poorly",' she said, and smiled, her eyes still closed. 'That's a nice word.' She opened her eyes, looking at him; she blinked in the light. 'I'm fine, really. Really I am. Just nerves; I'm a weepy female and I should probably be on valium, but fuck it. I'm riding it out, you know? I've things to get over. Sorry to be a bother.'

'It's no bother,' he said, and was at last pleased with the way he had said something; warm, strong, not patronising, but caring. Did she hear it that way, though? She nodded at him, eyes closing. She sniffed at the top of her dress, over her breasts.

'I'm sorry,' she said suddenly, eyes open again. 'I stink of some horrible aftershave.' Graham realised that indeed there was a strong smell of cologne from her. She smiled wanly at him and shrugged. 'I threw up. This was all I could find to cover the smell. I've brushed my teeth too, but I still taste it . . . God, this is awful, Graham. I'm using you like a nursemaid. I didn't mean to.'

'Don't . . . worry about it,' he said weakly.

Her eyes closed again. 'You wouldn't get the wrong idea if I asked you to put that light out, would you?' she asked. 'My eyes hurt.'

'Sure,' he said softly, and went to the door.

With the light off, cold yellow bands of light spread from the window. She was a black pool of shadow on the bed, a space of darkness. He sat down by her, and she raised one of her arms; he sat down beside her, muscles trembling. Her arm pulled him gently down. Her face was opposite his; close, indistinct.

'This is terrible, Graham,' she said, almost too softly for him to catch. 'You've been lovely and I'm leading you on but I can't deliver at the moment. You'll hate me.'

'I—' he began, but gulped that precipitous, too

instinctive and glib statement back. Too soon. 'No,' he insisted, 'not at all.' He put one of his hands out and took both of hers in his. They were warm. 'Just this is . . .' he shook his head, not knowing if she could see, or maybe feel the bed bounce slightly, '. . . it's really nice,' he gave a tiny, self-depreciating laugh on the last word, acknowledging its inadequacy. She squeezed his hands.

'Thanks,' she whispered.

They lay like that for a long time. His thoughts were in a strangely distant turmoil, as though they were no more the workings of his own mind than the far-below hubbub of the party was his own voice. In the end he gave up trying to analyse his own feelings, or even totally understand them, and lay there relaxed, listening for the slow, regular breathing of sleep, and wasn't sure if he detected it or not. The door opened briefly at one point and a young man's voice said 'Shit,' but Graham didn't even turn to look; he knew it could be nothing which would disturb them.

He held her in his arms, still and warm, and after a while in that darkness he felt as though he held nothing at all; it was like when a limb, having been left in the same position for too long a time, somehow loses all reference to the body, and for those instants before some willed movement the very location and attitude of that arm or leg is quite unknown. He held her, but he felt nothing; she was there, and in his consciousness distinctly other and different, but she was also like some relaxed part of himself; a silent mix of identities cancelled out, like the pale skin, white scar, dark clothes and black hair being equated and combined, and the resulting coalescence being clear, invisible . . . nothing.

Eventually she stirred, kissed him quickly on the forehead, and levered herself up, sitting on the side of the bed. 'I feel better now,' she said. She turned to look at him in the darkness; he stayed looking at her. 'I'd better go home,' she continued. 'Could you ring for a taxi? Come; we'll go back down.'

'Yeah,' he smiled.

The light was very bright when he switched it back on. She yawned and scratched her head, messing her hair still further.

In the hallway he called for a cab for her, going to Islington.

'Where are you going?' she asked him. 'Can you come as far as Islington, do you want to take the cab after that?' The party was slightly quieter, but there were still plenty of people about. A man and woman in punk gear lay asleep in each other's arms on the couch in the hall. Graham shrugged.

'Islington's a bit closer, I think,' he said. Was she inviting him back? Probably not. She looked pained.

'I can't invite you in or anything, I'm sorry.' He hadn't thought so, but his insides still ached briefly.

'That's all right,' he said brightly. 'Yeah, Islington's a bit closer. I'll pay half.'

She didn't let him pay half; he didn't protest too much. They got to the place where she was staying, a quiet cul-de-sac. The taxi drove off; he couldn't afford taxis. She looked at a big BMW bike parked by the kerb, then up at a darkened row of tall houses. In the yellow light, her face was like a ghost's. 'I keep saying I'm sorry this evening,' she said, coming closer to him. He shrugged. Would they kiss? It seemed impossible. 'I wish I could invite you in.'

'Not to worry,' he said, grinning. His breath made a cloud between them.

'Thanks, Graham. For staying with me, I mean. I'm such a bore; do you forgive me? I'm not always like this.'

'Nothing to forgive. It's been great.' She laughed quietly when he said it. He shrugged again, smiling hopelessly. She came to him, put her gloved hand behind his neck.

'You're lovely,' she said, and brought her face to his, kissing him; putting her lips to his just like that, soft and warm and wet, better than any kiss, better than his first real kiss, making him dizzy with the feel of it. He hardly knew what he was doing. His mouth opened slightly, her tongue touched his upper lip once, then slipped away again; she kissed him quickly on the cheek and turned, walked to a doorway, fumbling for a key in a small purse she took from her old fur coat.

'Can I see you again?' he croaked.

'Of course,' she said, as though it was a silly question. The key slipped in, she opened the door. 'I can't remember the telephone number here yet; Slater's got it. Ciao.' She blew him a kiss; her last few words, with the door open, had been whispered. The door closed quietly. He watched a light go on above, go out again.

It took him five hours to walk back to Leyton, where

he had a bed-sit. It was cold, it rained once, lightly, then turned to sleet, but he didn't care. That kiss! That 'Of course'!

The walk had been an epic. Something he would never, ever forget. One day, or night, he would do that walk again, retrace his steps for the sake of nostalgia. One day, when they were together and he had a good career, when he had his own house and a car and didn't need to walk and could afford taxis if he wanted them; he'd take that same route just for old times' sake, try to recapture the uncertain ecstasies of that dark, early morning trek.

Nearly half a year later, in the summer heat, he could still recall the feeling of the cold air on his skin, the way his ears became numb with the freezing cold, the way he kept bursting out laughing, holding up his arms to the cloudy dark orange sky.

He could smile at it now. He'd had more time to think, to get used to this slightly absurd rapture. He could accept it now. He still couldn't entirely believe it, in the sense that he could not believe that it was happening to him, that he was so vulnerable to such a common, almost hackneyed feeling. But it was there; he could not – in any sense – deny it.

Graham passed an abandoned workshop on Rosebery Avenue; posters advertised bands and their singles and albums. The traffic roared and the sun beat, but he remembered January, and shivered with the memory of that long walk.

Half Moon Crescent, he had repeated and repeated to

himself as he'd walked that night. She lived in Half Moon Crescent (he had checked the number and the street before he'd started out on his trek, so that even if Slater had lost or forgotten her number, she would not be lost to him). It became like a chant, a mantra for him; Half Moon Crescent, Half-Moon-Crescent, Halfmooncrescent . . .

A chant.

A litany.

Clerk Starke

Unemployed!

He sat in a plastic chair in a Job Centre. The chairs were all the same in these places; in every Social Security office and Job Centre he'd ever been in. Not exactly the same as each other; he'd seen different types, but they were all the *same* types. He wondered if any of the chairs provided protection against microwaves.

A woman had been talking to him, but she had gone away. She didn't seem to be able to cope with him. Probably they hadn't expected this. They hadn't prepared properly.

He had decided not to go straight home, or to go to the pub yet. That was what they would expect him to do.

Just sacked, or rather resigned, with all that money; of course, the obvious thing to do would be go home to his room or to have a drink. They wouldn't expect him to go to a Job Centre and sign on. So when he had seen the sign ahead of him in the street, he'd walked right in and sat down and demanded to be attended to.

'Mr . . . ?' a man said to him. Light suit, short hair, spotty face, but looking in charge. He sat down opposite Grout and clasped his hands on the large white blotter which almost covered the top of the small desk.

'What?' Grout said suspiciously. He hadn't been listening.

'Your name is . . . ?' the young man said.

'Steven,' Grout said.

'Ah . . . that's your first name?'

Grout leaned forward, put one fist on the table and stared into the man's eyes, his own narrowed and glinting as he said, 'How *many* do you think I've *had*?'

The young man looked confused and concerned. Steven folded his arms and leant back, feeling triumphant. That had floored him! Steven put his safety helmet further back on his head. This was quite good really. He felt he had the upper hand for once, and they hadn't been able to set up the Microwave Gun yet, either; he felt cool and relaxed. Of the two of them the young Job Centre man looked the more hot and worried.

'Can we start again?' the young man said, taking out a pen and tapping the end of it on his lower teeth. He smiled impatiently.

'Oh, yes,' Steven said cunningly, 'I'm an expert at starting again. Let's.'

'Fine,' the young man said. He drew a breath.

'What's *your* name?' Grout said suddenly, leaning forward again.

The young man looked at him for a while. 'Starke,' he said.

'Are you staring, or . . .'

'Look, sir,' the young man called Starke said seriously, putting his pen down, 'I'm trying to do my job here; now . . . are we going to approach this in a sensible manner or not? Because if not, there are plenty of people—'

'And you look, clerk Starke,' Grout said, and tapped one finger on the small desk. Starke looked at the finger, so he withdrew it when he remembered how dirty his fingernails were. 'I'm unemployed, you know. *I* don't have some nice safe little civil service job with pensions and . . . and things. I'm a victim of the recession. You may think it's all a joke—'

'I assure you—'

'—but I know what's going on, and I know why I'm here and why you're here. Oh, yes. I'm not stupid. You can't pull the wool over my eyes like that. I know what the score is, like they say. I may be thirty-sev – thirty-eight, but I'm "switched on" all right, and I know everything isn't "hunky-dory" the way people think it is. You may think it's easy for you, and it might be, but I'm not so easily fooled, oh no.' He sat back again, nodding emphatically. He didn't always express himself perfectly, he would be the first to admit that, but it wasn't what you said, it was the way you said it. Somebody famous had said that.

'Well, sir, I'm not going to be able to help you unless you let me ask you some questions.'

'Well then,' said Grout, throwing his arms wide and opening his eyes wide, 'get on with it. On you go; I'm ready. Ask away.'

Starke sighed. 'Right,' he said. 'What's your name?'

'Grout,' Steven said.

'That's your surname?' Starke said.

Grout thought about this carefully. He always got confused with this. Which was surname and which was Christian name? It was like net and gross; he always got them mixed up. Why didn't people just say first and second? Just to confuse him, no doubt. There was a way of working it out though. If you were a 'Sir' then the name just after that was your first name, so that must be the surname . . . and Christian name was easy because Christ had been Jesus Christ, so obviously therefore the Christian name was the second name . . . and that was how you could tell.

That seemed logical, but now he thought about it he wasn't sure that that wasn't the way to remember the way it wasn't, not the way it was. He decided to play safe.

'My name is *Mister* Steven Grout.'

'Fine,' Starke said, writing, '"Grout" as in that stuff you put between tiles and bricks and things, right?' He looked up.

Steven's eyes narrowed. 'What are you trying to insinuate?'

'I'm . . . I'm not—'

'I will not be insinuated against,' Steven said, and tapped the front of the desk. 'What business is it of yours to make insinuations against me, I'd like to know, eh? Answer me that.'

'I—'

'No, you can't, can you? And I'll tell you why. Because I'm not here because I want to be, that's why. There. I'm not one of your scroungers. I've never taken the easy way out, I'll have you know. It hasn't always been easy but I've always kept my self-respect, and I haven't let anybody take that away. I'm my own man and that's very important in these times, even if you haven't had the problems I've had, and you haven't, because that's perfectly obvious, you're sitting there and asking me the questions. You've got to realise, clerk Starke—'

'I'm not—'

'—that we're on opposite sides of the desk, as it were.' He tapped the desk to show what he was talking about. 'This is a symbol, you know.' He sat back to let this sink in. Starke looked at the desk.

'It's a desk, Mr Grout.'

'It's a symbolic desk,' Grout said, jabbing his finger at it. 'It's a symbolic desk because we're sat on opposite sides of it, and that's the way things'll always be. Like that. You can't tell me any different. I know the score, like they say.'

'Mr Grout,' Starke sighed, laying the pen down again, 'I'm afraid this interview isn't really getting us very far. You talked to my colleague Ms Phillips when you first came in—'

'I didn't find out her name,' Grout waved one hand dismissively.

'Well you didn't get very far with her either, did you? And now—'

'I didn't get very far?' Grout said, '*I* didn't get very far? It's not my job to get very far; it's yours. You're supposed to get far with me. You're the people who get trained in this sort of thing, not me,' Steven said indignantly, and tapped the desk once more, for emphasis. 'How often do you think I do this, eh? Answer me that. Do you think I make a habit of this sort of thing, is that it? Are you making insinuations again?'

'I'm not trying to insinuate anything, Mr Grout,' Starke said as he sat back in his chair, resigned. He shook his head, 'I'm trying . . . I was trying to conduct an interview, and now I'm trying to explain to you that you're not making it at all easy. First you made my colleague distressed—'

'I could tell she didn't like me. She was contemptuous. I won't have that,' Grout explained. Starke shrugged.

'Whatever. Now you've made it impossible for me to carry out an interview despite the fact I've been extremely patient—'

'I'm not stopping you from carrying on your interview,' Grout said, shaking his head. 'I'm not. You ask your questions, I'll answer. On you go. Just ask what you want. I'm very cooperative. I'm just not prepared to be contemptuated against or be the object of insinuations, that's all.'

The young man sat looking at him for a moment, then

raised his eyebrows, sat forward and took up his pen once more. 'Very well. We'll try one more time. Your name is Mr Steven Grout—'

'Correct,' Steven nodded.

'You've just left your previous employment, is that right?'

'Yes.'

'And you wish to—'

'Not,' Steven said, sitting forward and tapping the desk as Mr Starke sat back, slumping down with a sigh in his seat and shaking his head, smiling slightly, 'because I wanted to, either. They were out to get me from the start. They wanted rid of me all the time. I was hounded out. They forced me to leave. But I left of my own free will. I wouldn't give them the satisfaction. I resigned. I have my pride, you know. They can't kick me around.'

'Ah,' Mr Starke said, sitting forward in his seat and looking more interested, 'you resigned?'

'I certainly did. I wasn't going to let them—'

'Well, you do realise, Mr Grout, that by resigning you have made yourself ineligible for Unemployment Benefit for a period of—'

'What?' Steven said, sitting forward. 'What's this? I did the only decent thing I could do. If you think I was going to stand there and—'

'I'm sorry, Mr Grout, but I thought I ought to mention it. You still have to register as unemployed, but for the first—'

'Oh no,' Steven said, 'I'm sorry, that's just not good enough. I've paid my stamps. I've paid as I've earned. I'm not a scrounger or one of these social misfits. I'm a working man. Not just now, perhaps, but I am, I *certainly* am. I just wasn't going to let them sack me. I was not,' he tapped the desk, 'going to give them the satisfaction, you see?'

'I appreciate that you would rather terminate your employment yourself, Mr Grout, but the rules are that if you do then you have to—'

'Well, that's just not good enough, I'm sorry,' Grout said. They'd found him. He was starting to heat up. His collar felt itchy and he could smell some strange tense body-smell coming from his armpits. Mr Starke was shaking his head.

'Nevertheless—'

'Don't you "nevertheless" me, young man,' Grout said, raising his voice. People were looking at him. The sunlit Job Centre was quite crowded, he saw now. The sun was slanting in through the windows and heating the place up. But there was ordinary heat and there was microwave heat. He knew the difference well by now. Ordinary heat didn't itch the way microwave heat did. Ordinary heat didn't come from inside the way microwave seemed to, affecting you all at once. He decided to try ignoring it, and said, 'Don't you "nevertheless" me, oh no. I'm not having it.'

Starke gave a small laugh. A laugh! Just like that! 'I'm sorry, Mr Grout, but what you're not having is Unemployment Benefit. You get Supplementary Benefit instead for the first six—'

'*You're* sorry?' Grout said. 'Well, you don't suit your sorrow like they say. I want to know why I'm being victimised against.'

'You're not being victimised, Mr Grout,' Starke said. 'The rules are that if you leave your employment voluntarily you have to wait six weeks before you can claim Unemployment Benefit. If you are eligible, which I imagine you will be, you may claim Supplementary Benefit during the interim.'

'And what about my dignity?' Steven said loudly. 'What about that, I ask you? Eh? Supplementary Benefit, indeed! I've paid my stamps. I've paid my taxes. This isn't good enough.'

'I appreciate your position, Mr Grout, but I'm afraid that is the way things are set up. You probably will be eligible for Supplementary Benefit; first you have to register—'

'Well, it's *not* good enough,' Grout said, sitting straight up in his chair and fixing Starke with one eye, trying to turn the tables again so that he would stop feeling uncomfortable and Starke would go back on the defensive. 'I'm being victimised against and that's all there is to it. As though I haven't got enough crisises to have to put up with. But this won't be the last straw; they won't get rid of me that easy. I'm just not—'

'Well, if you feel you've been unfairly dismissed,' Starke said, 'you can go to the—'

'Ha!' Grout said, 'I'm unfairly everything. Employed, unemployed, housed, treated; everything. But you won't catch me complaining. I've learned better. Doesn't get you anywhere. I'd rather keep my dignity.' He was trying to explain, but he got the impression he was losing out now. Clerk Starke had the upper hand. It was so unfair. Those devils! They hadn't said anything to him at the depot; they hadn't told him anything about not getting unemployment money. They'd let him resign, just when they'd been on the point of sacking him. Maybe just a few more seconds and they would have fired him and he wouldn't be in this position now. Just a few more seconds! The swines!

'Well,' Starke began, and started talking about what Steven should do about registering as unemployed.

Grout wasn't listening. He watched the young man's face, now set in the sort of bored, practised, professional expression Grout had seen a hundred times before.

He heard the words 'P45' in Starke's speech, and his heart sank. That was what he'd dropped, wasn't it? Or was it? Ashton had shouted something which sounded like that, when he was running away from the depot. Oh-oh. A new salvo of microwaves hit him; he felt a rush of uncomfortable warmth slide all over his body, and he felt his face going red. His skin prickled and itched. Damn! He'd felt so pleased, victorious even, after leaving the depot, that he'd quite forgotten about dropping the form. But of course; Dan Ashton had chased after him with it.

Or at least, that was what they wanted him to think, he suddenly realised. *He* didn't remember being given that form; they had probably not even given it to him in the first place. If it was all that important then they almost certainly hadn't. It was like when his Giro cheques from the unemployment people hadn't turned up the last time he'd been out of work; it was all done to wear him down. They could talk all they wanted about incorrectly filled-out forms, wrong addresses and the like; he knew what was really going on. They were slowly trying to destroy him.

They probably didn't have to refer back to their superiors – those mysterious Controllers, be they human or not – for instructions, they probably had their contingency plans all ready and prepared. So even when he'd got the drop on them they could still count on messing him around somehow. Devious bastards!

Sometimes, he had to admit, he wished they would just leave him alone and let him live out this petty, pointless, insignificant life in peace. It might not be all that much, but it might be almost bearable if they didn't keep tormenting him. It was an ignoble, unworthy thought, he knew, but he was – now, anyway – only human, and therefore prey to human weaknesses, whatever sort of superhuman he'd been during the War. It was a measure of how well they had done that he even considered such an awful thing. They had so oppressed his higher thoughts, his own belief in himself, that he would almost trade the chance to return to his previous, glorious existence for some peace.

But he wouldn't give in! They *wouldn't* win!

All the same, he wished he'd paid a little more attention to what had gone on when he'd been leaving the depot, so that he could have spotted when they carried out that trick with the form he was supposed to have dropped. He wondered if they had some other sort of beam they could train on him, which would make him forget things, or make his attention wander. The trouble was, he thought, as Starke talked on, that it would be very difficult to spot when they were using such a subtly fiendish device. This needed more thought. But what to do *now*?

There was always Revenge. He could get back at them in some commando-style way.

Ever since he had been at high school he'd found some enjoyment and relief by getting back at them in ways they obviously didn't expect. He'd thrown rocks at windows of offices and works they'd sacked him from, he'd defaced buildings, scratched officials' cars and mutilated bonnet mascots (though that was largely for his own safety) and he'd made bomb-hoax telephone calls. It wasn't much, and they would take it in their stride, no doubt, but apart from the fact these revenge raids certainly did upset his Tormentors a little, making life and their cruel purpose just that little bit less easy for them, the greatest effect was on him. He relieved his frustration, he vented his anger and hatred. If he'd tried to bottle it up he would have exploded one way or the other long before now. They'd have been able to certify him insane, or he'd have done something so terrible and criminal they could have put him in prison, where he'd be sodomised and knifed; quietly disposed of without any fuss because the rules were different in there. At least out here they had to play according to some sort of standard of fairness, even if it was a standard they could change as they went along according to how it suited them (like doubling the bus fares just after he'd found that job way out in Brentford), but in prison, even more so than in a mental hospital, there were no real limits to what they could do to him.

Starke was still talking, taking bits of paper out of the drawers in the desk and showing them to Grout, but Steven wasn't looking or listening. His eyes were glinting as he thought about the revenge he could have on the Islington people. He could go and dig up the roadworks during the night, and get some cement made up in a small container and cement up the holes in manhole covers you used to lift the things up by. If he filled those in they'd have a devil of a job lifting them! And he could attack the filled-in holes they'd done in Upper Street earlier this morning. He'd leave the ones he'd done, so they'd eat their words about his way being inferior; that would be satisfying!

He stood up and pulled his hard hat down firmly over his head. Starke was looking up at him; 'Mr Grout?'

'What?' Steven said, looking down and seeing the young man again. He frowned and shook his head. 'Never mind. Sort it out later. I've got things to do.' He turned and walked away. Starke was saying something behind him.

He'd show them. He'd get back at them. He bumped into some people waiting to join the queue for the seats in the reception area (ha ha; he'd got in just before the rush!), and went out through the doors back to the street and the bright sunlight.

He'd sort this unemployment stuff out later. He should have gone to his local Job Centre anyway, where they knew him. Never mind. He at least had some ideas for Revenge. He'd go back to his room and change and wash, then . . . then he'd have a drink and think further about how to get back at them all. Maybe he would even mount a punitive expedition tonight, striking while the iron was hot, and all that. It was risky, especially considering he'd been out just that previous evening, putting sugar in car and motorbike petrol tanks, but it might be a good idea anyway. He'd have to think about it.

He drew a deep breath and headed for the nearest parked car.

Open-Plan Go

It took Quiss longer than he had expected to get to the castle kitchens; they'd changed some of the corridors and stairways en route from the games room to the lower levels, and Quiss, taking what he thought was the usual way, had found himself making an unexpected left turn and coming to a windy, deserted, echoing chamber which looked out over the white landscape to the tall wooden towers of the slate mines. He had scratched his head and retraced his steps, then followed his nose to the chaotic kitchens of the Castle Doors.

'You,' he said, and grabbed one of the kitchen helpers who was passing by carrying a heavy bucket full of some steaming liquid. The tiny scullion squealed and the bucket clattered to the floor, staying upright but letting some of its glutinous contents slop over the side. Quiss heaved the small attendant up by the scruff of its neck until its face was level with his. Its mask-face stared back at him with empty eyes. The green brim round its stained, spotted hood was like a giant washer, or a ring round a rather grubby planet.

'Put me down!' It yelped and struggled, the green cord round its waist waggling to and fro. 'Help! Help!'

Quiss shook it. 'Shut up you . . . spirochaete,' he said. 'Tell me where I can find the seneschal in all this racket.' He jerked the attendant's whole body and his own head to indicate the kitchen around them.

Quiss was standing at the foot of a flight of steps, on the outer edge of the pandemonium that was the castle's kitchens. The kitchens were buried deep in the structure, far from any outside wall. They were huge; there was a high ceiling, vaulted with cut slate on iron pillars, and standing where Quiss was, all the walls save for that immediately behind him were invisible, concealed by the rising steams, smokes and vapours from hundreds of pots, pans, vats, stoves, kettles, skillets, grills, tubs and cauldrons.

Light came from prisms hung in the roof; great cut slabs of crystal reflected light from the outside walls through long, empty light corridors and then down into the tumultuous kitchens. Also strewn across the complicated ceiling with the prism ports, obscuring whole sections of the barrelled structure, fume ducts writhed like immense square-flanked metal snakes, their grilled, barred mouths sucking the kitchens' vapours away to be vented high in some converted turret. The seneschal had told Quiss that the air circulation system was powered by one of the lowest ranks of the castle's diminutive attendants; they walked round inside treadmills linked to big watermill-like fans. Quiss felt his eyes start to smart in the fume-laden atmosphere, and as he peered through the grey, yellow and brown clouds of rising steam and smoke, thought of suggesting to the seneschal – if he ever found him – that he somehow persuade the scullions powering these airwheels that they should run rather than walk. It was, also, rather warm. Quiss could feel himself starting to sweat already, despite having left most of his furs lying at the top of the steps he had just descended.

'I don't know the way! I've never heard of him!' the squirming attendant said. Its little green-booted feet made running motions, though they were about a metre off the kitchens' slate-tiled floor.

'What?' Quiss roared, spraying spittle into the scullion's mask-face. He shook the thing roughly. 'What, you excretory wretch?'

'I don't know the way to the seneschal's office! I've never even heard of him!'

'Then how,' Quiss said, bringing the blank, sorrowful face closer to his own, 'do you know he has an office?'

'I don't!' came the yelped reply. 'You told me!'

'No, I didn't.'

'Yes, you did!'

'No,' Quiss said, shaking the attendant roughly so that

the crownless brim round its cowl fell off, 'I,' he shook it again, sending the thing's hood flying off its head and revealing the smooth continuation of the mask over the creature's skull, so that its little arms waggled, trying to put the hood back on again as Quiss finished, *'didn't.'*

'Are you sure?' the scullion said groggily.

'Positive.'

'Oh, heck.'

'So where is he?'

'I can't tell you; it isn't allowed. I – oh! Don't shake me again, please!'

'Then tell me where I can find the seneschal.'

'Waaah!' the small attendant said.

'You scrofulous tapeworm!' Quiss bellowed; he turned the attendant upside down and plonked its head into the bucket it had been carrying. The steamy yellow gruel in the bucket splashed out on to the kitchen floor. He let the minion struggle and kick for a little while, then hoisted it back out, shook it, and turned it the right way up again. His hands were getting messy; he wiped them on the creature's cloak.

'Now then,' Quiss said.

'That was *horrible*!' the attendant wailed.

'I'll do it again and leave you there unless you tell me where the seneschal is.'

'The who? No! Don't! I—'

'Right!' Quiss said, and dumped the scullion's head back into the now half-full bucket. He dragged it back out. The small creature's head lolled slightly on its shoulders and its arms flopped by its side.

'Tell you what,' it said, breathing with some difficulty, 'Let's both find somebody we can ask—'

'No!' Quiss shouted. He held the weakly struggling thing by one leg this time. He considered: surely things weren't so utterly disorganised in the kitchens that the scullions no longer knew who was in charge of them, or where his office was? Had things come to such a pass? It was a bad show, Quiss thought, shaking his head. The attendant had stopped struggling. He looked down, remembered what he was doing, said 'Oh,' and yanked the limp scullion out, dripping gruel. He shook it for a while until it gurgled and moved its head weakly. 'Are you willing to talk yet?'

'Oh, shit, all right,' the attendant said weakly.

'Good.' Quiss walked over to a large range of working surfaces, hotplates, sinks and racks; he sat the scullion down on a flat surface, only for steam to issue suddenly from its rear; it squawked and jumped up. Quiss apologised for setting it down on a hotplate, put it on a draining board instead, and splashed some water over its mask-face.

'It's like this, you see,' the scullion said, wiping its mask. 'We've started this new regime to make things more interesting down here. When people ask us a question some of us always tell the truth and some of us always tell the opposite. Some of us give correct answers and some of us give incorrect answers, but we're always consistent, you see?'

'No I don't see,' Quiss said, looking into the face mask. Sitting on the tall range, its small legs sticking out over the bright brass rail which acted both as a safety barrier round the hotplates and as a place to hang grubby kitchen towels, the small attendant's face was almost at the same level as the human's. Quiss waited for the scullion to draw breath, and looked round the kitchens again as it did so.

There were very few attendants visible. He was sure there had been more when he first arrived; they had been scuttling about all over the place, carrying implements, standing on stools stirring steaming mixtures, chopping things and throwing bits and pieces into cauldrons. Some of them had been mopping the floor; some washing plates and cups; some just running, not carrying anything, but speedy and purposeful all the same.

Now he could see only a few shadowy figures half-glimpsed through the mists of the cooking fumes. He wrinkled his nose at the smells, thinking that the cowardly little wretches were trying to keep out of his way. He hoped their cooking burned. The scullion on the draining board started talking again.

'Well, it means that you've got to approach the problem in a logical manner, you understand? It's another sort of game. You have to work out the right questions to find out what you want to know, see?'

'Oh,' Quiss said sweetly, smiling pleasantly, 'yes, I see.'

'You do?' the scullion said brightly, sitting up. 'Oh, good.'

Quiss picked up the small attendant by the front of its cloak and brought its blank face up to his own, scraping the creature's green boots over the surface of the draining board with a rattling noise.

111

'You tell me how to get to the seneschal's office,' Quiss said evenly, 'or I shall boil you alive, understand?'

'Strictly speaking, that isn't a well-formed question,' the scullion croaked, choking as Quiss's fist tightened the material round its throat.

'Strictly speaking, you're going to be *dead* very soon unless you give me the right instructions.' Quiss grabbed the scullion from the range, tucked it under his arm, and walked away from the entrance, straight ahead towards the centre of the kitchen.

The noises of the place went on around him, muffled only slightly by the mists and vapours; he could hear shouted instructions and curses, the clanking of ladles and giant spatulas, the hiss and splutter of frying, the sloshing of water and soups, the grating of giant pans being moved, the machine-gun chatter of chopping knives. Overhead, apart from the whispering air ducts, he heard a creaking noise, interspersed with a light clinking and clanking. Quiss looked up to see an overhead cable-car system of what looked like lengths of knotted string and bits of chain, running through little metal wheels set in the ceiling and carrying, on small hooks, cups and mugs and plates (so *that* was why they had a hole at the edge), forks and spoons and knives of every description. They sailed overhead and swayed with the slightly erratic action of the cableway holding them, bumping into each other now and again and so producing the clinking noise just audible over the din.

Quiss heard rapid footsteps approaching through the racket, and ahead of him he saw two small scullions running towards him out of the mist. The hindmost attendant was holding what looked like a large loaf of bread, and was using it to hit the minion in front, which was running almost doubled up, its little gloved hands held over its head, where the pursuing scullion was raining blows with the loaf.

Three metres in front of Quiss they saw the tall human and skidded to a stop, in unison. They looked intently at him, then at each other, then executed a smart about-face; the scullion with the loaf threw it at the other, who caught it and started to hit the other minion over the head with it as they ran back into the mist the way they had come, their figures – one crouched almost double, one striking out with the loaf of bread – and their running footsteps quickly absorbed by the rolling mists.

Quiss shook his head and marched on, the scullion tucked under his arm, not struggling. He caught sight of a few others, but they turned tail and vanished when they saw him through the mist. He called out to them, but they didn't come back. There must, he thought, be thousands of these small attendants, waiters, scullions, masons, miners, mechanics and general helpers and dogsbodies in the place and around it; he knew something about provisioning and logistics, and the castle's kitchens could have provided ten-course meals every few hours for an army of tens of thousands. It all seemed too large, too over-provided-for to feed them and the stunted attendants, even if there were a few more of them than they'd seen until now (and they were always complaining about being short-staffed, anyway).

Even the scale looked wrong. The kitchens appeared to have been designed for human use, judging from the height of the working surfaces and the sheer size of the ladles, pots and pans and other pieces of equipment. Hence the scullions having to use small stools to stand on when they wanted to do anything like wash up dishes, stir soups or work controls. They seemed to have their own stools, Quiss had observed; they carried them on their backs as they made their way from one range to another, and Quiss had seen quite violent fights and rows breaking out over the disputed ownership of one of the small three-legged platforms.

They came to a sort of crossroads in the kitchens. They were well out of sight of the broad flight of steps Quiss had entered the kitchens from, at a point where he could continue ahead into the mist, or turn either right or left, past huge fat stoves holding great rotund cauldrons of some bubbling, frothing liquid. The soot-black metal of the stoves was carved with grotesque faces from which a dark heat beat out at Quiss. A yellow-red light jetted out from the eye-holes of the distorted faces, like a bright beam shining through a keyhole in a door. Leaking wisps of smoke wormed their way out from the sides of the stoves' doors, adding a pungent aroma of something like burning coal to the medley of smells produced by the man-high vats bubbling away on top of the bulging, flattened-looking stoves.

Quiss looked around. He could see a few of the other scullions nearby, standing on their stools stirring pots, wiping stoves, polishing stove-fronts. They were all studiously avoiding meeting his gaze, though he thought they were watching him out of the sides of their eyes. He brought the minion he had under his arm out, lifted it up to look into its blank face. 'Which way?' he asked it. It looked about, pointed left.

'That way.'

He stuffed it back under his arm, marched off to the left past the heavy black stoves, through their radiated heat. The scullions ahead of him got down off their stools and waddled away, disappearing in the kitchens' foggy wastes. 'Are you sure you wouldn't like to ask more complicated questions?' the small attendant said, muffledly, from his side. He ignored it. 'I mean, "Which way?" is a bit basic, wouldn't you agree?'

'Now which way?' He brought it up, let it look about as they came to another junction, the cauldrons at their backs, great stone tubs set in the floor and covered with some sort of green scum on either side. The attendant shrugged.

'Left.'

Quiss went that way. The attendant under his arm said, 'That wasn't exactly what I meant; just adding a "now" on to the start doesn't really make much difference. With respect I don't think you've got the idea of the sort of questions you have to ask. It's quite easy once you get the hang of it. Really, I'm surprised you haven't encountered puzzles like this before. Think carefully.'

'Which way here?'

'That way.' The scullion sighed and pointed with its arm. It said, 'I'm probably saying more than I should, but as I'm giving you the information without you asking for it, I don't think it's covered by the rules. All I'd say is that what you have to do is to ask questions which although are apparently about what you want to do . . . where you want to get to, should really be telling you about the person you're—'

'Where now?'

'Left again. Do you see what I mean? What you're really finding out is the truth-telling status of the person you're getting the information from, so that—' Quiss half listened to all this as he watched, suspiciously, the same cableway of cutlery and cups squeak and rattle its way overhead, '– you can find out two things . . . no, wait a minute, come to think of it you're finding . . . hmm. Let me think about this.'

Quiss looked at the black stoves, the strange faces cast in hot metal, the giant vats of liquid. He made a rising, growling noise at the back of his throat and brought the scullion out from under his arm, looking into its mask-face again. 'We're back where we started, you lice-brained dwarf!'

'Well, I did warn you.'

'Cretin!' Quiss screamed into its face. He saw a cauldron to one side with its lid hanging above it, suspended on a pulley. He hoisted the scullion up and threw the creature into the huge vat. The scullion's whines and yelps disappeared in a series of gruelly splashes which spurted from the top of the big tub. Quiss slapped his hands together and turned. Almost immediately he was surrounded by what seemed like hundreds of the small attendants. They flowed from every avenue of the kitchen, a waist-high tide of grubby, grey-cowled figures rushing in towards him, their coloured boots, sashes and hat-brims swirling out of the mist. Quiss experienced the tiniest moment of fear, then savage anger, and was about to go down fighting – take as many of the little bastards with him as he could – when he realised that they were bowing and wringing their hands and making apologetic noises, not howling angry ones. He relaxed.

'I tell the truth! I tell the truth, honest I do!' one was shouting, and it and a few others tugged at the lower edges of the few furs he still had on and pulling on his under-breeches where they appeared out of the top of his boots. He let them lead him away, straight ahead between the rows of cauldrons. Other scullions were running in with ladders and lengths of rope, climbing up on to the big stove and scrambling up to the messy lip of the vat in which, judging by the amount of splashing and screaming, the small attendant still survived.

Quiss was led by the dwarfish scullions, through the banked ranges, past gleaming tubs, boiling vats, open fires and grills, past rows of massive, wing-nutted pressure cookers guarded by blast screens, under huge n-shaped pipes, bubbling and gurgling and leaking steam, and over the dainty, counter-sunk tracks of a narrow-gauge railway until eventually he saw a wall ahead, and was led up a rickety wooden staircase to a narrow gantry, then stopped at a small wooden door set into the wall. One of the attendants rapped on the door, then they all scampered off, a display of multi-coloured boots flashing along the wooden gantry until they vanished into the mist. The door was thrown open. The castle seneschal glared out at Quiss.

He was a tall, thin man of indeterminate age, with hairless grey skin and dressed in a long black robe without ornament save for a small silver fork with twisted tines which hung on a piece of string round his neck, and rested on the black breast of the robe. The seneschal's eyes were long, seemingly stretched out at either side as though the eyeballs within were the size of clenched fists. His right eye had two pupils in it, side by side in the grey whites. '*Now* what?' he barked when he saw Quiss standing there.

'Guess,' Quiss said, putting his hands on his hips and leaning forward, glaring back at the seneschal, who stood blocking the doorway into his office. 'There still isn't any heat up there; we're freezing to death and we can't see to play this absurd game. If you can't get more heat up there, let us move the games room down a few floors.'

'Not possible. The boilers are being repaired. Full power soon. Be patient.'

'It's difficult to be patient when you're dying of hypothermia.'

'The engineers are working as fast as they can.'

'So they can reheat our corpses?'

'I'll order more furs.'

'We can hardly walk for the weight of the ones we've got; what good will those do? Haven't you got any thermal underwear, or even *heaters*? Couldn't you build a fireplace? We could burn books. There are plenty up there.'

'Shouldn't do that,' the seneschal said, shaking his head. 'Aren't two the same. All unique. Don't have two copies of any of 'em.'

'Well they still burn – they would still burn well.' Quiss had to be careful. He'd already burned quite a few wall-fuls, and had come down, under protest, as much to keep Ajayi happy as anything else. She had complained about the waste, and said they shouldn't have to burn books to keep warm; it offended her. Besides, she had said, perhaps they would take more time repairing the heating system if they knew the two of them were able to keep warm without it. It was a bad precedent to set. He had grumbled but agreed. The seneschal said,

'Shouldn't be too long. I'll have some hot bricks sent up.'

'What?'

'Big hot bricks; glow red hot in the stoves; I'll have some sent up every mealtime; should last until next one; you can warm hands on them. Surprising amount of heat thrown out. When they've cooled down a bit you can put them in your bed, warm it up nice. You'll be as warm as toast.'

'*Hot bricks?* Is that all you can offer? Exactly how long until the boilers are fixed?'

The seneschal shrugged, studied the carving on the edge of the door he was holding, then said, 'Not long. You'd best get back to your game now.' The seneschal came out of his room, shutting the door quickly and taking Quiss by the upper arm. He led him back along the wooden gantry to the steps. 'I'll show you out.'

119

'Good,' Quiss said, 'there's a few questions I want answered. First of all, where does all this food go? You must make about a hundred times more than you need. What do you do with it?'

'Recycled,' the seneschal said as they came to the steps and went down them.

'Why bother making it all, then?'

'Never know who might drop in,' the seneschal said. Quiss looked at him to see if he was serious. One of the seneschal's two right pupils seemed to be looking at him. 'Keeps them in practice, anyway,' he continued, suddenly grinning at the tall old man as they walked between the levels of stoves and cookers and fires. Scullions ran about the place, carrying brooms and buckets and baskets full of hidden ingredients. They were all very careful, no matter how fast they were going and how urgent their task seemed to be, to avoid getting under the feet of Quiss or the seneschal. 'Yes. Keeps them occupied. Out of mischief,' the grey-skinned man said.

Quiss hmm'd to himself. Well, he could understand that, but he still thought it was a wasteful way of keeping the lower ranks occupied, and it didn't square at all with the continual excuses the seneschal and his minions kept making about being under-staffed. He would let it pass for now. 'Where does it come from? I've yet to see anything except weeds grow in this place.'

The seneschal shrugged. 'Where did *you* come from?' he said darkly. Quiss narrowed his eyes at the pupil which seemed to be looking at him, indeed out of the corner of its eye. He thought the better of pressing on that one too.

They came to the place where Quiss had seen the inset tracks of the narrow-gauge railway. A small train, hauled by a tiny steam engine and comprising double-bogied cars carrying three sealed, hissing cauldrons each, trundled slowly by, wheels screeching and clattering over a set of points. Quiss and the seneschal stopped, watching the train pass in front of them, disappearing into the steam and smoke of the kitchens with a cacophony of rattles, hisses and clanks, and a single, strangled whistle-blast. Then they walked on, Quiss swallowing a question concerning the train's destination.

There was a muffled explosion somewhere on their right, and a thick orange glow spread through the mist, like a setting sun. There was a clattering noise and some howls. The orange glow to their right faded but did not disappear. The seneschal glanced at it briefly but did not appear excessively worried, even when – after a few moments – the scullions running past and round them were all carrying pails of water and sand, fire blankets, cutting gear and stretchers.

'That's another thing,' Quiss said as they came closer to where he had dumped the mendacious scullion in the cauldron. 'With all this equipment for moving things about the place,' he gestured up towards the moving line of clinking cutlery above their heads, looping under the assorted ducting and swivelled prisms of the kitchens' ceiling, 'not to mention the clock mechanism and transmission set-up and the complicated plumbing for the floors and ceilings . . .'

'Yes?' said the seneschal.

121

Quiss scowled and said, 'Why can't you get the food to us while it's still hot?'

They were passing the vat Quiss had thrown the small attendant into. The scullion appeared to have survived the ordeal and was sitting, quivering and bedraggled, being wiped down by some of its colleagues. An under-cook was supervising the cleaning of the stove around the cauldron and the preparation of fresh ingredients to replace those lost. The seneschal stopped, looking at the work being done with a critical eye. The scullions worked even faster. The one Quiss had dumped in the gruel saw the huge fur-clad figure of the human and started shaking so hard that little flecks of soupy stuff flew off it, like water from a dog.

'Well,' the seneschal said, 'it's a long way from here to there.'

'So construct a dumb-waiter.'

'That would be . . .' the seneschal paused, watching one of the apprentice chefs dipping a long ladle into the cauldron the unfortunate attendant had just vacated. The apprentice put the ladle to its mouth, then nodded appreciatively and started back down the ladder as the seneschal continued, '. . . going against tradition. It is a great honour for our waiters to take our guests their meals. I certainly could not deprive them of that. A dumb-waiter would be . . .' the apprentice chef with the ladle was talking to the under-cook now, who also tasted the ladle's contents and nodded, while the seneschal said, '. . . impersonal.'

'Who cares if it's impersonal? These aren't necessarily the sort of . . . *persons* I want to have anything to do with anyway,' Quiss said, indicating the various attendants, waiters and scullions around them as the under-cook respectfully approached the seneschal, bowing to him. The seneschal stooped slightly as the under-cook borrowed a stool and stood on it to whisper something into his master's ear. The seneschal looked briefly at the quivering attendant being looked after by the others, then he shrugged and said something to the under-cook, who quickly got back down off the stool and turned to the others.

The seneschal looked at Quiss and said, 'Unfortunately there are not only your feelings to be taken into account. I have the welfare of my staff to think of. Such is life. I must go now.' He turned and left, ignoring the shouts and screams of the small wet attendant as – after the under-cook had gathered the other scullions round, pointed to the cauldron, the ladle and its own belly before nodding at the wet attendant – the kicking, howling creature was grabbed by the same scullions who had recently been comforting it, hoisted up the ladder still resting against the side of the great vat, and thrown back in. The lid clanged down, rattling on its pulleys.

Quiss stamped his foot in frustration, then marched back up the steps to retrieve the rest of his furs and make his way back to the castle's upper reaches.

Open-Plan Go had turned out to be a game of placing black and white stones on a grid to claim territory on an infinite board. It had taken him and the woman two hundred days – as they measured them – to work out and play the game. Again, they were nearly finished now, and here he was yet again, trying to get the heating improved. Since their last game, the heat and light had deteriorated.

'And now I suppose it'll be my fault the heating hasn't got better immediately,' he muttered to himself as he walked along the narrow passageway. She would blame him. Well, let her; he wasn't bothered. Just so long as they could finish this stupid game and get on to *his* answer. She might be better at thinking up things as stupid as their games (infinite pieces which were only infinite in one direction, *from a point*; you could hold one end but it was still infinite! Insane!), but he was certain he had the right answer, and a more direct and obvious one than hers had been. He should never have let her talk him into letting her give hers first when they had been deciding how to handle this whole situation. Her and her smooth-talking, 'logical' arguments! What a fool he'd been!

'We'll get it right now though,' he said to himself, as he ascended through the castle's twisted interior, and the light faded and the cold grew more sharp, and he gathered his furs more closely around him. 'Yes, we'll – *I'll* – get it right this time. Definitely.'

Muttering and talking to himself, the old, massive, motleyhaired man shuffled through the darkening levels of the castle, wrapped in his furs and hopes and fears.

Quiss's solution to the problem, his answer to the riddle 'What happens when an unstoppable force meets an immovable object?' was. 'The immovable object loses; force always wins!'

(The red crow, sitting on the balustrade of the balcony, had cackled with laughter. Ajayi had sighed.)

The attendant came back after a few minutes, its little red boots ruffling the hem of its robe. 'Much as I dislike being the bearer of bad news . . .' it began.

THREE

Amwell Street

A succession of heavy trucks rumbled down Amwell Street as Graham turned on to it from Rosebery Avenue; they were big grey lorries, stone or chippings carriers with great corrugated sides and a plume of dust trailing after them in the near-still air. Graham was heading slightly uphill now, and slowed his pace accordingly. He listened to the traffic, felt the warm air slip by, moved his portfolio from one hand to the other, and thought of her.

He hadn't been able to see Slater for two days after the party, and that time had passed in a daze for him. On the Monday, though, Slater had been in the small steamy café and sandwich bar on Red Lion Street which he usually spent most of his term days in, and Graham had supplied him with cups of tea and expensive rounds of smoked salmon on granary bread while Slater slowly, teasingly, told him about Sara.

Yes, they had been neighbours in Shrewsbury, but of course they had only seen each other during the school holidays, and of course they hadn't made friends over some grotty little terrace-house garden fence; he'd first noticed her from the tree house in his parents' garden while she was learning to ride her new pony in her parents' ten acres of mature woodland and well-kept pasture.

'A tree house?' Graham teased back. 'Wasn't that a bit butch?' Slater replied tartly: 'I was being Jane, sweetie, not Tarzan.'

Sara's best years, Slater continued, had been just after leaving school. She had been a scamp in those days, he said, sighing with exaggerated wistfulness. She drank Guinness, smoked Gauloises and would eat anything as long as it was loaded with garlic. Odour-free she wasn't. She carried a large handbag whenever she went out. It contained potatoes to stuff up the exhaust pipes of expensive cars, and a very large sharp knife for tearing holes in the hoods of convertibles. If it could be arranged, she threw up into the cars through the holes so created.

She got drunk a lot and once did a strip on top of the piano in a local pub. (Graham asked Sara about this, on one of their canal walks. She smiled, looked down at her feet as she walked, finally admitted, a little ashamedly, that it was all true; 'I was wild,' she agreed in her slow,

low voice, nodding. Graham felt a sort of ache then, as he had when Slater first told him; he wanted to have known her then, to have been a part of her life during that time. He was jealous, he realised, of time itself.)

She was three years older than Slater; twenty-three now. She had been married for the last two years, to a man who really was a sewage plant manager (Slater was quite hurt that Graham thought he'd invented this detail for the sake of a joke). She had married against the wishes of her parents; they hadn't talked since the marriage. She didn't get on well with them anyway; probably she married as much to get at them as anything else. It was a pity, because her parents weren't bad sorts; like his own, they just believed everything they read in the *Daily Telegraph*.

Sara had only one real skill, or talent. Not having done very well at school (not even allowed to sit the Oxbridge exams), she had nevertheless been diligent about her piano lessons, and was in fact quite good on the instrument. The horrible hubby had not encouraged this, however, and indeed had sold her piano one weekend when she was away staying with friends. That hadn't been The Last Straw; far from it. Selling the piano was only a few months into the marriage. She ought to have got out then, but she, the stubborn one, persisted.

Hubby wasn't happy when no kiddies appeared; blamed her. Sara had tried to be the good wife but failed; the other wifies she was supposed to socialise with to further hubby's career were dreadful, brainless bores. Social ostracism followed outbursts of silliness, hubby drank a lot, didn't hit her often but did bad-mouth her excessively, and took up fishing; went away for weekends with male friends she'd never heard of. Claimed to be tackling rivers but kept bringing home filleted sea fish on the Sunday night, and was always suspiciously careful to empty his pockets when he gave her his clothes to wash. She began to Suspect.

She had her own weekends, here in London, staying with Veronica, whose flat she was now looking after while its owner worked a year's exchange course at UCLA. On one of those weekends she had met Stock, a photographer who did a lot of work for one of the newspaper colour supplements, though always under assumed names, for tax purposes. Slater had seen him on his BMW bike, or just geting off it. Never seen him without his crash helmet on; could be an albino or a Rastafarian for all he knew. Looked a bit like Darth Vader without the cloak. Jealous, moody type, apparently; married too but separated. No idea why he appealed to the lovely Sara.

Anyway, he thought they would be drifting apart a bit now, perversely but predictably because they were seeing more of each other, not just weekends; Stock stayed the night at the horrible little place in Islington quite often, but Slater thought Sara might be getting bored with the black-leather macho man.

The thing round her neck? Scar tissue all right; a birthmark she'd had removed in early teens in case it turned malignant. Yes, he found it perversely beautiful too. 'La Cicatrice' had been his pet name for her.

Finally Slater divulged the flat's telephone number, and

Graham noted the seven numbers down carefully, double-checking them and ignoring Slater's snide remarks about quirky Sara with her terrible taste in men, and the unfaithful, untrustworthy nature of women in general. He'd offered to swap stories about what had happened once they had each paired off at the party, but Graham wasn't going to tell, and told Slater so as he carefully wrote her name by the side of the numbers: *Sarah Fitch*. Slater laughed, pointing and guffawing at what Graham had written. 'Not one big 'f'; two little ones. Like British industry, our Sara's undercapitalised. And no 'h' on the end of Sara,' he said.

Graham called her from the School that day, found her in. She said she was delighted to hear from him; he thrilled at the sound of her voice. She was free the following Thursday evening. She'd meet him in a pub called the Camden Head, at nine. Looking forward to it.

He whooped for joy as he left the phone cubicle.

She was late, as she always was, and they only had about an hour and a half to talk before she had to go, and he was nervous and she looked tired though still beautiful in bright red cords, Arran jumper and tattily magnificent fur coat. 'I think I might be falling for you, you know,' he said as they were drinking up at eleven.

She smiled at him, shook her head, changed the subject, seemed distracted, looking about as though for somebody she expected to see. He wished he'd kept quiet.

She walked with him to the bus-stop, would not let him walk her back to the flat, said not to follow her; she'd watch, be angry. She kissed him again, quickly, daintily.

'Sorry I haven't been great company. Call me soon; I'll be on time next time.'

Graham smiled to himself at the thought of that. Her sense of time didn't seem to be like everybody's else's. She kept her own time; some inner, erratic clock regulated her. Like some conventional caricature of female punctuality, she always arrived late. But she usually did turn up. Almost always. They met on weekdays, not weekends at first, in pubs never very far away from the flat. Small talk mostly; a slow process of discovery. He wanted to find out all she'd done and been, everything she thought, but she was reticent. She preferred to talk about films and books and records, and though she seemed interested in him, asking him about his life, he felt cheated as well as flattered. He loved her, but his love, the love he wanted to be *their* love seemed stalled, stuck at some early stage, as though hibernating until the winter had passed.

She wouldn't talk about Stock at all.

Graham walked up Amwell Street. How are you? he asked himself. Oh, I am well. He looked at his fingernails. It had taken him half an hour to get his hands and nails clean, using white spirit and a nailbrush as well as soap and water. A couple of specks of paint on his shirt had surrendered, besides. He had used a friend's Nivea to restore some moisture to the scrubbed, parched skin on his fingers. The only stains left on his hands were a few stubborn traces of India ink, left from the drawings of Sara he'd finished the previous day. Graham smiled; she was ingrained in him.

He passed the entrance to a courtyard. There was a banner slung slackly over it, advertising a fete. He gave the banner a second glance, fixing its curves and lines in his mind, storing the sight so that he could draw it some time. Tricks could be played, points made by drawing a drooping banner so that certain letters and words were obscured and altered by the folded fabric.

He remembered one time he'd walked up here, in May, after she had started seeing him in the afternoons and going for long walks along the canal-side. It had poured with rain; a total cloudburst, thunder cracking and grumbling in the skies above the city. He'd been soaked, and hoped that at least this might finally gain him entry to the flat; she'd never invited him in.

When he got there he pressed the button on the entry-phone, waiting for the crackle of her distorted voice, but there was nothing. He pressed and pressed. He stood back in the street, the rain stinging his eyes, wetting him to the skin, getting in his mouth and eyes; warm rain, huge hard drops, slicking and sticking the clothes to his body; erotic, making his heart beat faster in a sudden, squally sexual fantasy; she would invite him in . . . no, better yet, she would turn up in the street, having been out, also wet to the skin, she would look at him . . . they would go in . . .

Nothing.

He walked all the way to Upper Street, near the bus-stops, before he found a free phonebox. He stood in it, his clothes and skin steaming, dripping water into the urine-scented callbox, called her number, listened to it ring, called again, saying the numbers to himself like a chant, making sure his finger was in the right hole on the dial each time. The double ring: *trr-trr: trr-trr: trr-trr*. He listened to it, trying to will her to the phone; imagining her coming back to the flat after being out; she might hear the phone from the street . . . now she would put the key in the lock . . . now running up the stairs . . . now dashing in, dripping, short of breath, to grab the receiver . . . now . . . *now*.

Trr-trr: trr-trr: trr-trr.

Please.

His hand hurt, his mouth ached with the expression of tense anguish he knew he wore, water ran from his hair, over his face, down his back. Water dripped from his elbow where it bent, holding the phone up to his ear.

Be there: be there: be there: *trr-trr: trr-trr: trr-trr* . . .

There were people outside the callbox. It was still raining, though more lightly now. A girl outside tapped on the glass, he turned away, ignored her. *Please* be there . . . *trr-trr: trr-trr: trr-trr* . . .

The door of the callbox opened eventually. A wet-looking blonde in a rain-darkened coat stood there, glaring at him, ''Ere, wot's your game, eh? I've only been standin' 'ere twen'y minutes, 'aven' I? You ain't even put your bleedin' money in yet!'

He said nothing; he put the phone down and walked away to get a bus. He forgot to take his ten pence out of the slot where he'd had it ready, and he'd left a pile of tens and fives sitting on top of the directories. He felt sick.

She apologised, over the phone, the next day; she'd been hiding under the bedclothes, playing her favourite

David Bowie cassette at maximum volume on her Sony Walkman, trying to drown the noise of the thunder.

He laughed, loving her for it.

Graham passed a small hall; in its courtyard was a little stall selling cakes. He considered buying a cake to eat, but while he was thinking about it he kept on walking, and thought it would look stupid to turn back so far up the street, so he didn't, though at the thought his stomach suddenly rumbled. He'd last eaten about four hours earlier, in the same small café where he'd got Slater to tell him about Sara that January.

Graham crossed the road. He was approaching Clairmont Square, at the summit of the hill, where tall houses, once genteel, then decaying, now undergoing gentrification, faced over tall trees to the bustle of traffic on Pentonville Road. Graham shifted his plastic portfolio from one hand to the other. Inside were drawings of Sara ffitch, and Graham was proud of them. The drawings were in a new style he had been experimenting with recently, and now, he felt, he had got it just right. It was perhaps a little early to be certain, but he thought they were probably the best things he had ever done. This made him feel good. It was another sort of omen; a confirmation . . .

Once they'd had a conversation on two levels, from street to first-floor window; it had been in April; on the second occasion he'd visited her in the afternoon, for a walk along the canal.

* * *

She came to the window when he pressed the button on the entryphone, poking her head out of the lower half of the opened sash window, through dark brown curtains. 'Hello!' she'd called.

He went out into the middle of the street. 'Coming out to play?' he said, smiling up at her in the sunlight. Just then the window had slipped, the lower half falling down on her; she laughed and turned her head round.

'Ouch,' she said.

'You all right?' he asked. She nodded.

'Didn't hurt.' She wriggled. He shielded his eyes to see better. 'I think I can get back in. Hope so, or I'm stuck here.'

He gave a small, concerned laugh. He thought suddenly of how she must look, seen from inside the kitchen she was leaning out of; an ugly sexual idea occurred to him, and he looked about for the big black BMW bike, but it wasn't there. It never was when she invited him to meet her at the flat; she was keeping him and Stock out of each other's way. Sara was giggling.

'Things like this are always happening to me,' she said, and shrugged, put her elbows on the sill of the window and smiled down at him. She wore a loose, heavy tartan shirt, like some fake lumberjack.

'So,' he said, 'are you coming for a walk?'

'Where shall we go?' she said. 'Tempt me.'

'I don't know. You fed up with the canal?'

'Maybe,' she shrugged. Her eyes seemed to wander away from him, scanning the horizon. 'Ah,' she said, 'the Post Office Tower.'

He turned round, looking south and west, though he knew he couldn't see the tall building from the street. 'You want to go there?'

'We could go to the revolving restaurant,' she laughed.

'I thought they'd closed it,' he said. She shrugged, stretched her arms out, arching her back.

'Have they? How boring of them.'

'Bit out of my price range anyway,' he laughed. 'I'll buy you a Wimpy and chips if you're hungry. There; how's that for an offer?'

'The zoo,' she said, and looked down at him.

'Aardvark and chips? Chimpy and chips?' he said. She laughed, making him feel good.

She said, 'We could go to the zoo today.'

'You really want to?' he said. He'd heard it was quite expensive to get in. But he'd go if she wanted.

'I don't know,' she shrugged again, 'I think so.'

'The canal goes by the zoo. Might be a long walk, but it would be nice. Through Camden Lock.' His neck was getting sore from looking up at her. She gripped the edge of the window sill, seemed to strain up on the window across the small of her back. She's stuck, he thought, but she doesn't want to admit it. Proud; embarrassed. Like me. He smiled. Perhaps he would have to go and get a ladder; rescue her. The idea amused him.

'Did you know the canal goes right under this house?' she said.

He shook his head. 'No. Does it?'

'Straight underneath,' she nodded. 'Right below. I looked it up on the map. Isn't that amazing?'

'Maybe there's a secret passage.'

'We could build one. Tunnel.' Her voice sounded scratchy; he wanted to laugh at her but didn't. She was getting annoyed, embarrassed at being stuck out of the window, making conversation while she secretly strained, trying to heave the trapping window back up.

'You having problems up there?' he said, trying to keep a straight face.

'What?' she said, then 'No, no of course not.' She cleared her throat. 'So, what have you been doing with yourself.'

'Nothing much,' he grinned, 'just looking forward to seeing you.' She made a funny face, gave a snorting sort of laugh. He continued, 'I've done some more drawings of you.'

'Oh yes?'

'They're still not good enough, though. I'm going to tear them up.'

'Really?'

'You're difficult to draw.' He looked up and down the street. 'Will you pose for me properly some time?'

'You mean improperly,' she said. He laughed.

'Better still. But I'd settle for you sitting still for a while.'

'Maybe. One day. Well, all right; yes, definitely. I promise.'

'I'll hold you to it.'

'Do.'

'So, are you going to come down?' he said.

She really was stuck. She turned her head round, he

saw her shoulders tense and her back arch again. She muttered something which sounded like a curse. She turned to him again, nodded, 'Yes, yes, just a second.'

He grinned as she pushed up on the window sill, her head down, hair hanging blackly. He could just see her face as he walked over to the pavement beneath. She grunted; the window squeaked. He looked up into her triumphant face; she smiled broadly and then pushed herself back, waving once, saying, 'Ah, that's better. See you in a second.'

They walked to the lock at Camden; she didn't feel like walking very far. They spent most of the afternoon in a poster shop, looking, then in a café. She wouldn't walk back; they got the tube from Camden Town to the Angel.

In the train, in the tunnel, he asked her things he'd often wanted to ask, but never dared. There was a sort of noisy anonymity about the rattling carriage which made him feel safe.

He asked her about Stock; had she come to London for him?

She said nothing for a long time, then shook her head.

She had come to escape, to get away. The city was big enough to hide in, to become lost in and anyway she knew a few people here; Slater was one. Stock was here too, but she had no illusions, never had had any illusions, about the permanency of their relationship. She was here, she said, to be herself, to find her way again. Stock was . . . something she still needed, even yet; something to hold on to; a devil she knew, immovable in the change and flux of her life.

141

She knew they weren't suited to each other, really; she didn't love him, but she couldn't give him up just yet. Besides, he wasn't the sort it was easy to give up.

She stopped talking then, as though she thought she had already said more than she should have. She looked at Graham after a moment, put her hand to his cheek, said, 'I'm sorry, Graham; you're good for me, I love talking to you. That means a lot. You don't know how much.'

He put his hand on hers, held it. She gave a brave little smile. 'I'm glad I'm good for you,' he said (keeping his voice down; there were people nearby), 'but I don't want to be just like a brother to you.'

Her expression froze at that, and his heart seemed to sink into his guts as he realised he'd almost said the wrong thing. But she smiled again and said, 'I'd understand if you didn't want to see me any more,' and looked down, away from him, at her feet. She took her hand away. He hesitated at first, then put his hand on her shoulder.

'That's not what I meant,' he said. 'I love seeing you. I'd miss you terribly if . . . well, if you went away.' He paused, bit his lip lightly for a second, 'But I don't know what you're doing. I don't know what your plans are; if you're going to stay here or go or what. I just feel uncertain.'

'Join the club,' she said. She looked at him, touched his hand where it rested on her shoulder. 'I think I'll stay. I'm applying for the R.C.M. I had a place there if I'd wanted it, three . . . four years ago, but I didn't go. Now I might get a place there, this time. If they'll have me.'

He bit his lip. What to do; admit his ignorance and

ask what R.C.M. stood for, or just nod, make appreciative noises?

'What *exactly* will you do there?' he said.

She shrugged, looked at her long fingers, flexed them.
'Piano. I think I can still play. I'm not getting the practice I should, though. I've got this electronic one of
Veronica's; well, one of her ex-boyfriends' . . . and its
action is all right, but it isn't the same.' She shrugged, still
inspecting her fingers, 'We'll see.'

He breathed again, relieved. Royal College of Music;
that must be it. Of course; Slater had mentioned about
her being good on the piano. 'You should have a shot
on one of the pianos in a pub sometime,' he said. She
smiled.

'Well, anyway,' she said, taking a deep breath. He felt
her slim shoulder move under the thick fabric of the tartan
shirt, 'as much as I know anything at the moment, that's
what I think I'll be doing. Staying here probably, for the
next few years. I think. I've still to get myself sorted out.
But I'm glad you're here, you help me think.' She looked
into his eyes, as if searching for something in them; her
white face made the dark, heavy-browed eyes look lost
and empty, and after a while he could not look into them
anymore, and had to smile and look away.

Then, from nowhere, a kind of despair seemed to settle
on him, and he felt lonely and used and cheated, and for
a moment wanted to be far away from this slim, black-
haired woman with her tense white face and her slender
fingers. The moment passed, and he tried to imagine what
she was going through, how it felt to her.

The train shuddered and braked, slowing. Graham had a sudden, strange image of the train in its tunnel suddenly bursting through clay and bricks into the canal tunnel under Sara's flat; taking some ancient subterranean wrong-turning and missing the station entirely, smashing into the darkness and water of the old canal under the hill. He tried to imagine drawing such a scene, but couldn't. He shook his head, forgetting the idea and looking at Sara again as the train stopped in the station. She sat forward in her seat, smiling wryly.

'All my life people have liked me too quickly, Graham, and for the wrong reasons. Maybe you'll change your mind when you know me better.' The doors opened; she stood, and as he got to his feet, as they went out on to the platform, he grinned confidently and shook his head.

'No way,' he said.

And now, in June, how much better did he know her? A little better; he had seen her in a few more moods, some higher, some lower. Her attraction had only grown; he found himself trying to smell her hair when they sat together in pubs, he gazed out of the corner of his eye at her breasts under whatever jumper or T-shirt she was wearing, wanting to touch them, hold them.

But it never seemed right; she would kiss him, for not very long, at the end of each meeting, and he could hold her, feel his arms around her narrow back, his body briefly against hers, but he could feel her tense if his hands went lower than the small of her back, and when he tried to kiss her more deeply, or hold her tighter, she would break away, shaking her head. He had almost given up testing the limits.

But now what? It sounded as though Stock was no more, as though at last she was free, strong enough to do without him, to get rid of his influence and accept Graham as more of – and more than – a friend.

Don't get your hopes up, not too much, he told himself. It might not be all you hope for. He stood at the side of Pentonville Road, by a telephone junction-box with posters advertising *Woza Albert* on it, and he told himself not to expect everything. Hopes and dreams had a way of evaporating.

But he could remember the sound of her voice on the phone that morning, when he'd called her up from the School, too well.

'Why don't you come in this time?' she said, 'I'll get us a salad together, or something.'

'Actually come into the flat?' he laughed. 'You mean come oop and – 'ow you zay – zee you zome time?' he said, in a good mood, making a silly French voice which he started to regret almost as soon as he'd spoken. Her voice over the phone was cool:

'Well . . . why not, Graham?'

His throat went dry after that; he didn't recall what else he'd said.

Mrs Short

Social Insecurity!

He'd just remembered he owed Mrs Short a month's rent in a couple of days. He had plenty of money now, but what if they took a long time to give him this Social Security? Would he even get enough?

Grout stood outside Mrs Short's house in Packington Street, Islington. He didn't know whether to go in or not now; maybe he should go to the pub first; it was always easier to face Mrs Short with a drink in him. He decided not to be so stupid; he wouldn't really owe the rent until the end of the month, and it was only the twenty-eighth. Anyway, it being his birthday, he deserved favours. He let himself in.

It was dark in the narrow hall of Mrs Short's house; the small curved window over the front door was brown with grime, the walls were covered with dark brown wallpaper, and Mrs Short's supply of forty-watt lightbulbs appeared to have dried up once again. After the bright street, Grout was almost blind. He groped his way to the stairs and started up; his bed-sit was on the third, top storey. Mrs Short pounced on the second floor landing.

'Oh, Mr Grout, you're home early,' she said, coming out of the Television Lounge (hard chairs, monochrome set, lodgers to share licence fee and extra electricity, turned off at twelve o'clock). Mrs Short wiped her hands on her duster, then on her nylon dress; she was a stout, balding lady of about fifty. Her hair was so tightly tied back at the rear of her skull that Grout swore the front strands, over her forehead, were being pulled out by the roots, and that the tautened skin so produced was thus responsible for the expression of malevolent surprise she wore; he had the impression that when Mrs Short blinked her over-stretched eyelids didn't quite make it to the bottom of her eyes. That was why she blinked a lot and had such red eyes. 'You 'aven't been fired again, 'ave you Mr Grout?' Mrs Short said, and burst out laughing, bending at the waist and cracking her duster like a whip.

Damn! Grout hadn't thought about this. What was he to say? He had a few precious seconds while Mrs Short laughed and then dried her eyes, wiping her nose on the duster. She sneezed suddenly; more precious seconds! He stood there. The seconds ticked away.

'Ah . . . no,' he said. Well, it was succinct. Not all that

convincing, perhaps, he knew that, but unequivocal. He pressed his lips tight together.

'Well then, Mr Grout, what brings you back so early?' Mrs Short smiled. The subtle variations in the colour of the enamel on her false teeth, replaced one by one over the years as the originals gave up the unequal struggle against the mint humbugs Mrs Short favoured, drew Steven's eyes and he said quickly,

'Dentist.' Brilliant! he thought.

'Oh, you been or you going?' She poked her head forward, staring into his mouth. He closed it quickly.

'Going, soon,' he mumbled.

'What's he going to do, then? Take any out? Fill them? My niece Pam, she got hers drilled by her dentist the other day; hit a nerve! She bit him; didn't mean to but she closed her mouth, didn't she? End of the drill snapped off in her mouth! Right in the tooth!' Mrs Short doubled up laughing at this. Steven watched anxiously to see whether a way round her and up the stairs would present itself, but without reward. Mrs Short came upright again, searched for a hanky in her dress pocket, failed to find one and so used her duster again, blowing into it, inspecting the nasal hollow indented in it briefly, then looking back at Grout. 'Poor cow! Off work for a week she was. Had to eat through a straw!'

She mistook Steven's immobile expression for fear and said, leaning forward to flick his chest with her duster, 'Oh, there I go; I'm making you all frightened now, aren't I? Oh, Mr Grout, you men are all the same; least little bit of pain and you're off. You should have a kid sometime! Ha!' She laughed, tears coming to her eyes at the memory. 'Gawd, Mr Grout, I thought I was bein' torn in two! Scream? I thought I was goin' to die!' Mrs Short gave a long, in-sucking laugh, and had to hold on to the banister rail to prevent her mirth from toppling her to the ground. She flapped her duster weakly, then dried her eyes with it. Grout tried to estimate the distance between his landlady and the wall opposite the banisters to see if by grasping the latter she had left sufficient room for him to escape upstairs to his room. Not quite.

'Yes, well,' he said, edging forward to show that he wanted to go upstairs. 'Better get ready for the dentist.' He shuffled forward, turning to one side so that he could squeeze between Mrs Short and the wall.

'Oh, you got to go now then have you?' Mrs Short said, turning to look at him but not actually moving out of his way. 'Well I shall get on with my dusting then, I shall. You quite sure that I can't dust your room for you, Mr Grout? It wouldn't be any bother you know.'

'Ah, no, no thank you,' Steven said, trying to press himself back into the wall to get around Mrs Short's bulging hip. His back scraped against the peeling varnish of old wooden boards.

'Well, I should think you'd find it was much cleaner and less dusty in your room if I did your dusting for you, Mr Grout, really I do. Why don't we give it a sort of trial period?' Mrs Short nudged him in the ribs.

'No, honestly, no,' Steven said, rubbing the place where Mrs Short had nudged him. What did it feel like when your spleen ruptured? Mrs Short still wasn't moving to let him past. She frowned at his shoulder and used her duster to flick something off it.

'No, I really . . .' Steven said, and then sneezed.

'You wouldn't have that hay fever half as bad if you let me dust your room, Mr Grout.' She snapped her duster again. More of the shining motes which had made Steven sneeze the first time floated in the air around his face.

'Really must get to my—' he began, but Mrs Short said,

'No you wouldn't, Mr Grout.'

'Room!' Grout gasped. He pointed up the stairs, and with one mighty effort succeeded in squeezing through the tight space between Mrs Short and the wall, almost falling out on the far side. Mrs Short swivelled like a tank's gun turret and looked at him.

'The room, Mr Grout? You want me to do it, then?'

'No,' Steven said, backing off towards the next flight of stairs, but still facing Mrs Short and trying to smile without showing his teeth. 'No, honestly,' he said, 'really, I'll dust my own room, really. Thank you, but, no, really.'

Mrs Short was still shaking her head and shaking her limp duster when he finally got round the sheltering twist in the stairs; Steven wiped his damp forehead, turned and ran quickly up the rest of the steps, shivering and grimacing as he thought about Mrs Short.

In his room, he could relax. He sat by the window after he'd washed his face and upper body at the small hand-basin in one corner of his room. From the basin he had to negotiate four straights and three right-angled corners through his maze of books on the floor to get to the window, where he had a small chair and could look out into Packington Street.

He liked looking out the window (today he had it open; it was a nice day) and sometimes would spend entire Saturday or Sunday afternoons just sitting there watching the traffic and the people in the street, and a curious sort of peace would slowly take him over, like something hypnotic, like a trance; he would just sit there, not thinking or worrying or seething about anything, just sitting watching, mind blank and free of cares, and the cars would move and the people pass and talk, and for a little while, through that lack of thought, that temporary surrender of his own personality, he could start to feel part of this place, this city and people and species and society; feel like he imagined all the other, ordinary people, the people who were not him and were not there specifically to torment him, must feel all the time.

He dried himself with his small towel; it smelled a bit, but not offensively. Comforting, like his bed.

He looked over the maze-walls of books covering the floor of his room. The book-walls, which he tried to keep at roughly the same level, were up to mid-thigh level now, and he was worried that soon they would start to become unstable. Of course, if he wasn't going to be getting any money he wouldn't be able to buy any more paperbacks for a while, maybe not until he found another new job. But even so, it was depressing to think of the chaos which would result from the books becoming unstable through sheer height, and while there was one way round the problem (he was proud to have worked this out) by putting the books together like bricks in a wall instead of simply stacking them one on top of another, this would make it even more difficult to get at a book if he wanted to read it again.

He started to panic at the thought, and wound his way through the books to the door of the room. He locked it, and took his Sunday-best safety helmet down from the overloaded peg behind the door. He put the hat on, and felt better. He took a different route back to the chair by the window and sat down again. What would he do now? Go for a drink. That was what you did when you left work, or when you had lots of money. He took the money out. It was mostly in ten pound notes; there were lots. He looked at the big brown rectangles of paper; the Queen looked nice, the way he liked to think his mother must have looked. Florence Nightingale, on the back, on the other hand, reminded him of some of the nurses at the home he'd gone to.

He put the money away, stuffing it into his back pocket. He looked round his room, over the walls of books, the pile of clothes by the side of his bed, the hunchback of jackets and shirts and coat and ties on the back of the door, the large wardrobe where he'd kept all his books originally, and still had lots of them stored in shoeboxes, the small bedside cabinet with a plastic glass of water and his latest book lying on it. The room had an old, blocked-off fireplace, where his two-bar electric fire sat. On the mantelpiece was his collection of car mascots.

There were five Jaguars, eight Rolls-Royce silver ladies,

two old Austin signs, and a varied collection of leaping salmon, racing horses, pedigree dogs and one cricketer, wielding a bat. He still, to his disappointment, had no Bentley mascots. He kept the Mercedes signs in a big jar at one end of the mantelpiece. He wasn't really bothered about Mercedes signs, but somehow his original reason for hacksawing the mascots off cars – his own safety – had been complicated by the collector's urge to add depth and breadth to the collection.

Originally he had taken offence at Jaguar mascots; the leaping cat, no longer on every car, but still in actual, solid form on quite enough, seemed designed to disembowel him. The silver lady was little better, and some of the custom-made special mascots were even worse. He thought they were illegal, but when he went to the Police Station in Upper Street to complain that people were riding around in these lethally armed cars, the bored-looking sergeant had just looked at him and eventually said well there wasn't a lot he could do about it and sir would just have to look both ways before crossing the street (Steven had been disappointed about that, but on the other hand he was most impressed that a *policeman* had called him 'sir'). They weren't usually helpful, and of course it was obvious that at least some of them must be in on the whole secret of Grout's Torment, but even so, you couldn't help but admire them and look up to them, and to have one call him 'sir' was rather good. He went back a few weeks later to report the theft of a bi-cycle he didn't even own, just so that he could be called 'sir' again.

Taking the car mascots was often dangerous. Several times he had almost been caught by enraged owners when they heard some noises in the street outside, in the darkness, or heard feet crunch in a twilit driveway.

Steven had stuck to the immediate area at first; Islington, especially Canonbury, and the quiet streets around Highbury Fields. Then the pickings became leaner as people were careful not to leave their cars in shady spots and parked them only under lamp-posts, or were more conscientious about putting their cars in their drives or garages, and locking the gates.

Steven, hacksaw in pocket, had accordingly widened his area of operations, and now was liable to strike anywhere from the City to Highgate, capturing jaguars, kidnapping silver ladies and pocketing stars. He certainly felt a lot safer walking about the streets, holding his breath between the parked cars and trucks, keeping an eye out for low walls and raised doorsteps he could also use to escape from the lasers in the passing vehicles, knowing that a good few of those growling death-traps had been made that little bit safer thanks to him.

Then he had started to think about bikes; motorbikes could be pretty deadly, too. They were usually driven by suicidal exhibitionists, and just the sound of them had given Steven some terrible frights in the past, and made him hate the people who rode them.

So he'd started putting sugar in their fuel tanks; that was what he'd been doing the previous evening, down in Clerkenwell. He'd been out until two in the morning, and had been chased by a security guard who'd seen him fiddling with a bike's fuel tank in a car park. Steven had been very nervous and excited when he got back, and even though he felt very tired he had taken a long time to get to sleep. Maybe that was why he'd been on a short fuse this morning.

Well, he didn't care; that was their problem, back at the depot. They'd see, when those holes in Upper Street which he had repaired were still intact after all theirs had opened up again. Let them worry about all that. He didn't regret sugaring bikes' tanks and scalping car mascots in the least. He wasn't even just doing it for himself, after all. Although of course he was the most important person, he was doing everybody else – all these people walking in Packington Street, for example – a favour as well.

Steven hung the small towel on the back of the chair by the window. He looked through the pile of clothes hung on the back of his door until he found a cleanish shirt, and put it on. There was a can of Right Guard under his bed which he used to spray under his arms when he remembered, but it had run out last week and he kept forgetting to get a new one. He tucked his shirt into his trousers.

He took his Evidence Box out from the bedside cabinet and went to sit with it by the window. The Evidence Box was an old cardboard Black and White whisky case Steven had picked up somewhere. In it he kept a small radio-cassette recorder, a piece of estate agent's literature and a school atlas, along with dozens of fading yellow newspaper cuttings.

The cuttings were of the Strange But True type; fillers

and funnies, supposedly True Stories which Steven could tell were complete nonsense; made-up rubbish they taunted him with, trying to get him to stand up and challenge them, call their bluff. But he wasn't going to be so predictable or stupid; he would keep quiet, and he would collect the evidence. One day he might have a real use for it, but in the meantime it was reassuring.

He took out the cassette recorder, switched the tape on. He had recorded the noise of the so-called 'static' from the Short Wave band. But he knew what it really was; he listened to the grinding, deep, continuous roaring noise, and he recognised the sound of the War's eternal heavy bombers of the air. He was amazed that nobody else had noticed it. Those were engines, that wasn't static. He *knew*. This was a Leak, a tiny slip they had made which let part of reality slip through into this false prison of life.

He breathed deeply, looking out down Packington Street, trying to remember or imagine what those droning, immense-sounding noises represented; through what limitless airs and atmospheres did those huge craft power, what was their seemingly endless mission, what was the appalling cargo they carried, what dreadful enemy would suffer beneath them when they arrived over their target. He switched the tape off, rewound it.

The next piece of evidence was trickier. It was a sheet of paper with house-buying details on it; the evidence of the Leak came from the name of the firm. Hotblack Desiato was the name of the estate agents, and Grout *knew* that was a Leak. He was sure he could recall something about that name which related back to his previous life, his real life in the War. What that name actually meant, whether it was a name at all, and if so that of a friend or enemy or place or thing, or whether it was a phrase, order, instruction or what, he could not remember, no matter how hard he thought about it, or how hard he didn't think about it and just waited for his subconscious to come up with the right answer. But it meant something, he was sure. Something had happened to him, sometime, which related to that name.

Oh, and as usual, they were very clever, very subtle. If the name was not a Leak then it was a deliberate ploy by the Tormentors to taunt him, tease him. They had put that firm of estate agents in the area he lived in just so that he could keep seeing their signs and so be constantly distressed and frustrated by his inability to remember exactly when and where he'd heard the name before. Anyway, it was more evidence, even if it turned out just to be a Leak and they hadn't meant it. He folded the paper up again and put it back in the box.

He took out the atlas, opened it at a map of the World. He had drawn red-ink circles round places like Suez and Panama, Gibraltar and the Dardanelles.

He snorted with contempt at their ridiculous attempt to design a reasonable-looking planet. Who did they think they were kidding? Ho-ho, so the continents just happen to link on to each other, do they? Very handy. Any idiot could see it was all too carefully arranged to be natural. It had been designed. Whether he really was on a planet with those shapes on it he didn't know; he suspected not, but it didn't matter. Even if, as he rather suspected, the 'world' actually came to an end just outside Greater London, that wasn't the point. The point was that they were trying to get people – him – to believe this travesty of a map. The contempt they must feel for him, expecting him to accept this! It made him boil just to think of it. But they had made a serious mistake; they had underestimated him, and they would not break him, certainly not while he had evidence like this to back him up. He turned the atlas to the pages on South East Asia . . . yes, the island of Celebes still looked like a letter from some alien alphabet (and the more he thought about it, the more familiar it looked, too, so that sometimes he almost thought he knew what it represented, or the sound it made, if his human throat or brain was capable of forming such a foreign sound). He closed the atlas, smiling to himself and feeling better; justified and reassured. He put everything back in the Evidence Box and put it back in his bedside cabinet, where it fitted in neatly, then he made his way carefully back to the window, closed it, and threaded his way back through the walls of books to the door, making sure that he had his door keys and his money in his pockets.

He stopped at the door, faced with the choice of keeping his good hat on or putting on his usual safety helmet. He decided to keep the good one on. It was a lovely deep-blue colour, with almost no scratches or abrasions on it at all, and a nice real leather sweatband bit inside the front part of the inner webbing. Why not keep it on? Celebrate today. It was his birthday, after all. He wondered if it was worthwhile telling Mrs Short it was his birthday. It didn't seem right that nobody else knew. At least if he told Mrs Short there would be somebody to wish him 'Happy birthday' or 'Many happy returns'. That would be nice. Still undecided, he left the room, after first checking that he hadn't left the fire on or left a plug in a socket, or left the light on.

He didn't encounter Mrs Short on the way down the stairs, and found this something of a relief. He was walking quietly through the gloom of the front hall towards the door to the street when Mrs Short's door opened suddenly and she was there in front of him in the hallway, huge arms folded, the light reflected on her taut-skinned forehead.

'Aow, there you are, Mr Grout. Off to the dentist, then?'

'What?' Steven said foolishly, then remembered. 'Oh, yes, yes that's right. Umm . . .' He closed his mouth so that Mrs Short couldn't see into it, not that he expected her to be able to see anything in the darkness, but one never knew.

Mrs Short said, 'Don't suppose you'd like to give me my rent money now, would you, Mr Grout, in case I don't see you for a few days?'

Steven thought about this. Not seeing Mrs Short for a few days. What a pleasant thought. But unlikely. He shook his head and said. 'No, not just now, Mrs Short; I haven't got enough money just at the moment. I'll have it on . . . Friday,' he lied, starting to feel hot again. They were using the microwaves on him even now, even here! He had one of his hands behind his back, the fingers crossed because he was telling lies.

'Well, if you're sure, Mr Grout,' Mrs Short said, then looked down at his trousers. 'Only I thought I saw this bulge in your rear pocket, didn't I? An' me bein' me I just naturally assumed that it was pay.'

Steven felt his eyes widen. He didn't know what to say; Mrs Short had guessed! She must know! In fact – of course! – they'd told her. She had probably been informed by the depot immediately after he'd left. That was probably one of the first things that Mr Smith's secretary had done. Idiot! Why hadn't he guessed this?

Well, he would just have to brazen it out, he decided. There was no point in trying to come to some sort of compromise now. It was all or nothing. Mrs Short might know, but it seemed that it was not in the rules that she was allowed to tell him she knew, and she could only imply it.

'Friday,' Steven said, nodding briskly. 'Money on Friday. Definitely.' He edged towards the welcoming opening of the door, shaking his head as he passed her. She blinked rapidly at him. He had often wondered if this was some sort of code. He cleared his throat, said, 'That's all right, thank you.' He patted his back pocket; 'Dental card,' he explained. Mrs Short nodded sympathetically.

He was out! He stood on the doorstep, almost in the street, and he'd escaped. 'You mind how you go now, Mr Grout, won't you?'

'Oh yes,' he said, and turned, took a deep breath, and set off down the street.

'Sure I can't dust your room while you're out, Mr

Grout?' Mrs Short shouted from the still-open doorway when Steven was about ten yards away. He felt himself seize up; his legs stopped, his shoulders came up as though to tense for a falling blow. He turned round in the street, looked back at the stoutly smiling face of Mrs Short, and shook his head violently. There were no parked cars for about thirty metres; traffic was grumbling down the street in a ragged stream. He shook his head again.

'What's that, Mr Grout?' Mrs Short shouted, and put one chubby hand, cupped, to her ear. He stared at her, widening his eyes, shook his head as violently as he dared. 'Can't hear you, Mr G,' Mrs Short called to him. He was starting to run out of oxygen.

He put his head down and walked back to the doorway, stood up out of the level of the laser-axles, and said straight into Mrs Short's face, 'No, thank you, Mrs Short. Please don't dust my room. I prefer to do it myself.'

'Well, if you're sure,' Mrs Short smiled.

'Oh, completely,' Grout assured her. He waited there, to see if she would close the door, but she didn't. He took a deep breath, said 'Goodbye,' and turned away. He walked quickly, towards Upper Street, and had done perhaps fifty metres before he heard Mrs Short, far in the distance, shout at him. He didn't turn round, but heard her distant scream of 'Byeee!' with a sort of nauseous relief.

Spotless Dominoes

They sat on the balcony outside the games room of the Castle Doors. Inside was a blaze of light. The snow on the balcony had all melted and a warm, moist, salty breeze blew around them constantly, from the room over the balcony and out into the open air. Quiss and Ajayi sat with light tunics on, over the small wood-filigree table, shuffling plain white sticks of ivory over the cut surface.

It was now too hot in the games room. The boilers of the Castle of Bequest had been repaired only about thirty of their days ago, and according to the seneschal there was still a bit of 'fine tuning' to be done.

From where she sat, Ajayi could see the quarries. Small black figures moved up the snow-covered paths and roads

to the mines and quarries, and carts trundled to and fro;
the ponderous, laden ones disappearing from her view
behind an outcrop of – she peered, narrowing her eyes
to try and see better – well, either rock or the castle; she
couldn't tell.

The rest of the landscape was as near-flat and uniform
as ever. A gust of warm air from the baking heat of the
games room swirled round her, then unwound itself again.
She shivered briefly. No doubt all this heat, and the salt,
was playing even greater havoc with the castle's plumbing than usual, and before too long, once they did get
things back to normal, and an acceptable level of light
and heat, the whole system would break down again,
probably for even longer. In the meantime they were playing a game called Spotless Dominoes, in which plain pieces
of ivory had to be arranged in certain linear patterns.

Neither she nor Quiss had any idea when they were
going to finish the game, or even how well they were
doing at any stage, because although they knew that in
the original version of the game there were spots on the
ivory pieces, their pieces were blank. They had to lay
them out in lines each time they played, hoping that the
small table with the red glowing jewel at its centre on
which they played would recognise that the spot-values
it had – randomly, of course – assigned to the pieces before
each game were such that the pattern Quiss and Ajayi
produced was a logical one; one in which, if all the spots
suddenly appeared on the surfaces of the dominoes, the
pattern would make sense; a one would be matched with
a one or a double one, a two with a two or a double two,

163

and so on. It was the most frustrating game they had played yet, and they had been playing it for one hundred and ten days.

She deliberately did not think about how long they had been in the castle. It didn't matter. It was one instant of exile, that was all. She had no idea how much of it she would remember if . . . *when* she returned to her post in the Therapeutic Wars. It was a rare punishment and not one that people who had had to experience it were likely to talk very much about even if one did bump into them, so although she, like Quiss, had always known of the existence of the castle, what happened to those who successfully passed through it was not recorded.

No, it did not matter how long they were here, as long as they did not despair or go mad. They just had to keep playing the games and trying the many different answers, and eventually they would get out.

Ajayi looked over at her companion, without him seeing. Quiss was busy mixing the dominoes up, frowning deeply at them as though he could somehow bully the pieces of dead animal into forming a correct pattern. Quiss, Ajayi thought, seemed to be surviving all right. She still worried about him though, because his urgent, intimidatory style was not guaranteed to last for ever against the castle's so often impenetrably purposeless-seeming regime. She was afraid that what he had constructed for himself was something too much like armour, too much like what the castle itself represented. That armour might have to give in eventually, just as no fortress ever built could withstand *any* siege (they had discussed this ultimate vulnerability of the static, the hardened, before they gave their first answer to the riddle), whereas she had tried not to armour herself, she had tried to go with the castle's strange mood; adapt to it, accept it.

'Oh get *on* with it you two,' the red crow said from its perch on the stump of a flag-pole about three metres above their heads, 'I've had more fun watching snails fuck.'

'Why don't you go and do just that?' Quiss growled at it, without looking, as he took seven of the face-down dominoes from the shuffled log-jam of them in the centre of the small table. He held all seven of his pieces easily in one huge hand, the little bone-chips lost in the hard flesh's folds and creases.

'Listen, greybeard,' the red crow said, 'it's my appointed duty to stay here and annoy you bastards, and that's just what I'm going to do until you have the sense – not to mention the common decency, considering you've grievously overstayed your welcome – to do away with yourselves.' The red crow's voice twisted into an impersonation of Ajayi's least favourite teacher from her schooldays; 'Ajayi, you old bag, pick up your pieces and play. We haven't got all day, you know.' The red crow chuckled after this last sentence.

Ajayi said nothing. She selected seven of the dominoes, biting her lower lip as she did so. The bird's voice really did grate; it was ludicrous really, but the damn thing was an uncomfortably accurate mimic and commanded a repertoire of hateful voices from the past.

165

It was Ajayi's turn to start. She took one of the blank tiles and set it down in the middle of the table. She knew that there was something about the way she inspected her dominoes before placing them down which infuriated Quiss, who just picked out the first one that came to hand. Somehow, though, Ajayi needed this pretence; it was one of those little things which kept her going. She couldn't just pick up the dominoes, whack them down one after another, mix them up and do the whole thing again, even if that was the fastest way of getting through the games; that was too mechanical, too uncaring. It was important to her always to believe that this next game would be the right one, the one where everything fitted and all the junctions of all the pieces made sense, so giving them another chance to escape from here.

So she placed her piece down carefully, thoughtfully. Quiss slapped one of his down immediately after her. Ajayi paused for thought. Quiss tutted impatiently and tapped one foot. The red crow coughed from the stump overhead. 'Bugger me, here we go again. I hope you two get fed up soon and kill yourselves so we can at least get some people in here who'll be *fun*.'

'You're not the most gracious of hosts, crow,' Ajayi said, putting a domino down.

'I'm not your host, idiot,' the red crow sneered. 'Even you should be able to work that out. I know you've no balls but I thought you had the basic minimum of brains.'

Quiss snapped another of the white tiles down on the table, and Ajayi looked suspiciously at him, not sure if she could hear him suppressing a laugh or not. He cleared his throat. Ajayi looked up at the red crow. 'Oh,' she said, 'I think you are in a way, whether you like it or not. In some ways you are a very fitting host, because you help to epitomise what this place is about, so—' she looked away from it and studied the pieces of ivory in her hand when she heard the tap-tap of Quiss's foot on the balcony floor, '– while you might not like it, you do play the part well.'

(The red crow was looking out over the snowy landscape and quietly shaking its head.)

'Not pleasantly,' Ajayi concluded, 'but thoroughly.'

'What a load of bullshit,' the red crow said, looking down at her, still shaking its head. 'Bullshit from an old cow.' It looked away from her, out over the white plain again. 'You think *you're* being punished; I've got to stick around and listen to all this rubbish. I wonder why I bother sometimes, I really do. Must be easier ways of making a living.'

Ajayi was looking up at it, thoughtfully. She was wondering if there was some way of making a weapon with which they could shoot the red crow. If they did, what else would be added to their sentence, and would it be worth it? She could hear Quiss's boot going tap-tap again, but ignored it as she looked at the red crow. She had been aware of Quiss sniggering when the red crow was insulting her, and didn't see why she should hurry with her next domino just to please him. The red crow stared back at Ajayi, then after a few seconds shook itself furiously, spreading its wings briefly and stretching one leg out as though stiff. 'Come *on*, will you?' it shouted at her. 'Good god, woman, what got you in here? Prevarication or just plain stupidity? Or both? Get *on* with it.'

Ajayi looked away from the bird, selecting one of her dominoes and placing it slowly, carefully on the surface of the table. She felt her face flushing slightly.

'Don't tell me,' Quiss said, leaning close over the table to talk in a low voice as he put down his next piece, 'that our little feathered friend has hurt you . . .' he glanced into the old woman's eyes as he leant back again. Ajayi looked away from Quiss's eyes, then shook her head slowly as she chose between the remaining dominoes in her hand.

'No,' she said, taking one of the ivory pieces from her palm, leaning forward to place it on the table, then changing her mind, putting it back and reconsidering, rubbing her chin with one hand. An exasperated choking noise came from above their heads.

'This is ridiculous,' the red crow said, 'I think I'll go and watch some icicles form. It can't be any more boring than this.' With that, it opened its wings and flew off, muttering. Ajayi watched it go. Some other rooks and crows from higher battlements flew down and joined it as it flew off in the direction of the slate mines.

'Pest,' Quiss said after it. He drummed one set of stubby fingers on the table top and looked back at Ajayi, who nodded and put another domino down. 'No,' Quiss said, putting another piece down, 'it's just that I wondered if it had struck a bit close to the bone with that remark.

About how you ended up here.' Quiss darted a look at his companion, who watched him look away again and smiled to herself.

'Well,' she said, considering the choices in her hand, 'perhaps it's time we told each other why we're both here. What we did to be sent here.'

'Hmm,' Quiss said, apparently not all that interested. 'Yes, I suppose we might as well. Perhaps there's even some sort of clue to the right answer we should give; you know; something common to both our . . . reasons for being here which might help us out.' He raised his eyebrows at her, a 'what-do-you-think-of-that?' expression. Ajayi thought it politic *not* to remind Quiss that she had come out with exactly that argument for them trading stories not long after she had arrived in the castle. Quiss had been totally opposed to talking about their separate misfortunes at that point. She had decided all she could do – all she had better get used to doing – was be patient.

'Well, that might be a good idea, Quiss. If you're quite sure you don't mind telling.'

'Me? No, not at all, not at all,' Quiss said quickly. He paused. 'Ah . . . you first.'

Ajayi smiled. 'Well,' she said, taking a deep breath, 'what happened was . . . I was aide-de-camp to our Philosophy Officer, who in our squadron was of Marshal rank.'

'Philosophy Officer,' Quiss said, nodding knowingly.

'Yes,' Ajayi said. 'He was a terribly keen hunter, and – rather unfashionably – enjoyed getting back to the great

169

outdoors and the good old-fashioned ways of doing things, whenever he had the opportunity.

'I could appreciate the concept of getting back to one's roots and reaffirming one's integral relationship with nature – even if it was alien nature – all right, but I let him know I thought he took it too far. I mean, he would never take anything like communication gear or transport along, or even modern weapons. All we had were a couple of archaic rifles and our own legs.'

'You went along with him,' Quiss said.

'Had to,' Ajayi shrugged. 'He said he took me along because he liked arguing with me. So I used to go on these expeditions with him, and I became quite proficient at the art of rhetoric, and passably handy with the ancient, primitive weapons it amused him to hunt with. Also quite skilled at rejecting his rarely more than half-hearted advances.

'One day, towards dusk on this . . . place . . . we were trudging through a swamp trailing some immense wounded beast he'd just shot, beset by insects, tired, out of contact with the fleet until a fast picket rendezvoused with us at midnight, wet, fed up . . . well, I was anyway; he was having a great time . . . when suddenly he tripped on a submerged tree trunk or something, and as he fell his hand must have closed on the trigger – his gun was so old it didn't even have a safety catch – and he shot himself in the chest.

'He was in a bad way; still conscious but in a lot of pain (he didn't believe in taking modern medicines on these trips either). I thought I'd better move him out of the marsh and over to some rocks I could just about make out through the mists, but when I tried to move him he started screaming a lot; then I remembered reading some historical story about people being shot with these ancient projectile weapons and having bullets dug out of them without any anaesthetic, and what they used to do then, and I thought that what they did seemed oddly appropriate in the circumstances, even if it probably didn't do any real good, so I took a bullet out of my own gun and gave it to him to bite on while I dragged him over to the rocks.'

'And?' Quiss said, once Ajayi had stopped. She sighed.

'It was an explosive bullet. Blew his head off soon as he bit it.'

Quiss slapped his knee with his free hand and rocked with laughter. 'Really? Explosive? Ha ha ha!' He went on slapping his knee and swaying in his seat, howling with laughter. Tears came to his eyes and he had to put his three remaining dominoes face down on the table and hold his belly with both hands.

'I knew I could count on your sympathy,' Ajayi said drily, putting down another ivory tile.

'That's beautiful,' Quiss said, voice weakened with laughter. He wiped the tears from his old cheeks, took up his dominoes again. 'I take it he was dead.' He played one of the pieces.

'Of course he was dead!' Ajayi snapped. It was the first time she had ever spoken loudly or harshly to Quiss, and he sat back, looking surprised. She tried not to scowl as much as she felt like doing, but went on, 'his brains were spread over half the swamp. And me.'

'Ho ho ho!' Quiss said sympathetically. 'Ha ha ha!' He shook his head, grinning widely, and sniffed.

'What about you? What did you do?' Ajayi asked. Quiss was quiet all of a sudden. He frowned at the two remaining dominoes in his hand.

'Hmm,' he said.

'I've told you mine,' Ajayi said. 'Now you tell me yours.'

'I don't know that you'd really be interested,' Quiss said, not looking at her. He shook his head, still looking at his hand. 'It's a bit of an anti-climax after yours.'

He looked up, a look of pained apology on his face, to see that Ajayi was glaring at him, not only more furiously than he had ever seen her looking before, but also rather more furiously than he would have thought her capable of looking. He cleared his throat.

'Hmm. Well, on the other hand,' he said, 'I suppose it is only fair.' He put down his dominoes on the table, put his hands on his knees and stared over the top of Ajayi's head. 'Strangely similar to yours, in a way . . . might be a common link. There was this gun involved . . . anyway.' He cleared his throat again, putting his fist to his mouth and coughing. He was still staring over his companion's head, as though the red crow was still on the broken flagpole above them and he was addressing it, not the woman.

'Well, anyway . . . suffice to say that after a long . . . ahm . . . and strenuous campaign . . . and not one we had expected to survive really, I might add, I was with others of our guard corps on the roof of . . . this big palace in this city. There were celebrations; the . . . ahm . . . this dignitary . . . well, a prince actually; this was one of those backward places as well, and we were limited by the rules to fairly crude weapons and equipment and stuff . . . well this prince was due to appear on . . .' Quiss looked briefly at Ajayi, then around at the balcony they sat on, '. . . on a sort of balcony thing like this,' he said lamely. He cleared his throat again.

'Well, there was this huge crowd waiting to greet the prince; maybe a million locals, all armed to the mandibles with pitchforks and muskets and things – but all more or less on our side, and anyway glad the fighting was over – and we were guarding the palace roof with a few unobtrusive missiles, just in case there was some desperate last-ditch aircraft attack, not that that was very likely, we thought.

'We were all a bit . . . umm . . . happy, I suppose, and we were celebrating too, and in high spirits anyway, glad to be alive, and we had some drink . . . and two of us – this other captain and me – were having a lark, daring each other to walk along this sort of balustrade thing on the roof, looking over the crowd, above the balcony where this prince and his cronies were going to appear, and we were closing our eyes and walking along, and standing on one leg and drinking, and using these big machine-guns to balance ourselves . . . sounds a bit undisciplined, I know, but like I say . . .' Quiss coughed.

'This other captain and myself, we collided while we were walking along the parapet; walked right into each other while our eyes were closed . . . of course, our comrades thought it was a great laugh, but while the other fellow was falling towards the roof and into the arms of these other drunken types, *I* was falling the other way, over the edge of the roof. All there was down that way was the balcony about ten metres down, and then the ground about twenty metres beneath that. I was off-balance, going over, my comrades were out of reach; I mean that was it; I was going to plummet right down to my death. I was a goner.' Quiss looked briefly at Ajayi, his expression one of pained sincerity, then he looked away again and continued.

'But ... well, like I said, I was holding this big machine gun, and just sort of without thinking about it, pure instinct I suppose, I . . . I brought this big machine-gun round, and pointed it down the way, and fired it off.' Quiss cleared his throat loudly, shaking his head and narrowing his eyes. 'Thing was set on anti-aircraft rate; just about leapt out of my hands. Could barely control it, but the recoil was enough to bring me upright again, let me get my balance on the parapet before the magazine ran out of bullets. So I was saved.

'Only trouble was, the prince and his retinue had just come out on to the balcony beneath me as this was happening, and got caught in this hail of fragging AA shells that bugger of a gun had sprayed all over the place. Killed the prince and quite a few of his pals, not to mention several dozen in the crowd underneath.

'Crowd got very annoyed. Pandemonium; riot and mayhem. Palace was sacked. Cost us forty days and half a brigade to calm the upset. That's it.' Quiss shrugged, looked down at the table.

'Yours sounds more dramatic,' Ajayi said, trying not to sound amused. 'Back from the brink of death.' She played a domino.

'Oh, yes,' Quiss said, and his eyes took on a misty, distant expression as he looked up, 'I felt really great for about half a second.'

Ajayi smiled, 'So, it would appear we share an element of slightly thoughtless irresponsibility, and projectile weapons.' She looked up at the ramshackle heights of the castle above them. 'The links don't seem *all* that close, but there you are. Here we are. Does any of this actually help us?'

'No,' Quiss said, shaking his great grey head sadly, 'I don't think so.'

'Still,' Ajayi said, 'I'm glad we both know now.'

'Yes,' Quiss said, placing his second last piece. He coughed. 'Sorry I ah . . . laughed. Shouldn't have. Bad form. Apologies.'

His head was down, so he did not see Ajayi smile at him, a look of real affection on her old, lined face. 'As you say, Quiss,' she said, smiling quietly.

Her stomach rumbled. It must be nearly mealtime. A waiter would probably appear soon. Sometimes the waiters took their orders and brought what was ordered, sometimes they brought something quite different, sometimes they didn't take their orders but arrived with what they probably would have ordered anyway. Often they brought far too much food and stood around looking confused, as though looking for other people to serve. At least the times of the meals were relatively

175

predictable, and the food satisfying, usually.

She wanted a break from the games anyway. She could take only so much of this purposeless placing of ivory pieces. After a while she got bored and restless and wanted to do something else.

For a while, when her stiff back and sore leg permitted, she had explored the castle, going off for long walks, at first always with Quiss, who knew the rough lay-out of the place better, then later mostly by herself. Her bones and joints still complained about climbing stairs, but she ignored the pain as best she could and anyway took frequent rests, and trudged through vast areas of the castle, exploring its turrets and rooms and battlements, shafts and halls. She preferred to keep to the upper levels, where there were less people around and the feeling of the castle was more . . . sane, she supposed.

Lower down, Quiss had told her, things got more chaotic. The kitchens were the worst, in some ways, but there were even stranger places, places Quiss didn't like talking about (she suspected this was just him enjoying the feeling of power which exclusive knowledge gives to people, but perhaps in some clumsy way he thought he was protecting her from something. He meant well; she would allow him this).

Eventually, though, the attraction of the castle's tortuous internal geography palled on her, and now she restricted herself to only very occasional sallies, mostly conducted – as near as possible – on the same level, just to stretch her legs. The very inexhaustibility of the castle's ever-changing topography depressed her after a while, whereas at first it had seemed encouraging that one could never know the place perfectly, that it would never be boring, that it was always constantly changing; falling down, being rebuilt, altered and redesigned. Stuck all the time in a human frame which would not change, imprisoned in this one age, this cage of cells, the analogue of organic change and growth and decay which the castle exhibited seemed somehow unfair; an unpleasant reminder of something she might never have again.

Now she filled up her spare time with reading. She took books from the interior walls of the castle and read them. They were in many different languages, most of them tongues from the nameless planet which was the castle's Subject and from where all the books seemed to originate. These languages she could not understand.

Some of the books, however, appeared to have been produced on this single globe as translations into other – alien – languages, some of which Ajayi could to varying degrees understand. She often wondered, as she read, if perhaps the name of the Subject world was some sort of clue; it had been carefully removed from any and every book in the castle which mentioned it, the word cut out from each page it had been written on.

Ajayi read the books she could. She took them from the littered floor of the games room, or from deteriorating walls and columns, only glancing at most of them, dropping or replacing those whose languages she couldn't understand, scanning the remainder and keeping to read later those which sounded interesting. Only about one in twenty or thirty was both comprehensible and intriguing.

Quiss wasn't happy with her new pastime, and accused her of wasting not only her own time, but his as well. Ajayi had told him she needed something to keep her sane. Quiss still grumbled, but he was hardly blameless himself. He still went for his long walks through the castle, and sometimes didn't come back for several days. She had tried asking him what he did, but the reaction was always either blank or hostile.

So she was reading, and gradually, with the use of some picture books she had discovered in one not-too-distant gallery, she was trying to teach herself one of the languages she kept encountering in the books which appeared to be written in one of the Subject world's own tongues. It was difficult – almost as though by design – but she was persevering, and after all, she had plenty of time.

THE CAT SAT ON THE MAT. Well, it was a start.

Ajayi put her last domino down. Quiss hesitated before completing the pattern, suddenly unsure which end of the line of tiles to put his last one on.

The woman was getting restless, and soon, he guessed, it would be time to eat. And this would be another wasted, stupid game, like all the others, no matter what way he put this piece down. They should have come up with a solution by now, a good pattern, a logical arrangement that would satisfy whatever subtle mechanism existed within the small table. But they hadn't. Were they doing something wrong? Had something escaped them in their attempt to escape? They had checked and re-checked and didn't think so.

Perhaps they were just unlucky.

Already they had gone through three sets of the pieces; three times he had become so frustrated with the whole idiotic exercise he had just thrown the dominoes away, out over the balcony; once while still in their ivory box, once lifting the table and shaking it over the edge of the balcony (Ajayi had almost died of fright, he remembered with a grim smile; she thought he was going to throw the table away too, and there was only one table; no replacements. If it was destroyed or badly damaged then they were not allowed to play any more games, and therefore could give no more answers), and once he had just cuffed the bone pieces off the table surface and sent them scattering through the pot-bellied slatework of the balcony's balustrade. (However, now the seneschal was saying he would have the table bolted to the floor.)

Well, what did they expect? He was a man of action. This constipated, decaying puzzle-palace wasn't his sort of place at all. Ajayi seemed to enjoy it at times, and he would have to sit sometimes, fidgeting, while she expounded on some philosophical or mathematical idea she thought might get them out of their predicament. He wasn't going to challenge her on what was more or less her home ground, but from the little that even he knew of philosophy, he thought that her smug positivism sounded too soulless and logical to be much use in the real world. What the hell was the point of trying rationally to analyse what was fundamentally irrational (or a-rational as she, splitting hairs as usual, would sometimes admit)? It was a way to arrive at personal madness and despair, not some universal understanding. But he wasn't going to put this to Ajayi; she'd smile tolerantly and shoot him down in flames, without a doubt. Know your strengths; don't attack where you're weak. That was his sort of philosophy; military. That and an acceptance that life was basically absurd, unfair and – ultimately – pointless.

The woman read a lot. She was going downhill, even trying to understand one of the common languages she had found in the books on the games room floor and in the walls. It was a bad sign, Quiss was sure. She was starting to give in, not taking the games they were playing seriously. Or taking them too seriously; the wrong way. The appearance was taking over the reality. She was getting caught up in the surface of the games, not their real meaning, so that instead of getting the games over with as quickly as possible and so getting to their real goal – another crack at the riddle – she was starting to behave as though the playing, the motions and apparent choices, mattered.

He wasn't going to give up, but he did need to escape this dead, desperate feeling the games and the woman gave him. He had escorted her round the castle for a while, showing her the odd places he had discovered, the one or two odd characters who existed in the place (the neurotic barber was his personal favourite), but gradually she had gone off more and more by herself, then seemingly become bored with it (or frightened, somehow, he wasn't sure), and stopped.

He still visited the castle's lower floors and storeys, journeying down to the kitchens and even beyond, so far below he guessed he was almost down to the level of the snowy plain itself, deep inside the rocky crag the castle proper stood upon. There were a few strange things down there, and, past a certain level, a suspicious number of locked, stout, metal-banded doors.

He had a few attendants he had partly befriended and partly terrorised into acting as guides for him. He told them he would put in a good word for them with the seneschal if they did what he wanted, but that if they didn't he would have them transferred to the slate mines or the ice-gathering expeditions. Apart from these bribes and threats (none of which he could deliver on as he had no influence whatsoever with the seneschal in such matters) he relied entirely on personal charm.

The stunted minions led him to new places in and under the Castle of Bequest, and even told him things about themselves; that of course they too were exiles from the Wars, but from a somewhat lower scale than he and Ajayi. They even coyly revealed the secret of their physiology; Quiss listened patiently though in fact he knew all about their physical make-up, having taken one of them apart not long after he first arrived in the castle, trying to torture the truth out of it. So he knew that these failed soldiers had no solid bodies at all; he had peeled layer after layer off the one he was interrogating, robe after robe after vest after vest after tunic after tunic, taking off finer and finer layers of gloves and little socks and clothing, taking off mask after mask only to find smaller and smaller masks inside, and a sort of ubiquitous gooey stuff which permeated all the fabrics and in places acted like some silicone mixture, flowing easily but cracking when hit sharply. This whole, weird stripping process was accompanied by the gradually diminishing screams of the wretch he had tried his experiment on. The bits of it he tore off and threw to the ground moved weakly of their own accord, as though trying to reassemble themselves, while the bit he still held, slowly getting smaller and weaker and thinner as he went on, struggled hopelessly.

Eventually he was holding nothing more than a sort of squidgy sack, like a sort of sticky fabric balloon from which a clear, odourless fluid wept, while all the rest of the layers and pieces of clothing trembled and spasmed on the glassy floor around him, their movements attracting the slowly writhing shapes of the luminescent fish in the waters below. He hung the whole scrappy assemblage out to dry, eventually, on a makeshift washing line. The wind moved the pieces so that he could not tell whether the thing was still in some dismembered way alive, or not. A few crows had pecked at the remains, but not for long. When he brought the bits back in to try and reassemble them, they had started to smell, so he just threw it all away.

He had asked the minions if they knew of anything the castle kitchens produced – or any other part of the castle produced, for that matter – which could get a chap *merry*? You know; drunk, happy, smashed, out of one's box? Did they?

They looked at him, mystified.

Drink? Fermented something-or-other. Brewed or distilled; boiling off vapours to leave alcohol behind, or even freezing water off . . . fruit, vegetables, grains . . . no? Any plants they knew of which, when you dried the leaves . . . ?

The minions had never heard of such things. He suggested they investigate, see if they could set something up. He met a few of them every now and again, and was even fairly confident that he could have picked them out in a crowd of the things. They weren't all identical, after all; they had slightly different patterns of stains and scorch-marks on their little robes which helped one to identify them, and of course their boots seemed to be colour-coded to their precise duty in the castle's service structure. The ones he had made contact with, this gullible gang, tried to do what he asked them. They stole food from the kitchens and hid bits and pieces of kitchenware under their cloaks. They tried to set up a still and a fermentation vat, but it didn't work. They produced a liquid at one rendezvous which made Quiss throw up just from the smell, and when he ordered them to take him to their equipment so that he could look it over and set it up properly, they explained that they had set it up in the only place they thought was safe from the prying eyes of the seneschal; their own quarters, where the cramped scale of their tiny cells and corridors made it impossible for the seneschal – and, alas, Quiss – to enter. They refused to set it up anywhere else. The seneschal would do *much* worse things to them than what Quiss was threatening. This was all strictly illegal and against the rules, didn't he know?

Quiss was depressed by this. He had thought it would

be possible to find *some* way of getting out of one's skull in this place. Perhaps it was thought that here in Castle Doors reality itself was so strange that there was no need for any substance to make it more so. That was Ajayi's sort of thinking; logical but out of touch, even naïve.

Then, by chance, he found something which really did do just that; alter reality. But not in the way he had expected.

He had been exploring alone, deep down, well underneath the level of the kitchens and the great central clock mechanism. The walls were of naked slate, blasted and scraped out of the rock on which the castle stood. Light came from transparent pipes set in the ceiling, but it was cold and still quite dark. He came to one of the heavy, metal-strapped doors he had seen time and time again on his travels in the lower levels, but unlike all the rest, this one was open very slightly. He could see a glint of light as he passed; he stopped, looked around, then pulled the door towards him.

It was a small, low-ceilinged room. The ceiling was like that of the upper reaches of the castle, made of glass, with a few dim specimens of the light-fish swimming slowly to and fro. The floor was rock. The room had one other door, on the far wall, also constructed of wood and metal strapping. In the centre of the room, alone in the place, stood a small stool. Above it was what looked like a hole in the glass ceiling.

Quiss looked up and down the dark corridor. There was nobody about. He slipped into the room, observing as he did so that the door had in fact been locked, but somehow the bolt had missed the hole it ought to have slipped into. He let the door swing to behind him, so that it caught on the extruded bolt, but was as closed and as unobtrusive from the outside as possible. He explored the small room.

The far door was locked securely. There was nothing in the place except for the small stool under the hole in the ceiling glass. It looked like the stools the scullions employed to bring themselves up to the right level to attend to their duties in the kitchens. The hole above the stool was dark; something seemed to be shielding the inside of the hole from the glow of the light-fish. A large, shadowy shape filled a circle nearly a metre in diameter around the hole, which was ringed with what looked like some sort of fur, like a collar, and which was just about big enough for a human head to go through. Warily, Quiss went up to it. He stood on the stool.

There were two metal bands, hoops of iron which extended from the lower surface of the glass ceiling's iron reinforcing bands, with leather pads on them. The U-shaped pieces of metal were on either side of the hole, a little over half a metre apart, and hanging about a quarter of a metre down from the ceiling. Looking at them more closely, Quiss saw they were adjustable; they could be lowered or raised slightly, and set further apart or closer together. He didn't like the look of them. He had seen pieces of torturing apparatus which looked vaguely similar.

He peered up into the dark hole in the glass ceiling.

He carefully touched the fur surround. It seemed ordinary enough. He took the end of his loose-fitting fur sleeve and poked the pinched cuff up into the hole. It came back down unscathed, and he inspected it carefully. He grimaced, stuck a small finger into the gap. Nothing. He put his whole hand in. There was the faintest of tingling feelings, like blood going back into a cold limb after a winter's walk.

He looked at his hand. It too seemed undamaged and the tingling had disappeared. He put his head tentatively up towards the hole, the fur tickling his grey-haired head. The hole smelled of . . . fur, if anything. He stuck his head up inside, not the full way, and only briefly. He had a very vague sensation of tingling on his skin, and an even more vague impression of scattered lights.

He put his hand in one more time, felt the tickling, tingling on it, then checked the door again. He stood on the stool and put his head fully up into the hole.

The tingling disappeared quickly. The impression of tiny scattered lights, like a rather too consistent starfield, stayed, and it made no difference whether his eyes were open or not. He thought for a moment he could hear voices, but wasn't sure. The lights were unsettling. He felt he could make them out individually, but at the same time felt there were too many – far too many – to count, or even for him to be able to see separately. Also, he had the disturbing impression that he was looking at the surface of a globe; all of it, all of it at once, in some way spread out in front of him so that no part of it hid another part. His mind swam. The lights seemed to beckon him, and he could feel himself starting to slide down towards them, then pull back as he fought the impulse. He arrived back at some still point.

He got down out of the hole again. He rubbed his chin. Very odd. He put his head back in. Temporarily ignoring the lights, he snapped his fingers, outside, in the room. He could just hear the small sound. He felt for the iron loops and put his arms through them, supporting himself there as one was obviously meant to.

He felt the pull of those lights again, and let himself go towards them, sliding down towards one area. He found that just by thinking about them he could head for other areas. It was as though he was parachuting, able to steer however he wanted as he fell.

As he approached the area of lights he was sliding towards, he got the impression of them also being strangely globe-like yet spread out. He still had the impression that he could see too many, that they should not look so individual for their apparent size, but he ignored this as he approached the surface of whatever the lights were placed upon. He tried to convince himself that he was floating towards the outside of the sphere, that he had started at the centre and worked his way out, but for some reason he felt he was falling down the way, on to a convex surface.

A single light approached; an orb of shifting, multi-coloured hues, like something cellular, dividing and re-dividing within a single membrane, yet with the patterns in the sphere somehow like distorted pictures, images thrown haphazardly on an unfixed screen. He felt himself float round this odd, scaleless thing, the other lights still apparently as far away as they had always been, and he felt oddly attracted to this globe of light, and that he could somehow, without damage to it or himself, enter inside it.

He was still, when he thought about it, aware he was standing in the room. He snapped his fingers, felt the edge of his tunic sleeve where it still hung at his side, then willed himself to enter the glowing, slowly pulsing sphere.

It was like walking into a room filled with babbling voices and lit with chaotic, ever-changing images. His head was full of confusion for a moment, then he thought he started to glimpse patterns and real shapes within the inchoate mix.

He let himself relax slightly, ready to watch, and just then all the images and noises seemed to coalesce, become part of some single feeling, which included the impression of touch and taste and smell as well. Quiss reacted against this, and was back in the noisy, gaudily chaotic room-feeling. He relaxed again, just a little more warily and slowly. The strange crystallisation of sensation occurred again, and slowly Quiss became aware of some sort of other thought-process, a set of feelings which was at once intimately close but still utterly cut off from him.

The truth of what was going on suddenly hit him, stunning him. He was inside somebody else's head.

He was so amazed he didn't have time to be revolted or really shocked before the novelty, the sheer interest of it all, took him, excited him. He shifted his body slightly, feeling in a very distant sort of way, like something in a dream, his feet move on the small stool he stood on, his armpits settling a little more comfortably into the leather-softened hoops.

He felt a moment of dizziness as the light and sound swelled around him, then a sudden, sharp feeling of anxiety; fear and distress. He smelled burning, heard loud, crude engine noises, saw metal wheeled vehicles frighteningly close (the fear increased, he felt dizzy again, sensed he was somehow losing contact), then he looked up, or the person whose head he was in did, and saw a blue, blue sky, like some polished, blue, shining sphere, some immense, smooth and flawless jewel.

The dizziness made him stagger (he only then realised he – or his host – was walking), and a wave of fear pulsed at him, sending him out and away, breaking off, back into the strange, dark, light-speckled space again, his heart beating wildly, his breath quickened.

He collected himself, snapped his fingers a couple of times, back in the real room inside the Castle Doors.

He vaguely considered giving up his little experiment; that experience had been frightening and alien, but he decided to persevere. This was much too fascinating to abandon now, he might not get another chance to explore so, and anyway he wasn't going to give in to some undisciplined streak of cowardice, not him.

He let himself fall gently towards another of the soft-looking orbs of shifting colours, and entered it as before. There was the same feeling of dizziness, but no fear this time.

He was looking at a pair of hands, holding small stalks

in one hand, taking a stalk at a time from the bunch and planting them quickly, accurately, into holes in brown earth. His back was sore. The arms were brown, like the earth. They were his arms, the arms of the person he was inside, and he wore some sort of loose, filmy covering. The arms were very slim. He – or rather the other person – stood up, straightening that sore back, putting one arm behind their back and stretching again. The view was of lots of women doing the same thing he was; stooped, putting shoots into the ground. The landscape was fiercely lit by a high sun. The ground was brown, he could see distant shacks and what looked like thatched roofs. There were some hills in the distance, green, cut with terraces like map contours made solid. Tall trees with naked trunks and all the leaves in a round bunch at the top. The sky was blue. A thin white vapour-trail stretched across it. There were a few clouds, pure white. His belly rumbled, and he thought of – what? The child in his belly.

The woman whose body he had invaded bent back to the soil. Why yes! Now he thought about it he could feel the weight on her chest; tits! The child must be small, because his/her belly felt normal, if a bit empty (and at the back of her mind the woman, he realised, was looking forward to a small meal of some stored, baked grain in another few hours, after which she still would not feel full; she would still be hungry. She had always been hungry. She always would be hungry. Probably so would this child, like all the others). A woman! Quiss thought. A peasant; a hungry peasant; how odd! How strange to be in this way inside her body, there but not there, here but not here, listening in. He tried to sense her own feelings about her body, as the woman bent to her task again, methodically planting the small green shoots. She was chewing on something, her mouth working on some substance, she was not actually eating; something numbing, something which helped to deaden thought and make the work easier.

How very, very singular, Quiss kept thinking. And although this was a woman's body, strangely it didn't feel all that different to being inside his own; less than he would have imagined. Maybe he just wasn't making full contact, he thought, but somehow he got the impression he was. The woman didn't seem totally aware of herself. Not specifically as a woman. What about her – ?

The woman's hand moved, involuntarily, towards her sex, actually brushing the gathered-up material of her clothing between her legs. She stood up, puzzled almost, then stooped back to her work. A pain or an itch, she thought. Quiss was amazed; just by thinking something he had made the woman do it.

He imagined that she had an itch behind her right knee. She scratched there, quickly and hard, hardly breaking the rhythm of planting and stooping. Fascinating!

Then something was pulling at the woman's leg, but she ignored it. In fact she didn't seem aware of it. Quiss didn't understand; he could feel the tugging. It was quite urgent and insistent . . . then he remembered where he was really standing. His head swum slightly for a moment as he re-oriented himself mentally, then he was aware again of the weight under his arms and on his feet. He took his arms out of the loops and ducked down, back into the room under the Castle Doors.

'Don't do that! Don't do that!' a small attendant squeaked, jumping up and down as it tugged on the hem of his tunic. 'You can't do that! It isn't allowed!'

'Don't tell me what to do, you . . . nanobrain!' Quiss kicked the attendant square in the chest, sending it tumbling away from him over the slate floor. It quickly picked itself up, pulled its loosened cowl-brim back down tight and glanced at the opened door. It put its little hands together, the yellow-gloved fingers meshing.

'*Please* get out of here,' it said. 'You really shouldn't be in here at all. It isn't allowed. I'm sorry, but it just isn't.'

'Why not?' Quiss said, hanging on to one of the iron loops and leaning forward, glaring at the small attendant.

'It just isn't!' it screeched, jumping up in the air and waving its arms about. Quiss found something funny about the thing's antics juxtaposed with the frozen expression of aching sadness shown on its mask. He got the impression from its sheer anxiousness that it was in some way responsible for leaving the door open. It wasn't pleading with him to leave just for his sake; it was frightened stiff.

'Actually,' Quiss said lazily, letting the iron hoop he was holding take his weight as he leaned back underneath the open hole in the glass ceiling and looked inside, 'I've found this to be a quite fascinating experience. I don't see why I should stop now just because you tell me to.'

'But you must!' the attendant shrieked, flapping its

arms about and running forward towards him. It thought the better of tugging at his tunic again, however, and stayed about a metre away from the stool, hopping about from foot to foot and wringing its hands. 'Oh, you must! You aren't supposed to see any of this. It isn't allowed. The rules—'

'I'll go if you tell me what it is,' Quiss said, glowering at the small figure. It shook its head desperately.

'I can't.'

'Fair enough,' Quiss shrugged, and made as though to put his arms back through the hoops again.

'No no no nonono!' the attendant wailed. It ran forward, throwing itself at his legs as though tackling him. He looked down at it. It cuddled his hosed shins like a tiny lover; he could feel it trembling. It was terrified; how delightful!

'Get off my legs,' Quiss said slowly. 'I'm not going to go until you tell me what this is.' He glanced back up at the dark shadow inside the glass which surrounded the hole. He shook his right leg, and the quivering attendant rolled along the floor. It sat on the slate, put its head in its hands, then it glanced towards the door which Quiss had found open. It got up quickly and took a key out of its pocket, put it in the lock, twisted it, shoved the heavy door to with some difficulty, then locked it.

'You promise?' it said. Quiss nodded.

'Of course. I am a man of my word.'

'All right, then.' The attendant ran forward. Quiss sat down on the little stool. The attendant stood, facing him. 'I don't know what it's called, or even if it has a name.

It's a fish, they say, and it just sits there and . . . well
. . . *thinks.*'

'Hmm, it thinks, eh?' Quiss said thoughtfully, rubbing
his neck. A little bit of fur from the hole's collar had stuck
to his tunic neck; he picked it off and fiddled with it.
'What, exactly, does it think about?'

'Well . . .' the attendant looked agitated and confused.
It kept shifting its weight from one yellow-booted foot
to the other and back again. '. . . it doesn't actually think
so much as experience. I think.'

'You think,' Quiss repeated, unimpressed.

'It's a sort of link,' the attendant said desperately. 'It
links us up with somebody . . . in the . . . on the Subject
world.'

'Ah-ha!' Quiss said. 'I thought so.'

'There, that's all there is to it,' the small attendant said,
and started tugging at his sleeve, its other hand indicating the door it had just locked.

'Just a moment,' Quiss said, and jerked the sleeve away
from the creature's grasp. 'What is the name of this Subject
place, this planet?'

'I don't know!'

'Hmm, well I suppose I'll find out soon enough,' Quiss
said, and started to get up off the stool, looking up at the
hole. He stood and grasped the iron hoops, put one foot
on the stool. The attendant jumped up and down, its little
yellow gloves made into fists and jammed together at the
small hard mouth of its face mask.

'No!' it shrieked. 'I'll tell you!'

'What's it called then?'

'"Dirt"! It's called "Dirt"!' the hopping attendant said. 'Now will you go, *please*?'

'Dirt?' Quiss said incredulously. The attendant beat its gloves on its head.

'I . . . I . . . I think . . .' it spluttered, 'I think it loses something in the translation.'

'And this thing,' Quiss nodded up at the ceiling, at the shadow round the hole. 'It forms a link from here to this place called Dirt. Is that right?'

'Yes!'

'And are all the people on this planet . . . accessible? Are all those lights you see initially individual people? How many? Can you get into any of them? Are they all unaware of people looking in on them? Can they all be affected?'

'Oooh no,' the small attendant said. It stopped jumping and bouncing around, seemingly collapsing in on itself. Its shoulders dropped, it looked forlornly down at the slate floor. It went and sat with its back to the door. 'All the lights you see at the start are individuals.' It sighed, talking more slowly now in a small, resigned voice. 'They are all available, and can all be influenced. There are about four billion of them.'

'Hmm. Their bodies look quite similar to ours.'

'Yes, they're supposed to. It is our Subject, after all.'

'That's where all the books come from?'

'Yes.'

'I see,' Quiss said. 'Why?'

'Why what?' the small attendant said, looking up at him.

'Why the link? What's it all for?'

The small attendant put back its head and laughed. He had never heard one of them laugh before. It said, 'How am *I* meant to know *that*?' It shook its head, looked back at the floor again, 'What a question.' Suddenly it sat bolt upright. It turned quickly and pressed the side of its head to the door. It spun round to face him. 'Quickly; it's the seneschal! You must get out!'

It quickly unlocked the door and pulled it open, its small boots sliding and skidding on the slate floor with the effort. Quiss was on his feet, but he couldn't hear anything. He suspected the small attendant of trying to trick him. It looked at him, held out its little hands, pleading with him. 'For your own sake, man. You'll be here for ever; you must go now.'

Quiss could hear a sort of deep rumbling noise from beyond the open door. It sounded like one of the main driveshafts from the great clock, heard through one of the thinner walls. It hadn't been there when he entered the room from the corridor outside. He went quickly to the door and outside. The attendant ducked out with him, and he helped it close the heavy door. The rumbling noise stopped. From along the corridor, as Quiss and the attendant went in opposite directions (the small creature scurried to a tiny door on the far wall and disappeared through, slamming it), a tortured squeaking, squealing noise came. Quiss was walking slowly towards the source of this cacophany; it sounded like metal scraped over metal. A wedge of light came from the side of the wall, and from a large square room with metal gates which squeaked and squealed as they were concertinaed to one side, and which Quiss realised must be a lift, the seneschal emerged with an entourage of black-cloaked minions. They stopped in the corridor when they saw him. Quiss looked at the small figures surrounding the seneschal, and for the first time felt genuinely apprehensive of the castle's dwarfish inhabitants.

'May we escort you back to your own levels?' The seneschal's voice was cold. Quiss got the impression he had little choice; he entered the elevator with the seneschal and most of the small minions, and they let him out a few storeys below the games room level. Nothing else was said.

He had tried since to find either the attendant he had met in the room, or the room itself, but without success. He thought they had probably rebuilt some of the corridors down there; a lot of building work had been going on in that area recently. He was fairly sure, too, that even if he did ever find himself in the same place, the door would be locked.

He hadn't said anything to Ajayi about this. He enjoyed having knowledge she didn't. Let her read, and complain about not having the name of this mysterious place; he knew!

Quiss placed his last domino down. The two of them sat looking at the irregular construction of flat, placed ivories, as though expecting it to do something. Then Quiss sighed and went to scoop them up for another game. He might persuade Ajayi to give it another go before she broke off for food or a book. Ajayi was leaning forward, putting out one hand to stop her companion from starting another game. Then she became aware that the dominoes weren't moving. Quiss was trying to prise them from the surface of the small table, and growing annoyed.

'Now what the—' he began, and went to pick up the table. Ajayi stopped him, putting her hands on his forearms.

'No!' she said, and met his gaze. 'This might mean . . .'

The old man realised, and quickly got up from his seat and went into the hot, bright space of the games room. By the time he came back from calling for an attendant, Ajayi was leaning over the table with a smile on her face, watching as a pattern of spots slowly appeared on the dominoes they had placed there.

'There, you see!' Quiss said, sitting down, bright-faced with sweat and triumph. Ajayi nodded happily.

'Gosh,' said a small voice, 'it's awfwy hot in here.'

'That was quick,' Quiss said to a waiter as it appeared from the games room's bright interior. It nodded.

'Welw,' it said, 'I was on my way here to see what you wanted fo' wunch. But I could take you-wanswer, if you wike.'

Ajayi was smiling at the waiter, finding its speech impediment more funny than she knew she ought. She was just in a good mood, she supposed. Quiss said, 'Certainly you can; it's . . .' he glanced at Ajayi, who nodded, and Quiss continued, '. . . they both disappear in a blaze of radiation. Got that?'

'"They bofe disappea' in a bwaze of wadiation." Yes, I fink I've got that. Twy not to be too wong; see you water . . .' It turned and waddled back through the games room, head down, mumbling the answer to itself, its little blue boots sparkling with reflected light from the fish under the glass floor, its steps and voice dopplering oddly as it passed a clock face.

'Well . . .' Quiss said, and leaned back in his chair, taking a deep breath, putting his hands behind his head and resting one booted foot on the balcony balustrade, 'I think we might just have got it this time, you know that?' He looked at Ajayi. She smiled and shrugged.

'Let us hope so.'

Quiss snorted at such faint-hearted lack of belief, and looked out over the blank white plain. His thoughts returned to that odd experience in the room deep in the castle's bowels. What was the point of that hole, that absurdly named planet and the link between here and there? Why the ability actually to make those people do things? (He had, reluctantly, discounted the idea that it was only he who had this intriguing capacity.)

It was most frustrating. He was still in the process of trying to get his contacts in the attendants to talk about this new aspect of the castle's mystery. So far they had been quite unforthcoming, despite all his cajoling and threats. They were frightened, no doubt about that.

He wondered just how immutable the castle's society really was. Might it be possible, for example, for them – him – to carry out a *coup*? After all, what god-given right did the seneschal have to run the place? How had *he* come to power? Just how closely did the two sides in the Wars supervise the castle?

Whatever the answers, at least it gave him something else to think about apart from the games. There might be another way out. There just might; never assume things were set and certain. That was a lesson he'd learned long ago. Even traditions change. Maybe this run-down heap was approaching some sort of catastrophe curve-edge, some *change*. Once, no doubt, it had been all its architects had intended, perhaps full of people, intact, not crumbling, fortress as well as prison . . . but now Quiss felt its pervasive air of decay, tottering senility made it – if he could find the right key, or weapon – easy prey. The seneschal was only slightly impressive; nobody else was at all. He – along with the woman – was the most important person in the place, he was sure. It was all for them, it revolved around them, only really made sense if they were here, and that itself was a kind of power (as well as a comfort – he liked to feel he was, as he had been in the Wars, part of an elite).

Ajayi sat, wondering whether to wait for the small waiter to return before she went on reading her book. It was a strange story about a man, a warrior, from an island near one of the planet's poles; he was called Grettir, as far as she could make out from the translation she was reading. He was very brave except for being afraid of the dark. She wanted to go on reading, no matter what the response was to their riddle-answer. Either way she couldn't imagine anything happening for a while.

They were both sitting there, quiet, absorbed, a few minutes later when, from the bright, air-shimmering depths of the games room a small voice said,

'Sowwy . . .'

FOUR

Penton Street

Outside the Belvedere pub, in Penton Street, a table stood on the pavement, guarding the pub's open cellar doors. They must be expecting a delivery from the brewers, Graham thought. The table, wood and formica, standing over the two opened traps of the cellar, reminded him of the chair in the corridor of the School, just before he left.

He was almost at the top of the low, building-disguised hill now; the road had all but flattened out. A few cars went along Penton Street, but it was quiet after the bustle of Pentonville Road, which he had just crossed. He looked over to the far side of the street, at some shops, a café. The area seemed unable to make up its collective mind whether it was run-down or not.

A copy of that day's *Sun* newspaper tried to wrap itself round Graham's feet, caught in a sudden dusty gust of wind. He stepped out of it and let it flatten against some roadside railings. He smiled, recalling Slater's apoplectic reaction to *Sun* readers. The best time, Graham thought, was when – only a few weeks ago – they had been sitting in Hyde Park. Slater had decided that as they were all going to be around during the summer anyway, they should arrange days out, and had therefore organised a Saturday afternoon picnic, having made up his mind on the Friday that the following day would be hot and sunny, which it was.

Slater had invited Graham, Sara, and a young man Graham assumed was Slater's latest conquest, a short, muscled ex-soldier called Ed. Ed had short fair hair and wore cut-off jeans as shorts, and a green Army T-shirt. He sat on the grass slowly reading a Stephen King novel.

They had talked, at Slater's instigation, about what they would do if they won a million pounds. Sara refused to play; ask her if she ever did win, she said. Ed thought carefully, and said he'd buy a big car, and a pub somewhere in the country. Slater didn't know what else he'd do, but he'd had this great idea for using at least some of the money; go to the American South, hire a crop-dusting plane and a willing pilot, fill the tanks with a mixture of chilli sauce and indelible black ink, then fly over the biggest Ku Klux Klan march of the year. *That* would make their eyes water; *paint* the mothers! Yippee!

Graham said he would use the money to create an

ultimate work of art . . . it would be a map of London, with every single street and house shown, and on it would be traced – in black ink, funnily enough – the path, the route that each individual person in London took that day, whether by train, tube, bus, car, helicopter, plane, wheelchair, boat, or on foot.

Sara laughed, but not unkindly. Ed thought it would be difficult to arrange. Slater pronounced the idea boring, and said that it would be boring even if the map was coloured and/or you used different-coloured inks for the trails, and anyway, his was a much better idea all round. Graham thought Slater sounded a bit drunk, and didn't reply – he just sat with a knowing smile on his face, and grinned briefly at Sara, who smiled back.

She wore a light summer dress with a high, elegant neck, and a big white hat. She had on white shoes with round toes and rather old-fashionedly large clumpy heels, and silk or silk-look stockings, or tights, which Graham thought were unnecessary on such a warm day. She leant against a tree, looking beautiful. When she put her head back, and put her arm behind her neck, he kept glancing, quickly, ashamed, at the dark length of curled hair in the exposed armpit.

Slater, in white trousers and striped blazer, complete with battered boater (real straw, Graham noticed), sat cross-legged on the grass holding a plastic cup full of champagne (he'd told Graham and Sara each to bring some food; he'd bring a Magnum).

From money, they had gone on to politics:

'Edward,' Slater said. 'You can-*not* be serious!'

Ed shrugged and lay back in the grass, one arm propping up his cropped head as he read the paperback gripped, spine broken, in his other fist. 'I reckon she's done all right,' he said. He had a vaguely East London accent. Slater bounced the heel of his free hand off his forehead.

'My *God*! The stupidity of the English working class never ceases to amaze me! What do those murderous, money-grabbing, self-seeking . . . *bastards* have to do to you before you start getting angry? Good grief! What are you waiting for? Repeal of the Factory Safety Act? Compulsory redundancy for all trade unionists? The death penalty for cleaning windows for gain while claiming the dole? I mean, *tell* me!'

'Don' be daft,' Ed shrugged. 'It isn' her fault; it's the recession, isn't it? Bleedin' Labour couldn't do no better; just nationalise everything, wouldn' they?'

'Edward,' Slater sighed, 'I think there's a place on the Editorial Board of *The Economist* just waiting for you.'

'Well, you can come out with all these smart answers,' Ed said, still reading, or at least looking at the paperback, 'but most people just don' see things the way you do.'

'Yes,' Slater said, hissing. 'Well, there's an open sewer at the bottom of Chancery Lane you can blame for that.'

Ed looked puzzled. He looked round at Slater. 'What's that, then?'

'Oh, good grief,' Slater said. He collapsed back in the grass melodramatically, but left his hand holding the champagne sticking up. 'Bingo!' he gasped.

The general election was in a few days. Slater couldn't

believe that people really were going to vote the Conservatives back in. Graham wasn't so sure it was such a bad thing, but he kept this private; Slater would have exploded. Graham agreed slightly with Ed; he didn't think anybody could do very much about the economic situation of the country. Certainly he thought the Tories spent too much on arms, especially nuclear weapons, and maybe they should spend more on things like the Health Service, but he admired Mrs Thatcher a little, and she had had a famous victory in the Falklands. He knew it was all rubbish, but he had felt a sort of grudging pride when the Army marched into Port Stanley. Ed didn't seem bothered about letting Slater know what he thought; Graham wasn't sure whether to admire him or feel sorry for him. He felt somewhat put out when he realised that Ed probably wouldn't care what he thought.

Ed stood up. 'Well, I think I'll go an' hire a boat. You want to come?' he looked at Slater, then Graham, then Sara, who shook her head. Slater lay on the grass while Graham looked at him.

'There's a terribly long queue,' Slater said. They had already discussed hiring a boat.

'If we don' queue we won' get a boat,' Ed shrugged. He stuffed the paperback into the rear waist of the denim shorts, against the small of his back. Slater said nothing, stared at the sky. 'Well,' Ed said, 'I can queue anyway. You come down later when I'm nearer gettin' a boat, if you like.' He stood there.

'Sometimes,' Slater said, addressing the sky, 'I think

it would be nice if they just got the war over with now. One ten-megaton over Westminster now, and we'd hardly know a thing . . . just vaporised dust mixed up with the grass and the soil and the water and the clay and the rock . . .'

'You're a right bleedin' pessimist,' Ed said. 'You sound like some of them C.N.D.-ers sometimes, you do.' He nodded down at Slater, hands on hips.

Slater kept staring at the sky. Then he said, 'I do hope you're not now going to tell me once again what a fine bunch of lads you met in the Army.'

'Shit.' Ed turned away, shaking his head, and started walking off towards the Serpentine and the boat houses. 'Well, if you don' want to fuckin' defend yourself . . .'

Slater lay there for a moment, then jerked upright, spilling a little of his champagne. Ed was about ten yards away. Slater shouted after him, 'Well, when it *does* fall, and you *do* fry, I just hope you remember what a fucking wonderful idea you thought it was!' Ed didn't react. People in nearby deckchairs and other groups of people also sunning themselves did, though, looking over.

'Sh,' Sara said lazily. 'You won't do any good shouting at him like that.'

'He's an idiot,' Slater said, collapsing back on the grass.

'He's entitled to his views,' Graham said.

'Oh, don't be stupid, Graham,' Slater snapped. 'He reads the *Sun* on the bus every morning going to work.'

'So?' Graham said.

'Well, my dear boy,' Slater said, talking through rictused lips, 'if he spends half an hour each day shovelling shit into his brain, you can't expect his ideas to do anything else but stink, can you?'

'He's still entitled to his views,' Graham said, feeling awkward under Sara's gaze, her cool regard. He played with a few blades of grass, twisting them in his fingers. Slater sighed.

'If he had any of his own, I might allow you that, Graham, but the question is: are the proprietors of Fleet Street entitled to Edward's views? No?' He came more upright, leaning on one elbow and looking at Graham. Graham made a face and shrugged.

'You expect too much of people,' Sara told Slater. He looked at her through hooded eyes, one eyebrow raised.

'Do I indeed?'

'They're not all like you. They really don't think the way you do.'

'They just don't think, period,' Slater snorted. Sara smiled and Graham was glad she was talking; it let him look at her, drink her in, without either of them feeling embarrassed.

'That's just it,' Sara smiled. 'They do, of course they do. But they believe in different things, they have different priorities, and a lot of them wouldn't want some perfect socialist state even if you could bring it about.' Slater snorted with derision at this.

'Great, so they're now getting ready to vote themselves five more years of cuts, poverty and exciting new methods of incinerating millions of our fellow human beings. Certainly a long way from your ideal socialist state; what is this, the de Sade school of political sociology?'

'So they get what they deserve,' Sara said. 'Why do you pretend to care so much more about them than they do themselves?'

'Oh, fuck,' Slater said, 'I give in.' He collapsed back on the grass. Sara looked at Graham, smiled and raised her eyebrows conspiratorially. Graham laughed quietly.

She hurt his eyes. She sat in the shadow of the tree, but the whiteness of her skin, the bright shoes and stockings and dress and the hat all reflected sunlight from the brilliant sky, and he could hardly look at her for the glow which struck his eyes.

He drank his champagne. It was still cool; Slater had brought the bottle inside a cool-bag, and it lay by the tree trunk, in shadow like Sara. Slater had been genuinely offended when Graham, told to bring glasses, turned up with only plastic cups. He thought Graham would *understand*.

Graham had been a bit worried about Slater meeting Sara; the last time either of them had seen her had been earlier that same week, and he thought Slater might have mentioned it. They had gone together up to Half Moon Crescent, on a day when Sara had suddenly cancelled their afternoon walk along the canal. She'd been abrupt, even distressed over the phone, and he had been worried. He had decided to walk up that way anyway, just to be there, in case there was anything obviously wrong. Slater had been concerned, too, both at Graham's obvious agitation, and at Sara's state as Graham described it. Graham didn't mind his friend coming along: he was glad of the company.

* * *

They started out walking, but then on Theobald's Road Slater insisted on getting a bus. Graham pointed out that a 179 only went as far as Kings Cross, which wasn't very far and not even in exactly the right direction. Slater said it was in roughly the right direction, and anyway his new shoes were tight and he didn't want to walk all that way. At King's Cross he got them a taxi. Graham said he couldn't really afford . . . Slater told him not to worry; he'd pay. It wasn't far.

In the taxi, Slater suddenly remembered something; he had a present for Graham. He dug into his jacket pocket. 'Here,' he said, and handed Graham something hard wrapped in tissue paper. Graham unwrapped it as the cab went up Pentonville Road. It was a small glazed china figurine of a woman, naked, with large breasts and her knees bent, feet under her buttocks, legs spread out. Her tiny face was set in an expression of ecstasy, her shoulders were thrown back as though she was forcing her conical breasts higher, and her hands were down at her hips, open and delicate, each finger carefully moulded. Her genitals, in the quick glance Graham gave them, seemed rather exaggerated.

'Is this supposed to be some sort of joke?' he said to Slater.

Slater took the figurine back with a grin and produced a pencil from his inside pocket, 'No,' he said, 'it's a pencil sharpener; look,' and he inserted the pencil between the model's legs.

Graham looked away, shaking his head. 'It is just a little bit tasteless.'

'I have more taste than anchovies in garlic butter, you young pup,' Slater said. 'I was just trying to cheer you up.'

'Oh,' Graham said, as the taxi turned left. 'Thanks.'

'Huh,' said Slater, sitting forward in his seat to make sure the taxi driver went the right way as they approached Half Moon Crescent. 'I spent several days making that for you.'

'I said thanks,' Graham said, then, 'Oh, tell him to stop here; don't want to get too close.' He checked the street to make sure Sara wasn't around; they were still in Penton Street, but you never knew.

The taxi stopped. 'Let's have a drink,' Slater said.

'I'll tell you one thing,' said Graham, as Slater led him across the street into a pub called the White Conduit,

'What?'

'You forgot about how to get the shavings out.' Graham held the china figure up in front of Slater's face. Slater frowned, looked at the over scale-sized orifice. His lips tightened.

'It's your round; I'll have a pint of lager,' he said, and went to sit at a window seat looking down the short stretch of Maygood Street to Half Moon Crescent.

They heard Stock's bike ten minutes later. They both stood up and looked over the top of the window curtains, which hung from a brass rail halfway up the window. A large black BMW bike turned down Maygood Street. The person riding it wore black leathers and a black, full face helmet with a heavily tinted visor. 'Yup,' Slater said, 'that's our man.'

Graham caught a glimpse of the bike's number: STK 228T. It was the first time he had seen the bike since that night in January when he first met Sara, when they had arrived here in the taxi. He hadn't thought to look at the bike properly then, and had always avoided coming up this way when he knew Stock was about. The rider straddling the machine got off it, took its key out and went – not entirely steady on his feet, Graham thought – to the door of Sara's flat, and put a key into the lock. Seconds later he was gone.

'Did you think he looked six foot?' Graham said, looking at Slater as they sat down. Slater nodded, took a drink.

'Easily. Looked a bit tipsy, I thought. What a hunk, though, eh?' He waggled his eyebrows up and down theatrically. Graham let his shoulders slump, and looked away.

'*Do* you mind?' he said. Slater nudged him.

'Don't take it so hard, kid. I'm absolutely certain it'll all work out. Believe me.'

'Are you really?' Graham said, turning to his friend.

Slater looked into Graham's face for a few seconds, watching him bite his lower lip, then his own lower lip trembled and finally a smile burst out over Slater's face as he turned away, shaking his head, sniggering.

'Well, to be honest, *no*, but I was trying to be encouraging. Good grief, how on earth should I know?'

'Jesus,' Graham breathed, and finished his half pint of bitter. He stood up, sighing. Slater looked at him unhappily.

'Oh God, you're not going out in a huff, are you?'

'I'm just going outside for a little bit . . . to have a look round. I won't be too long.'

'You know,' Slater said, weakly slapping the table top beside his drink, 'Oates, you're going to have to get those lines right before we hire the ice-breaker.' The last few words were barely comprehensible as Slater collapsed, forearm on table, head on forearm, his back shaking as he laughed, muffled grunts of mirth echoing off the floor beneath him. Some of the older customers in the bar looked at him suspiciously.

Graham frowned deeply at Slater, wondering what on earth he was talking about, then left and went for a quick, stealthy walk round the back of Half Moon Crescent and up a little side alley, listening for any shouts or arguments from inside the flat. There was nothing. He went back to the pub, where Slater had bought him a pint. As Graham sat down Slater started to shake and his face went red; tears appeared in his eyes, and finally he had to splutter, 'Fucking Norwegian bastards!' He fell sideways on the bench seat and doubled up with silent, spasmic laughter. Graham sat, feeling terrible, hating Stock and Slater and feeling sick about Sara and what she might be doing right now, and half-wishing that the pub landlord would throw Slater out.

Luckily, despite his threats, Slater did not tell Sara he and Graham had been there that day. They sat in the park later that week, getting slightly drunk on the champagne, and Slater talked about lots of things, but not that.

'I've just had this great idea,' he announced from the

grass, holding up his plastic cup. They had almost finished the champagne.

'What?' Sara said. She sat against the tree, Graham's head on her shoulder. He was pretending to be asleep so that he could keep his head there, near her soft, warm-scented skin.

'Interdopa,' Slater said, waving the cup around at the still blue sky. 'This *hippy* turns up on your doorstep, bums a fag off you and shoves a lump of crumpled silver paper into your hand . . .'

'Put me down for the inaugural run,' Sara laughed gently. Graham wanted to laugh, too, but could not; better to rest here, feel her lovely body shake, tremble under his head and touch . . .

He still remembered that feeling; weeks later he could still shiver at the thought of it. It was like the first time he had ever spent a night with a girl, back in Somerset. The next day, with his friends in the pub at lunchtime, watching a local football match in the afternoon, having dinner with his parents that evening, later watching a film on television at a friend's house, he kept having flash-backs; a flesh-memory of the feeling of that young woman's skin would suddenly make him shudder and his head swim. He recalled with some shame that he had been naïve enough at the time to wonder if this feeling was love. Luckily he hadn't talked to anyone about it.

He could see the White Conduit ahead now, and he remembered how wretched he had felt that afternoon. Since then he had been back here once again when he knew he wasn't expected. He'd said to Slater he was going home, when they parted at lunchtime in the sandwich bar in Red Lion Street, but in fact he came up here, and saw Stock arrive on the bike not long after he started watching. This time Sara was visible, moving about in the room she usually greeted Graham from when he pressed the entryphone buzzer. Stock had let himself in, and Sara had not reappeared.

Graham felt sick, and left soon afterwards. He got throwing-up drunk all by himself in Leyton that night.

The day in the park had been good, though. He had kept his head on Sara's shoulder for ages, until his back and neck ached, but she hadn't appeared to mind, and once had even stroked his hair, absently, with one caressing hand. Ed had come back later on; he'd had a half-hour's row on the Serpentine.

'You should've come down when I was nearer the front of the queue, you should,' he told them. He had bought some small dumpy cans of McEwan's Export, and handed the others one each. He sat down to read.

'You see?' Slater said loudly, still lying down, his voice slightly affected by the champagne he'd drunk. 'This man is a fucking socialist at heart and even he doesn't realise it!'

'Give it a rest, Dick,' Ed told him mildly.

Slater poured the last of his champagne over his own forehead. 'He calls me *Dick*,' he gasped in a strangled voice, and rolled over on to his face. 'Me: the communal ranger, superhom, the pinko pimpernel, the man in the

Fabergé mask; I'll scratch the mark of Zero on your fore-skin, you—'

'Shush now,' Sara ffitch said, her voice resonating in her chest, buzzing Graham's head with glorious sensation. Slater went quiet; he started snoring lightly a few minutes later.

A pretty girl, blonde, wearing a short bouncy skirt and a thin pink top through which Graham could just make out the outlines of her nipples, passed him on Penton Street. He watched her walk by, but didn't make it obvious.

He had always worried about this. He didn't want to be sexist, but how the hell did you *not* look at attractive women? He didn't say anything to them, or try to touch them; he'd never dream of that; he despised the stupid idiots who did that sort of thing; they made him ashamed to be a man; they were the sort Slater accused of 'carrying their brains in their scrotums' (or did Slater say 'scrota'?); but looking . . . as long as it didn't embarrass the woman . . . that was all right.

Especially now, or maybe, with a bit of luck, until now. It had been a strange, awkwardly sexual time for him. It had been worrying – of all things! – about masturbating.

He found it difficult, almost unpleasant to think of Sara at night, in bed, before he went to sleep. But to think of other women, previous sexual encounters, seemed wrong too. It was absurd, it was crazy, it was like being pubescent again, or worse; it didn't even make much sense in terms of the beliefs he had worked out long before about sexual fidelity, but there it was. He hated the idea of pornography, even soft pornography, but he had almost come round to the idea that it might be better to buy one of the glossy girlie magazines and accept the inhuman, labial beauty of those seductive image-women; it would at least absolve the release of his sexuality from the responsibilities of the real world.

'Most people's ultimate sexual fantasies, their idealised desires, are built of clay,' he recalled Slater saying. Slater had just discovered that most of the weight of a glossy magazine came from kaolin, the same clay used in a morphine mixture to clog up people's guts when they had the runs. Graham seemed to remember Slater had been talking about gay photo-mags, but the point was the same.

Anyway, what did it matter now? It might all be over soon; all the worrying and waiting and empty desiring. He was opposite the pub now; he would turn the corner on to the short length of Maygood Street, and there would be Half Moon Crescent.

The name fascinated him.

He made a symbol of it:

$$\frac{)}{2}$$

Half. Moon. Crescent.

Mr Sharpe

Drunk!

He sat on a park bench in the small triangular piece of ground which was called Islington Green. Mr Sharpe sat by his side; they were both drinking from large bottles of cider. Mr Sharpe was smoking a cigarette. Steven felt quite drunk.

'I mean,' Mr Sharpe said, stabbing at the air with his cigarette, 'they don't 'ave to stay where they fackin' well are, do they? 'Course they don't . . . do they?' Steven shook his head in case Mr Sharpe was really asking him a question. Most of the questions seemed to be rhetorical, though. He couldn't remember what Mr Sharpe was talking about now. Was it the Jews? The Blacks? Scroungers?

Mr Sharpe was a small man of about fifty-five. He was going bald and his eyes looked yellow in the grey-pink skin of his face, which was lined with grey stubble. He wore a big old coat and working boots. He had approached Grout in the pub he had gone to, the Nag's Head. Steven usually avoided pub drunks, and it was fairly obvious Mr Sharpe was the resident PD in the Nag's Head that lunchtime, but Steven was quite drunk himself, and apart from Mr Sharpe seeming to be encouragingly worried about conspiracies – Grout hadn't entirely given up the idea of finding a fellow exile and cooperating to escape together – Mr Sharpe had also displayed what appeared to be genuine good-heartedness when Steven told him it was his birthday. A few small tears had come to his eyes, in fact, when Mr Sharpe shook his hand for a long time and wished him many happy returns several times in a loud voice.

Steven had bought most of the drinks from then on, as Mr Sharpe wasn't working and didn't have very much money, but Steven didn't mind. He showed Mr Sharpe all the money he had, explaining that he had been paid off that day.

'The cans,' Mr Sharpe had said, spitting inadvertently, 'the fackin' cans; I bet it was them unions, wasn't it?'

Grout hadn't been sure about that, but he told Mr Sharpe he wasn't sorry anyway. He did say he couldn't spend all the money, of course, he had to keep some by for his rent and food and things, and he had to wait for his unemployment money. Mr Sharpe said he was quite right, but to watch out; there were plenty of smart jewboys and big black muggers around; the jewboys would swindle it off you and the niggers would slit your throat as soon as look at you.

After the pub shut at three, they went over to the Green with a couple of bottles of stout they had bought to carry out. Steven had bought Mr Sharpe a packet of cigarettes, too, and some matches. 'You're a gent, Steve, that's what you are; a gent,' Mr Sharpe had said, and Steven felt almost as good as when the policeman had called him 'sir'. He sniffed, eyes tingling.

They drank the bottles of stout, then Mr Sharpe said why didn't they nip over to the off-licence in Marks and Sparks on Chapel Market and get a couple of bottles of cider? It was cheap. In fact, if Steve would lend him the money; a fiver, say . . . no, make it a tenner, seeing as he felt generous and Steve was a real pal . . . he'd get the drink himself, seeing as Steve had been so generous in the pub and all. He'd pay him back next Wednesday, when his Giro came through.

Steven thought this sounded fair, and so he gave Mr Sharpe two ten pound notes. 'Have twenty,' he said. Mr Sharpe was taken aback and said again what a gent Steven was. He went off to the shop and got four bottles of cider and a carton of cigarettes.

Although he felt drunk, Steven didn't feel all morose like he usually did when he'd had a lot to drink; he felt quite happy, sitting on the bench under the trees of Islington Green with the traffic rushing harmlessly by all around. It was nice to have somebody to talk to, somebody you felt was on your side, who didn't laugh at you or show contempt for you, who felt sympathy for the way you were treated but not pity for who or what you were; somebody who wished you happy birthday. He didn't mind that Mr Sharpe was doing all the talking.

'You take the likes of my old boss, right?' Mr Sharpe was saying, drawing smoky patterns with the cigarette he held between his fingers. 'Good bloke, good bloke, you know; strict but fair; wouldn't stand for any nonsense or people turning up late or anyfink, but straight, know what I mean? In the textile trade 'e was; 'ad to mix with a lot of Jews. Didn't like it, of course, but that's business, innit? 'E went bust last year, didn't 'e? 'Ad to lay me an' the rest of the lads off, see? Recession, it was, basically, but also the fackin' unions. 'E used to give them short shrift, I can tell you; wouldn't 'ave them in the place, an' quite right too, say I, but 'e reckoned they'd got at 'im be'ind 'is back, like, an 'e's a smart bloke, right? Anyway, it was the recession what really did it, 'e said, and 'e said 'e was really choked 'e 'ad to let us go on account of 'ow we'd all stood be'ind 'im. An' we did; when 'e explained to us what was 'appenin' a couple of years ago, we didn't take no pay rise, did we? We even took a pay *cut* last year, that was 'ow much we was prepared to look after our jobs, see? Not like these fackin' union cans; we was responsible, we was. Yeah, 'e was really choked, Mr Inglis was. That was 'is name, was'n' it? "Inglis by name and English by birth, and proud of it", 'e would say.' Mr Sharpe laughed.

Steven took his blue safety helmet off and wiped his brow. He would have to go for a pee soon. It was lucky there were toilets at one end of the Green. 'Yeah, 'e's a good bloke, that Mr Inglis. An' you know wot 'e told me? 'E told me 'e didn't even make a profit the last *five years*. These fackin' Troskyists, they talk about bosses an' that, but they don't know nuffink, do they? I know, 'cos one of my nephews; 'e's a Troskyist, isn't 'e? Little can; I nearly knocked 'is bleedin' teeth out last time I saw 'im; only tryin' to tell me I was one of them racialists, wasn't 'e? I said, "Lissen, son," I said "I've worked with blacks an' I've even made friends with some of them, which is prob'ly more than you've ever done, an' I quite liked some of 'em; they was Jamaicans – not these little Pakkie cans – and they was okay, some of them, but that don't alter the fact there's too many of them over 'ere, an' that don't make me your racialist, now, does it?" Little can. That's wot I told 'im. Straight, I did.' Mr Sharpe nodded aggressively, reliving the confrontation.

Steven was toying with the leather sweatband of the hard hat. He was hot. It was probably safe to take the hat off; there was no scaffolding nearby. He put the hat down on the bench, between him and Mr Sharpe, who went on,

'Where was I? Oh, yeah; Mr Inglis, 'e said 'e 'adn't made a profit for *five years*, but people think just because 'e rides round in a Rolls-Royce, people fink 'e's bleedin' rich, don't they? *They* don't know, see, that it don't even belong to 'im; it's 'is company's. Even 'is 'ouse isn't 'is; it's 'is wife's, innit? 'E'd just as soon drive a Mini, but people in the trade wouldn't take 'im seriously, would they? Specially them jewboys.'

Steven shook his head, thinking this seemed to be

required. He wasn't all that happy about this mention of a Rolls-Royce. He considered telling Mr Sharpe about the dangers of disembowellings by Rolls-Royce mascots, but he thought he'd better not.

'But I'm glad to say,' Mr Sharpe said, smiling, lighting another cigarette, 'e's managed to get back on 'is feet again. I 'appened to see 'im the other day when I was looking for a job; 'e's got a new place up in Islington Park Street making dresses an' all an' repairing machines. 'Course, the place is full of these little wog wimmin, but, like Mr Inglis says, 'e'd love to 'ave whites working for 'im but people've got lazy, 'aven't they? 'E can't find white wimmin to work for them wages, an' why? Cos the fackin' money they're gettin' from the government an' from workin' on the side's too much, that's why. Mr Inglis, 'e'd love to take me an' the lads back on for the machines, but the fackin' unions they've priced us all out of a job, 'aven't they? Mr Inglis can't afford to take on more than a couple of experienced blokes an' all the rest are these YOPs or wotever they're called; you know, them young kids wot the government pays you to train, an' that.'

Steven nodded. He watched the reflections of the trees above him as they slid and swayed about the shiny blue surface of his safety helmet. It really was the most lovely shade of blue. He took it off the bench and put it on his lap.

'An' that stupid young nephew of mine, 'e'll tell you they don't take our jobs! Little poof. I think 'e's on that canopus stuff; I bet if you looked at 'is arms you'd find them pot-marks. I tried that stuff, you know; when I was in the navy I did, out in wogland somewhere; some fackin' place . . . but it didn't do nuffink for me an' anyway I wasn't that stupid to take enough to get me 'ooked, was I? Not me, mate; give me a pint an' a fag an' I'm quite 'appy.' Mr Sharpe puffed on his cigarette and took a drink of his cider.

Grout was thinking about beer crates. He'd had one, once; he remembered coming down Essex Road, on the very bit of pavement they could see in front of them, over the grass. The crate had seemed like such a good idea at first; a way round searching for parked cars all the time. He had taken the beer crate, which he'd found behind a pub one night, with him when he went to look for work one day, about a year ago. Whenever he was running out of breath and there were no parked cars or low walls to protect him from the laser-axles, he simply had to put the crate down on the ground and then stand on it. Safety at last!

It had been a brilliant idea, but people treated him like some sort of maniac. Young men shouted at him, women with children avoided him, a gang of kids started to follow him. He threw the crate into the canal eventually, cruelly hurt not just by the reaction people had exhibited, but also because he knew he didn't have the strength of character to resist them; he couldn't take that much scorn, he couldn't keep up such a high profile for long.

Yes, it had hurt, but he liked to think he had learned from the experience. He knew how cunning they were now, how carefully they made sure that he had no easy ways out. Mere ingenuity wouldn't help him live any easier here. He had to concentrate on escape, on finding the Key, the Way Out. Maybe he should ask Mr Sharpe about Hotblack Desiato. He seemed to know the area a bit, though Steven couldn't remember having seen him before either in the Nag's Head or anywhere else . . . but he said he lived locally. Maybe he would have some idea.

Yes, he supposed, the beer crate hadn't been such a good idea; it had shown them too obviously that he was on to them, that he felt contempt for them. He had to be more subtle.

'. . . what a little can, eh? Calling me a can . . .' Mr Sharpe was saying. Steven nodded. He really must go to the toilet soon. He took the safety helmet and hung it on the end of the bench. He put his bottle of cider down on the tarmac at his feet; it wobbled and fell, and rolled away spilling cider from the top for a couple of seconds before he could get hold of it again. He set it down more carefully.

'Oops-a-daisy,' he said.

''Ere, Steve,' Mr Sharpe said, nudging him with his bottle, 'you wanna watch that. That's precious stuff, that is. You can't afford to go wasting precious stuff like that, now can you? Not on your burfday even you can't, eh?' Mr Sharpe laughed. Steven laughed too, and got up from the bench. His tummy hurt a bit. He staggered slightly as he left the bench, and his right foot hit the plastic carrier bag with the rest of the drink and the carton of cigarettes Mr Sharpe had bought. 'Steady on,' Mr Sharpe laughed, putting out one hand to catch Grout.

'Just going to the lav,' Steven said. He patted Mr Sharpe's hand and started off.

''Ere, Steve, do one for me!' Mr Sharpe shouted after him, and laughed. Steven laughed too.

He didn't feel too bad, but he couldn't stand up properly; it was like having appendicitis or something like that. He walked bent over. Luckily it wasn't too far to the public toilets.

In the gents he had a good long pee and felt much better. He was quite drunk, he knew, but he didn't feel sick. Actually he felt pretty good. It was nice to have somebody to talk to, somebody who seemed to understand. He was glad he had met Mr Sharpe. Steven combed his hair slowly and carefully. It was a pity there was nowhere to wash his hands, which were a bit sticky, but never mind. He took some deep breaths to clear his head.

Outside the toilet, he stood looking at Jim's Café, across the street. Maybe he would treat Mr Sharpe to a meal. That would be nice. He swayed slightly as he went back into the little park. There were quite a few other men in the park. Some of them looked very poor and dead-beat, and Grout felt sorry for them.

When he got back to the bench, Mr Sharpe had gone.

He stood looking at the bench, swaying, staring at it, trying to work out if it really was the right bench. At first, though it seemed to be in the right position, he thought it couldn't be, because his good blue hat wasn't there, hanging on the end of it. The carrier bag and everything else had gone, too. He looked, mystified, at the nearby benches. Just a few tramps. He scratched his head.

What could have happened? Maybe it wasn't the right bench, maybe he was in completely the wrong place. But no, here was quite a lot of grey cigarette ash on the ground, and an empty cider bottle lying behind the bench, against the concrete kerb which separated tarmac path from green grass. His own bottle had gone.

He looked round. Traffic buzzed down Essex Road; buses moved redly up and down Upper Street. What could have happened? Had the police mistaken Mr Sharpe for a tramp and taken him away? Surely not the Tormentors; they wouldn't dare do anything so flagrant, so against the rules, would they? Just because he and Mr Sharpe had been getting on so well?

He kept looking around, thinking that suddenly he would see Mr Sharpe waving from another bench, beckoning him to come and finish his cider and stop being so stupid. Maybe Mr Sharpe had moved to another bench; that must be it. He looked round all the other benches, but all he saw were tramps and dead-beats. Had they done something to Mr Sharpe?

It *had* to be the Tormentors. It was one of their tricks, one of their filthy tests. He didn't believe it was the Jews, like Mr Sharpe had said; he knew it was the Tormentors. They had done this. He'd get them, though, he swore. He'd get to the bottom of this, right now!

He went to the nearest tramp, an old man lying on the grass. He had very long greasy black hair and a collection of plastic carrier bags spread out on the ground around him.

'What happened to my friend?' Grout said. The tramp

opened his eyes. His face was very tanned and dirty.

'I didnae do anythin', honest I didnae, son,' he said. A bloody drunken Scotsman! Grout thought.

'What happened?' Grout insisted.

'What, son?' The Scot tried to lever himself up off the grass, but couldn't. 'I didnae see anythin', honest. I've just been sleepin', honest. I havnae touched anythin', son. Don't you accuse me. Honest. It's no crime to sleep, you know, son. I've been abroad, you know, son, to foreign countries.'

Grout puzzled over this last statement, then shook his head. 'You're sure you didn't see anything?' he asked carefully, showing this drunk Scot that he at least knew how to speak correctly. He put some menace into his voice as he finished. '*Quite* sure?'

'Aye, I'm sure, son,' said the Scot, 'I've been sleeping; that's what I have been doing.' He seemed to be waking up, making an effort with his speech. Grout decided the man probably knew nothing. He shook his head and went back to the bench, standing beside it, looking about.

A tramp a couple of benches further up towards Upper Street was waving at him. Grout turned and went up the path to the man. This one was even older and grubbier than the Scot snoring on the grass, cuddling one of his carrier bags. Where on earth were all the clean people, Grout thought.

'You lookin' for yer frand, muster?' My God! This one was Irish! Where were all the English people? Why didn't they send some of *this* lot back where they came from?

'Yes, I am looking for my friend,' Steven said coldly,

carefully. The Irishman nodded towards the apex of the small triangle of park, towards the bus-stops on the far, north-bound side of Upper Street.

'He wen' up that way. Took all yur stuff,' the Irishman said.

Grout was puzzled. 'Why? When?' He scratched his head again.

The Irishman shook his head. 'I dunno, muster. He just up 'an wen' as soon as you wen' down to the toilets; I thought you'd had an argument or somethin', so I did.'

'But my hat . . .' Grout said, still unable to fathom why Mr Sharpe would do such a thing.

'That blue thing?' the Irish tramp said. 'He put that in huz bag.'

'I don't . . .' Grout said, his voice trailing off as he walked slowly up in the direction the Irishman had pointed.

He left the small park, waited for the traffic to clear, then crossed the road, over to the other side of Upper Street, keeping down by the roadside rather than going up the stepped curb on to the raised section of pavement, because he was afraid of things falling off buildings and he didn't have his hat. A horrible knotted feeling, a pain, started to eat at his guts; he felt the way he had in the home, when all the children he'd befriended were adopted or sent away, and he wasn't; the way he had when he got lost down by the sea at Bournemouth, on an outing. This can't happen to me, not on my birthday, he kept thinking. Not on my birthday.

He went down the side of the street, round the parked

cars nose-in to the slanted curb, down to the bus-stops, looking all the time for Mr Sharpe. For some reason he kept thinking that Mr Sharpe would be wearing the blue hat, and he found himself looking for that all the time instead of Mr Sharpe, who, he now realised, he probably couldn't have described very well if a policeman had asked him to. He wandered down, the terrible feeling growing in his guts like a live thing, wringing him, squeezing him. People mobbed about him, on the pavement, by the bus-stops, down ramps and out of buses; blacks and whites and Asians, men and women, people with shopping trolleys or bags of tools, women with children in push-chairs or dragged along from one hand. Older children ran by, screaming and shouting. People ate hamburgers from polystyrene boxes, chips from bags, they carried shopping or parcels, they were old and young and fat and thin and tall and little, dull and gaudy; he started to feel dizzy, as though the alcohol or the sultry air was dissolving him, as though the pain inside was wringing him out like a wet towel, twisted and squeezed. He staggered, pushed past people, looking for the blue helmet. He could feel himself being dissolved, his identity sapped from him, lost in this siege of faces. He got to the side of the curb, made sure there were no buses coming, then stepped out on to the in-set bus lane, turned round and started to head back the way he had come, further out from the crowd now, staggering and swaying his way back. He looked over his shoulder, but there were still no buses coming, ready to swing into the bus-stop lane and crush him, only traffic from the lights further down charging up the street, engines roaring. He heard a bike engine, revving, coughing. He kept going, heading back for the park; maybe Mr Sharpe would have come back. The holes he had repaired were around about here . . .

Rough, screaming engine noises shouted at him. He ignored them. A bike engine, spluttering, a diesel engine, revving. He felt suddenly dizzy and disoriented for a moment, filled both with a sudden panic and an unsteadying conviction he had been here before, seen this all before. He glanced up at the sky for a second, and felt himself stagger. His head cleared and he did not fall into the stream of traffic, but it had been close. He heard a great thundering noise then, a noise like a car hitting something, but probably just the sound empty lorries or trucks make when they go over those speed-ramp things, or holes in the road, too fast. He turned round slowly, still feeling strange, to see if it was one of the holes Dan Ashton and the squad had done. He bet it was.

A woman screamed from the pavement.

He looked up again, into the blue, blue sky, and saw something sailing out of it, like a reflection sliding over a globed, shiny blue surface.

A spinning cylinder.

A bike and a flat-bed truck flashed by on one side. He stood, transfixed, thinking; my hat . . . my hat . . .

The tumbling aluminium beer barrel hit him right on the top of his head.

Chinese Scrabble

They sat, covered in their furs, in a small open area near the summit of the Castle of Bequest.

A few decrepit towers and decaying fractions of floors with rooms and chambers rose into the shining grey sky to one side of them, but most of the apartments were empty and useless, only good for rookeries. Stones, great slabs of slate, lay tumbled all around the small cleared area where they sat. A few stunted trees and bushes, little more than overgrown weeds, poked out from the mass of fallen, fractured masonry. Ruins of arches and columns lay about them, and while they played Chinese Scrabble, it started to snow.

Quiss looked up slowly, in surprise. He couldn't recall

it snowing for . . . a long time. He blew some of the small, dry flakes off the surface of the board. Ajayi hadn't even noticed; she was still studying the two small remaining plastic tiles balanced on the little bit of wood in front of her. They were very nearly finished.

Nearby, perched on a pitted, flaking column, the red crow sat, puffing on the green stump of a fat cigar. It had taken up smoking at about the same time they had started playing Chinese Scrabble. 'I can see this is going to take some time,' it had said. 'I'd better find some other interests. Maybe I can contract lung cancer.'

Quiss had asked it, casually, where it got the good cigars from. He should have known better, he told himself later: 'Fuck off,' the red crow had said.

'I liked that other game you played,' the red crow announced suddenly, between puffs, from the column. Quiss didn't deign to look at it. The red crow balanced on one leg and took the short stump of the cigar out of its beak with the other foot. It looked pensively at the glowing end of the cigar. A flake of the quietly falling snow landed on it and hissed. The red crow cocked its head, looking up accusingly at the sky, then went on, stuffing the cigar back into its beak (so that its words came out oddly distorted). 'Yes, that Open-Plan Go was all right. I liked that board, the way it seemed to stretch for ever in all directions. You two looked proper twats, I can tell you, standing in the middle of an infinite board, cut off at the waist. Real dickheads you looked. Those dominoes were just stupid. Even this is pretty boring. Why don't you just admit defeat? You aren't going to get the answer. Throw yourself off the edge over there. Doesn't take a second. Dammit, at your age you'll probably die of shock before you hit the fucking ground.'

'Hmm,' Ajayi said, and Quiss wondered if she had been listening to the bird. But she was still frowning deeply at the tiles on her little ledge of wood. Talking to them, or herself.

In a few days, if Quiss had counted correctly, they would have been together in the castle for two thousand days. Of course, he recalled proudly, he had been there longer than she had.

It was good, counting up the days, working out the anniversaries so that they could celebrate them. He had started working them out in different number-bases. Base five, base six, seven, eight, of course, nine, ten, twelve and sixteen. So two thousand days would be a quadruple celebration, as it was divisible by five and eight and ten and sixteen. It was just a pity Ajayi didn't share this enthusiasm.

Quiss wiped his head slowly, dislodging some small cold flakes of snow. He blew some more off the board. Perhaps they would have to go back in soon, if the snow kept up. They had got bored with the games room, and the weather had seemed milder, so, after much cajoling of the seneschal, they did finally get permission to have the small table with the red jewel in it unbolted again from the floor (an apparently simple job which absorbed three – sometimes more – constantly arguing attendants armed with oilcans, screwdrivers, hammers, bolt-cutters, tweezers, wrenches and pliers for all of five days) and transported up through the upper levels of the castle to what was, by default, thanks to the crumbling architecture of previously higher storeys, the castle's roof. In this sort of elevated courtyard, surrounded by stunted trees and fallen stones and distant turrets, they had played the game of Chinese Scrabble for the past fifty-odd days. The weather had been kind; no wind, slightly warmer than before (until today) and the sky still grey, but bright grey. 'Maybe it's spring!' Quiss had said brightly. 'Maybe this is high summer,' Ajayi had muttered dourly, and Quiss had got angry with her for being so pessimistic.

Quiss scratched his scalp. It felt funny since the castle barber had cut his hair. He wasn't sure if the hair was growing back or not. His chin and cheeks, which had been grizzly with mottled stubble for nineteen hundred days in the castle, now felt smooth to the touch, though still lined with age.

Quiss made a funny little laughing noise as he thought of the castle barber, who was neurotic. He was neurotic because he had the job of shaving every man in the castle who didn't shave himself. Quiss had heard of this odd character long before he met him; the seneschal had told him of the barber shortly after Quiss had arrived in the castle, in answer to his inquiry whether there were any other relatively ordinary human people in the place. Quiss hadn't believed the seneschal at first; he thought the grey-skinned man was joking. A barber who shaves everybody who doesn't shave himself? Quiss said he didn't believe such a person existed.

'That is the provisional conclusion,' the seneschal had said gravely, 'that the barber has arrived at.'

Quiss met the barber much later, when he was exploring the middle levels of the castle. The barber had a huge, splendidly equipped, almost totally unused barber's shop with a fine view of the snow-filled plain. The barber was taller and skinnier than the seneschal, and had deep black skin. He had white hair, and was half-bald. He shaved the right side of his scalp, to the skin. The left side had a fine head, or half-head, of curly white locks. He shaved his left eyebrow off, but left the right intact. He had half a moustache, on the left-hand side. His beard was very full and bushy, on the right side only; otherwise he was clean-shaven.

The barber wore thick white spotless overalls, and a white apron. He either didn't speak the same language as Quiss, or had forgotten how to speak, because when Quiss had entered the brass-railed, red-leather-chaired barber shop he just danced around Quiss, pointing at his hair and beard and twittering like a bird, his hands and arms fluttering about as he danced. He flapped a big white dusty towel at Quiss and through pleading, imploring motions tried to get him to sit down in one of the chairs. Quiss, wary and suspicious of people who shook and trembled a lot even at the best of times, but especially so when they wanted to come near him with anything resembling long scissors and a cut-throat razor, had declined. Later, though, he found out that the barber had a steady hand when actually carrying out his duties. The seneschal's hair still grew, and he had it cut by the barber.

A hundred or so days ago, Quiss had sent an attendant to tell the barber Quiss would be coming down soon to have his hair cut. Either the minion got the message wrong or the barber misunderstood it, or couldn't wait, because he arrived in the games room a short time later, carrying a portable barbering kit. Quiss let him cut his hair while Ajayi looked on. The barber had seemed pleased, gibbering away to himself quite happily as he skilfully trimmed Quiss's mottled hair and shaved off his beard.

The red crow had watched, too, which was a pity, because it had kept telling Quiss the barber would cut his throat just as proficiently if he asked him to nicely; after all, what was the alternative? Madness, or a slip on the stairs one day . . .

Quiss stroked his chin, still finding – after a hundred days – the smoothness novel and pleasing.

He had no luck in getting the attendants to brew or distil something alcoholic from the kitchens' supplies. And he never had found that open door again, or any open door. All of them were closed and locked these days. The last interesting thing he'd found was another stupid joke, and one he didn't even fully understand.

He'd been deep in the castle's lower levels, looking for the door, or for the small attendant who had discovered him in the room (he still had dreams about those alien brown arms, that blue sky with the contrail across it; that *sun*!), and he had heard a steady, monotonous thumping noise far away, down a network of tunnels and corridors.

* * *

He followed the pounding sound until he came to an area where the floors of the corridors and alcoves were covered with fine grey dust, and the air was hazed with the same dry stuff. The floor shook rhythmically to the pounding. He went down some broad, worn steps to a cross-corridor, and sneezed on the dust.

A small attendant wearing grey boots and no cowl-brim scuttled along the broad corridor the steps led down to. It stopped when it saw him.

'Can I help you?' it squeaked. Its voice was very high, but at least it was civil. Quiss decided to take advantage of this.

'Yes, you can,' he said, holding a bit of his furs over his mouth and nose to keep the swirling dust out. His eyes smarted. The pounding was closer, down the corridor where large double doors faced him. 'What the hell's that noise? Where's all this dust come from?'

The attendant regarded him quietly for a moment, then said, 'Come with me.' It walked off towards the double doors. Quiss followed. The double doors were made out of plastic, with clear plastic inserts at about human head-level. On one of the doors there was a large symbol like this: D. It reminded Quiss of a half-moon. On the other door, the right-hand one, there was this symbol: P. The attendant swept through the doors in a cloud of dust. Coughing, holding the furs tighter over his mouth, Quiss held one door open and looked through.

Inside a huge cavern of a room, hundreds of minions scurried about in the grey mist. There were conveyor belts, overhead cranes and hoppers, buckets and wheelbarrows, and a narrow-gauge railway system with rails – where they could be seen through the piles and drifts of dust – which looked very similar to those Quiss had noticed in the castle kitchens. The whole place was filled with clouds of fine grey swirling dust, and shook and echoed to the continuous pounding, crashing noise he had heard more distantly earlier. The noise was being produced by a single gigantic machine in the very centre of the room. The machine appeared to be made up largely of great man-thick metal columns, tangles of wire and cables, and a cagework of constantly rising and falling gates of metal mesh.

In the centre of the machine something massive-looking flashed silver in time to the pounding noise. Above the centre of the machine, also in time to the beat, a silver metal cylinder rose and fell. Grey, oddly crafted blocks or sculptures went in at one side of the machine; dust blew out at the other side. Dust and rubble. The rubble was carried away on a conveyor belt to huge vats Quiss could just make out in the powder-hazed distance. The dust was apparently meant to be sucked up by extractor ducts in the ceiling (again, similar to the system in the kitchens), but a lot of the dust seemed to be evading the intakes. Quiss could see – through all the dust in the air – great drifts of it piled like frozen waves around vats and conveyor belt housings. In several places grey-booted minions were shovelling the grey dust into wheelbarrows or small hopper-like wagons on the narrow-gauge railways. Other minions were wheeling full, grey-heaped barrows up perilously narrow planks and gantries to the lips of the giant vats, and tipping the dust in; a lot of it billowed out again.

As far as Quiss could make out in the grey gloom, from the vats large overhead buckets scooped up grey, viscous fluid, which was poured into moulds on conveyor belts which disappeared into long, hissing machines; at the far end of the machines the moulds were stripped off the grey sculptures which were then minion-handled or trolleyed to another conveyor belt which led into the pounding machine in the centre of the room . . .

'What in hell's name is *this*?' Quiss said incredulously, choking on the dust.

'This is dee pee,' the attendant said primly, standing in front of him, arms folded. 'This is the nerve centre of the entire castle. Without us, the whole place would simply grind to a halt.' It sounded proud.

'Are you *sure*?' Quiss said, coughing. The minion stiffened.

'Have you any other questions?' it said coldly. Quiss was looking at the objects which he thought of as sculptures as they moved steadily along the conveyor belt to their destruction. They were funny shapes: 5, 9, 2, 3, 4 . . .

'Yes,' he said, pointing at the shapes, 'what are those meant to be?'

'Those *are*,' the attendant said pointedly, 'numbers.'

'Don't look like numbers to me,' Quiss said.

'Well, they are,' the minion said impatiently. 'That's the whole point.'

'The whole point of *what*?' Quiss said, laughing and choking in almost equal parts. He could see he was annoying the small minion, and thought this was good fun. He'd certainly never seen numbers that shape before, but of course they could easily be numbers in some alien language or system. Ajayi might even have recognised them.

'The whole point of what we're *doing* here,' the attendant said, as though trying to be more patient than it really felt. 'This is the number-crunching room. Those are numbers,' it said, enunciating clearly as though for some small and wilfully obtuse child, and motioning behind it to the conveyor belt with one arm, 'and this is where we *crunch* them. That machine is a *number-cruncher.*'

'You're crazy,' Quiss said into the fur over his mouth.

'What?' the attendant said, stiffening still further and then jolting forward, drawing itself up to its full – if still modest – height. Quiss coughed.

'Nothing. What do you make the numbers out of? What's that grey stuff?'

'Plaster of Salt Lake City,' the minion said, as though only an idiot would ask such a question. Quiss frowned.

'What the hell's that?'

'It's like Plaster of Paris, except duller,' the minion said, then turned and stamped off through the drifts of grey powder. Quiss shook his head, coughed, then let the plastic doors swing to.

Ajayi was still looking at the board and her two remaining tiles, staring from one to the other. Then she put her elbows on her knees, her chin in her hands, and closed her eyes, looking thoughtful.

The snow collected in the thin grey hairs of her head, but she still did not notice it was snowing. Her expression of concentration intensified. They were nearly finished.

Chinese Scrabble was played on a gridded board, a little like an infinitely small square section of the Go board they had played on hundreds of days ago, but in Chinese Scrabble one placed small tiles with pictograms on them into the squares formed by the grid of lines, not small stones on the interstices. They hadn't needed to come up with any complicated things like infinitely long pieces this time, but the problem had been the choice of pictograms they had been saddled with at the start of the game. Apart from anything else, they had had to learn a language called Chinese.

That alone had taken them over seven hundred days. Quiss had nearly given in several times, but Ajayi kept him going somehow; the new language excited her. It was a key, she said. Now she read even more.

Ajayi opened her eyes and studied the board again.

The meanings and possibilities of the pictograms in front of her filled her mind as she tried to fit the last two tiles somewhere into the network of skewed pathways she and Quiss had created on the small board.

Chinese was a difficult language, even more difficult than the one she had started studying, the one called English, but they were both worth all the effort. They were even worth the effort of having to drag Quiss along the same educative road. She had helped and cajoled and prompted and shouted and insulted until he could get by in the language they had to play the game in, and even once he had just about grasped the basics she still had to keep helping him along; she'd been able to work out roughly what tiles he still had on his side as the game had entered its final, most difficult, stage, and had deliberately left him easy openings so that his imperfect grasp of the language would not prevent him getting rid of the last of his tiles. The result was that now she was stuck, unable to see where she could put the last two pictograms she had left. If she couldn't place them somewhere, make one or two or more new meanings, they would have to start again. The next game wouldn't take as long as this one, which had lasted thirty days so far, but she was worried that Quiss would get impatient. He had already grumbled several times that she hadn't taught him the language properly.

But the language had been a marvellous, magical gift for her. To enable them to play the game properly, they of course had to understand Chinese, a language from the castle's Subject place, the still un-named planet all the books appeared to originate from. The seneschal had therefore provided them with a dictionary which gave Chinese pictograms and their equivalent in one of the languages common to both sides in the Therapeutic Wars, an ancient, long-deciphered battle-code so elegant its utility as a language had ensured its survival after its secrecy had evaporated.

With that key Ajayi could unlock any of the languages original to the un-named globe. It had taken her only a few days to find a Chinese-English dictionary, and after that she could read the books she found far more easily. She learned Chinese, for the game, and English, for her own reading, alongside each other, becoming relatively fluent in the Indo-European system long before the more tricky Oriental tongue.

It had been as if the whole, massive crumbling ruin of the castle suddenly became transparent; now there were so many more books she could find and take and read and enjoy; a whole culture and entire civilisation was spread out before her, for her to study as she wished. She was already learning French, German, Russian and Latin. Soon Greek, and from the Latin, Italian shouldn't be too big a step (her English was already helping her with the ancient Roman language). The castle was no longer the prison it had seemed before; it was a library, a museum of literature, of literacy, of language. The only thing which still worried her was that she could not find any way to translate the markings on the slates. Those cryptic, buried symbols still meant nothing. She had scoured wall after wall of books but never found a single mention of the strange, simple markings somehow etched inside the grained rock.

But that was a small worry in comparison to the immense satisfaction she felt with her discovery of the key to the castle's original tongues. She had started methodically to read all the classics of the un-named planet's past, having discovered long before a book which acted as a guide to the literature of that world. Apart from the occasional foray further forward in time – to whet her appetite – she was being quite strict with herself in keeping to a chronological exploration of the books she had discovered and stored in her rooms. She was now, at the end of this first and – she hoped – last game of Chinese Scrabble, just starting the age of the Elizabethan dramatists in England, and was already starting to get excited about reading Shakespeare, desperately hoping he hadn't been over-praised in the later critical works she had already encountered.

Even having only got that far, she had still missed out a lot; there were still books she had to find, or go back and read, once she had read through to the last era books were still printed in (or the castle's records stopped; she didn't know what had happened; did some cataclysm overwhelm the world, did they move on to some other form of communication, or did the castle only contain works up to a certain period in the world's history?).

'Come on, Ajayi,' Quiss said with a sigh. 'I finished ages ago. What's keeping you?'

Ajayi looked up at the old, mottle-haired man, with his smooth cheeks and broad, lined face. She arched one eyebrow, but said nothing. She would have liked to have thought that her companion was making a joke, but she was afraid that he was serious.

'Yeah, get a move on,' the red crow said. 'My cigar's getting put out by this fucking snow.'

Ajayi looked up then, and realised it was snowing. Somehow she had been aware that Quiss kept blowing the board in front of her clear every now and again, but she had been so involved with trying to find a niche, or two, for the remaining tiles on her side of the board that it hadn't got through to her properly that what he was blowing off it was snow.

'Oh,' she said, suddenly aware of it. She looked around, seemingly confused for a second. She pulled the collars of her furs up closer around her neck, though if anything it had become slightly milder since the snow started to fall, not colder. She frowned at the board, then looked up at Quiss again. 'Should we go back to the games room, do you think?'

'Oh gods no,' the red crow said in an exasperated voice, 'let's get this over with. Shit.' It pulled the cigar from its mouth, glared at its wet, black end, then tossed it away with a flick of its skinny black leg. 'No point in asking either of you bastards for a light,' it muttered, then shook its head fiercely, stretched its wings half-out, and fanned its tail. It shook itself free of the snow gathering on its back. A couple of small red feathers floated down to the soft ground, like strange flakes of blood in the white fall.

Ajayi went back to staring at the board.

Quiss had given up all hope of carrying out some sort of *coup-de-château*. The seneschal was in an impregnable position, he discovered, because he was beyond time. Five hundred days ago some of the scullions Quiss had befriended were working in the kitchens when a temporary stove collapsed, sending a huge vat of boiling stew crashing down on the seneschal, who was walking by it at the time. Half a dozen scullions saw what happened next; one second the seneschal was there, walking, the next he was disappearing under the gigantic metal cauldron as it fell and cracked and split, flooding an entire section of the kitchens with molten stew. Two of Quiss's little attendants were only metres away, and had to jump for their lives into the sink with the dishes they were cleaning to escape the tidal wave of steaming, bubbling broth.

A moment later, the seneschal was walking past on the *other* side of that sink unit, telling the section undercook to find out who had been responsible for the building of the temporary stove, get them to construct another, and then burn them alive in it. He went on to his office as though nothing had happened. No body was ever discovered when the remains of the shattered stove and cauldron were cleared up. One – still stunned – scullion said the seneschal had simply materialised, right in front of it.

Quiss wasn't a fool. There was no way you could go against power like that.

He had also given up the idea of trying somehow to short-circuit the process which occurred when they finished a game and gave an answer to the riddle they had been set. The red crow had told him what happened – the last creature in the castle Quiss would have expected to be so forthcoming, but it had obviously decided that by telling him it would discourage him still more and thus send him a little further along the road to self-destruction.

Quiss couldn't recall the whole story now, but it went on for a long time and involved the waiter whispering the answer in a room full of bees which then built some sort of nest which something called the message crow ate and then started flying.

After that there were some more funny beasts, most

of which seemed to end up eating each other, then a place on the surface of wherever-they-were with thousands of tiny lakes which thousands of animals marched on to and spontaneously combusted, melting the ice of the lakes in a certain sequence which some sort of organic communication satellite with a message laser recognised . . . after that it got even more complicated.

It was, in other words, foolproof. Impersonating or somehow coercing the waiter who did the whispering was pointless too; as a final check whoever or whatever arrived to take them away from the castle would ask the rooks and crows what they had seen, to make sure there had been no tricks employed.

The whole thing, of course, happened in some sort of time warp, which was why, despite the labyrinthine complexity of the answering process, they always found out the response to their answer within a matter of minutes. Quiss found it all very depressing.

Well, they were about to finish this game. Perhaps, he told himself, they would get it right this time. They had only about one good answer left to the riddle, which was worrying in one way but encouraging in another. Maybe this one *had* to be the right one, maybe they would finally say the right thing and get away from here.

Quiss tried to think of the things he used to try not to think about; the things he had missed so much at first that it had really hurt to think about them. He could think of them quite easily now, quite painlessly. The good things in life, the many pleasures of the flesh and mind, the joy of battle, plot and drunken reminiscing.

It all seemed so far away now. It felt as if it had all happened to somebody else, some young son or grandson, some other person entirely. Could it be that he was starting to think like an old man? Just because he looked like one was no real reason, but perhaps there was a sort of back-pressure, a feedback cycle of effect and cause which made his thoughts gradually fit the husk they filled. He didn't know. Maybe it was just all that had happened here in the Castle Doors, all the disappointments, all the missed chances (those brown woman-arms, that bright promise of a contrail, that sun, that sun in this overcast place!), all the chaos and the order, the seemingly purposeless, apparently directed insanity of the castle. Maybe it just got to you after a while.

Yes, he thought, the castle. Perhaps it makes us as we are, as we are to be. Perhaps it moulds us, like those numbers ever circling to destruction, reincarnation. Indeed: disintegration and break-up, an epilogue at birth . . . why not? He would even be sorry to leave, in some ways. The small minions he used as contacts in the kitchens were hardly the crack troops he was used to, or even battle-honed mercenaries, but they had their own nervous, inefficient attraction; they amused him. He would miss them.

He laughed at the thought of the barber, he recalled meeting the master mason, and the superintendent of mines; both surly, proud, impressive men he would like the time to know better. Even the seneschal himself was interesting once he could be persuaded to talk, ever disregarding his ability to evade catastrophe.

But a lifetime, or more than a lifetime, here?

Unbidden, the thought suddenly filled him with deep, awful despair. Yes, he would miss this place, in some strange, twisted way, if they were able to leave at last, but that was only natural; as a prison it was very mild indeed, and anywhere not unendingly unpleasant could inspire nostalgia given enough time, sufficient scope for the processes of memory to select the good and neglect the bad. That was not the point, that was simply not the point.

To stay here would be to fail, to give in, to compound and affirm the error he had made in the first place which brought him here. It was duty. Not to his side or even his comrades; they were not involved here. It was duty to himself.

How strange that only now, in this odd place, he should understand fully a phrase, an idea he had heard and dismissed all the way through his education and training!

'Ah!' Ajayi said, breaking Quiss's thoughts. He looked up to see the woman reaching over the board, cupping her hand and blowing in to the half-bowl it formed, directing her breath down on to an area of the playing surface and scattering the snow flakes which had settled there. 'There,' she said, placing the two tiles down together in one corner of the board, then smiling proudly at her companion. Quiss looked at the two newly set-down tiles.

'That's it, then,' he said, nodding.

'Don't you think it's good?' Ajayi said. She pointed.

Quiss shrugged noncommittally. Ajayi suspected he didn't understand exactly the new meanings she had made on the board.

'It'll do,' Quiss said, looking not particularly impressed. 'It's finished the game. That's the main thing.'

'Well, thank Kryste for that,' the red crow said. 'I was just about falling asleep.' It flapped from its perch on the broken column and hovered over the board, inspecting it.

'I didn't know you could hover,' Ajayi said to the bird; its wingbeats, just above them, disturbed the snow falling on them and the board, making artificial flurries.

'I'm not supposed to,' the red crow said absently, eyes fixed on the board. 'But then crows aren't supposed to talk either, are they? Yes, that looks all right. I suppose.'

Quiss watched the red bird, flapping energetically above them. He made a face when it gave its disdainful approval of their game. The red crow made a sound like a sneeze, then said, 'What's your contribution to the wit and wisdom of the universe this time, then?'

'Why should we tell you?' Quiss said.

'Why not?' the red crow said indignantly.

'Well . . .' Quiss said, thinking, '. . . because we don't like you.'

'Good grief, I'm only doing my job,' the red crow said, sounding genuinely hurt. Ajayi coughed on a laugh.

'Oh, tell it,' she said, waving one hand dismissively.

Quiss gave another sour look, first at her, then the bird, cleared his throat and said, 'Our answer is "You can't . . ." no, I mean "There is no such thing as either."'

'Oh,' the red crow said, still hovering, unimpressed, 'wow.'

'Well, have you got any better answers?' Quiss said aggressively.

'Plenty, but I'm not telling you bastards.'

'Well,' Ajayi said, standing up stiffly and dusting the powdery white snow from her furs, 'I think we should get inside and find an attendant.'

'Don't bother,' the red crow said. 'Allow me; it'll be a pleasure.' It cackled with laughter and flew off. '"No such thing as either"; ha ha ha . . .' its voice trailed back to them as it flew away.

Ajayi picked the small table and the board up slowly and together she and Quiss made their way through the tumbled masonry of the roof towards the intact floors, some way off. Quiss watched the red crow flap slowly through the snow-filled air until he lost sight of it.

'Do you think it's gone off to tell somebody?'

'Maybe,' Ajayi said, holding the small table carefully and watching where she put her feet.

'Think we can trust it?' Quiss said.

'Probably not.'

'Hmm,' Quiss said, stroking his smooth chin.

'Don't worry,' Ajayi said, stepping over some cracked slate blocks as they made their way towards the shelter of a broken arcade, 'we can always tell somebody ourselves.'

'Hmm, I suppose so,' Quiss said as they entered the arcade, stepping over some of its fallen columns and the remains of part of the roof. They came under the shelter of the roof where it was still good, and as they did so Quiss slipped on a patch of ice, crying out as he slid, putting out both hands, trying to steady himself on a column on one side and Ajayi on the other. He knocked the board.

Tiles scattered. Quiss fell heavily to the ground.

'Oh, *Quiss*!' Ajayi said. She put the board down quickly to one side. She went to the old man, lying on the ground, spreadeagled over the ice he had slipped on, eyes fixed on the vaulted roof of the arcade. 'Quiss!' Ajayi said, kneeling down painfully by the man's side. 'Quiss!'

Quiss made a strangled, choking noise; his chest moved up and down quickly. His face was grey. Ajayi put her hands to the sides of her head for a second, shaking her head, tears coming to her eyes. Quiss gurgled, his eyes popping. She took his hand in hers, held it with both her hands as she leant over him. 'Oh Quiss . . .'

The man sucked a huge, laboured gust of cold air into his lungs, his arms came up and he thumped his chest, then he tried to roll over on one side. When she saw what he was trying to do Ajayi helped him. He propped himself up on one elbow, then, with Ajayi's help, sat up. He banged his back with his clenched fist, weakly. Ajayi did it for him, harder. He nodded, his breath coming more regularly now.

'Just . . . winded . . .' he said, shaking his head. He wiped his eyes. 'Okay . . .' he sucked in more air. He looked over at the board; the pattern on it broken and spilled. 'Oh, shit,' he said, and put his head in his hands.

Ajayi kneaded his broad back through the heavy robes and said, 'Never mind about that, Quiss. As long as you're all right.'

'But the . . . board, it's all . . . messed up . . .' Quiss gasped.

'I can remember how it looked, Quiss,' Ajayi said,

leaning close behind him and talking into his ear, trying to sound confident and encouraging. 'I studied it for long enough, goodness knows. It's engraved on my memory! Don't worry about it. Are you all right? Are you sure?'

'I'm all right; stop . . . fussing!' Quiss said irately, trying to shove Ajayi away with one hand. She knelt back from him, her hands falling to her lap, eyes lowered.

'I'm sorry,' she said, getting up slowly from her knees. 'I didn't mean to fuss.' She bent, sitting on her haunches, grunting with the effort, and started to pick the fallen Scrabble tiles out of the snow to one side, drifting in under the roof of the arcade, and off the ice-crusted surface of the slate slabs.

'Fucking ice,' Quiss said hoarsely. He coughed, rubbed his nose. He looked round at the woman, carefully picking the pieces up from the ground and putting them on the board again. 'Have you got a nose-rag?' he said.

'What? Yes,' Ajayi said, reaching into her furs and bringing out a small handkerchief. She handed it to Quiss, who blew his nose loudly and handed the kerchief back. She folded it and put it away. Ajayi sighed. She wanted to tell him to get up; he'd catch cold sitting on the freezing slabs like that. But she didn't want to fuss.

Quiss got up with some difficulty, grunting and cursing. She watched him out of the corner of her eye as she picked up the scattered pieces, ready to help if he asked, or reach out quickly if he started to fall back again. Quiss stood, rubbing his buttocks and back, leaning against a column.

They could so easily die, she reminded herself. They

might be fixed in one age, but it was an old and fragile one, a weak and accident-prone age. So far they had not fallen really badly, or broken any bones, but if they did injure themselves they would take a long time to get better. She had asked the seneschal about that, long ago. His advice had been: 'Don't fall'.

She thought she had all the tiles. She counted them, all the ones on the board, and found there was still one missing. She got up, still stiffly, arching her pained back and looking round in the snow and on the slate flagstones.

'Got them all?' Quiss said. His face was still pale, but not as grey as it had been. Ajayi shook her head, still looking round about her.

'No. One missing.' Quiss looked quickly over the slates.

'I might have known it. They won't let us answer the riddle now. I bet we'll have to start all over again. I bet it. That's what'll happen. This is just *typical*.' He turned quickly away and slammed an open palm into one of the columns, staying facing away from her, breathing deeply, head hung down between his shoulders.

Ajayi looked at him, then lifted up the small table, to see if she had placed it on top of the missing tile when she put it down to help Quiss. But the tile wasn't there. 'We'll find it,' she said, gazing into the drifted snow. She didn't feel as sure of it as she hoped she sounded. She couldn't understand it; the tile couldn't have bounced so far, could it? She counted the tiles on the board again, then once more.

She began to get angry; at Quiss for falling in the first

place and then for trying to shove her away; at the missing tile; at the castle itself, the red crow, the seneschal, the attendants; all of them. *Where* could the stupid thing be?

'Are you sure you've counted them properly?' Quiss said in a tired voice, still holding on to the column.

'Of course I have, several times; there's one missing,' Ajayi snapped, her voice clipped. 'Now stop asking stupid questions.'

'No need to bite my tongue off,' Quiss said huffily. 'I was only trying to help.'

'Well, look for the tile,' Ajayi said. She could hear herself, and she hated herself for it. She shouldn't lose control like this, she oughtn't to snap at Quiss; it did no good. They ought to be sticking together through all this, not quarrelling like schoolkids or growing-apart couples. But she couldn't help it.

'Look,' Quiss said angrily, 'I didn't hit the fucking board on purpose. It was an accident. Would you rather I broke my neck?'

'Of course not,' Ajayi said carefully, trying not to snap or shout. 'I didn't say you did it deliberately.' She wasn't looking at Quiss, she was moving her head from side to side, still scanning the snow and slates, seemingly intent on finding the missing tile, but her mind was all caught up in the words; she knew she wouldn't have seen the tile even if it had been quite obvious; she wasn't concentrating on the search.

'Maybe you'd rather I did, eh?' Quiss said. 'Eh?'

She looked up at him then. 'Oh, Quiss, how can you

say that?' She felt as though he'd kicked her. There had been no need for him to say that. What made him say such things?

Quiss just snorted. He pushed himself away from the column with one slightly shaking arm, and as he did so, the missing tile fell out of one of the bottom hems of his furs, where it had lodged when it and he fell. At the same moment a small figure appeared at the far end of the arcade, from a door which led back into the main body of the castle. They both looked first at the fallen tile, then at the small attendant. It waved and called out in an excited voice:

'Did you say, "There's no such thing as either"?'

They looked at each other again. Ajayi tried to answer, but had to stop, and patted the top of her chest with one hand; her throat seemed to have dried up, she couldn't get any words out. Quiss nodded enthusiastically. 'Yes!' he shouted. He kept nodding his head.

The attendant shook its head. 'No,' it said, and with a shrug disappeared back into the castle.

Somewhere far away, beneath them in the ruins, a familiar voice cackled, crowing with distant laughter.

FIVE

Half Moon Crescent

On the corner of Maygood Street and Penton Street there was an employment office, where people went to sign on for dole money. A sign said: Door C surnames A-K, Door D surnames L-Z. Graham walked by, looking down to Half Moon Crescent itself; the curve of tall houses where Sara ffitch was living. His stomach seemed to lurch, tensing with nervous anticipation. He felt shivery, keyed up; the vaguely sultry, dulling air seemed suddenly sharpened. Colours stood out, smells (cooking, asphalt, exhaust fumes) became more vivid. The buildings – ordinary Victorian three-storey terraces, now mostly converted into flats – were strange and alien.

His heart beat faster when he saw a bike parked outside

one of the houses in Half Moon Crescent, but it was outside the door next to Sara's, and it was a red Honda, not a black BMW. He took deep breaths to try and slow his heart down. He looked up at the window Sara leaned out of sometimes, but she wasn't there.

She will be there, though, he told himself. She won't be out. She will be in. And she won't have changed her mind.

He went to the entryphone. He pressed the button for her flat firmly. He waited, staring intently at the grille from which her voice would come. Very soon.

He waited.

He put his finger on the button, about to press it again, then hesitated, uncertain whether to wait a little longer or not. She might still be waking up, or having a shower; anything. There could be lots of reasons for her not answering yet. He licked his lips, kept staring at the grille. He leaned forward on the button once more, closing his eyes as he did so. He let the button go.

There was still plenty of time. Even if she wasn't in, he could wait; she would probably just be out getting something for the salad she'd said she would make for them.

He wondered whether he ought to press the button again. His stomach was feeling heavy, sick. He could just imagine someone from the houses on the corner of Maygood Street watching him now, looking at his back as he stood at the entryphone grille, waiting and waiting. The grille made a clicking noise. 'Hello?' said a breathless voice. It was her!

'It—' he said, and choked on the words, throat dry.
He cleared his throat quickly, 'It's me. Graham.' She was
there, she was there!

'Graham, I'm sorry,' she said. His heart seemed to sink,
he closed his eyes. She was going to say she had changed
her mind. 'I was in the bath.' The buzzer on the entryphone sounded.

He stared at the door for a moment, then at the entryphone, then at the still buzzing door. He pushed it
quickly, just before the buzzer stopped sounding. The
door swung open, and he went in.

There were carpeted steps down to a basement flat, a
door straight ahead to the ground-floor flat. He went up
the stairs; cheap but cheerful carpet, white paint on the
banisters, fading pastel wallpaper. He could hear an old
Beatles record being played downstairs. He got to the
first-floor landing. There were more steps up to another
flat, but the door on the first floor, into her flat, was open.
He knocked and went in, looking around with obvious
trepidation, just on the off chance it wasn't the right flat,
or she hadn't meant to leave the door open. He heard
water from a room to his right. Light showed under the
door. 'Graham?' she said.

'Hello,' he called out. He put the portfolio down
against the wall and closed the door on to the landing.

'Go on in, to your left.' Her voice was soaked up by
the sound of the running water. He took the portfolio up
again, went round to his left, into a small, cluttered room
with a couch, chairs, television, hi-fi, bookcases and a
small coffee table; at the far end, raised up a few inches,

separated from the main part of the room by small wood railings which each extended a third of the way across the area, was a kitchen section; cooker and fridge and sink, a larger table, and behind it, main curtains drawn, white lace ones floating out slightly on a faint breeze, was the window.

He put his portfolio down by the side of the couch. A small table at one end of the couch held the telephone; he recalled the time it had rung and rung, and she was under the bedclothes, hiding from the thunder. He crossed the room to the raised kitchen section, stepping up on to its worn linoleum surface and going to the sink. He rinsed his hands under the cold tap, splashed some water on his forehead. He dried his face and hands on a dishcloth; there was no hand towel. He was shaking.

He went back down on to the carpeted area and stood, heart beating quickly, in front of the bookcase beside the television. He saw a book there which he hadn't read but had seen televised. *The Restaurant at the End of the Universe* was the second part of the story begun in *The Hitch-Hiker's Guide to the Galaxy*; Slater had told him that when the BBC made the series they just lumped the two books together. Graham took the slim volume out, flipped through it, looking for one bit in particular. He found it, in about the middle of the book. The scene involved a character called Hotblack Desiato, who was spending a year dead for tax reasons. Desiato was a firm of Islington estate agents, Graham had seen their signs; Douglas Adams must have lived in the area.

He put the book back. Although it was funny, it was

rather *light* reading; he wanted Sara to find him reading something more impressive.

There were a lot of books on best things and worst things; books full of quotes, criticisms, collections of hyperboles and euphemisms, lists of lists, books full, simply, of facts; books on what had happened on each day throughout the year, books about last words, famous mistakes, most useless objects. Graham knew what Slater thought about such works. He took a very dim view indeed; they were yet more signs that the End was In Sight. 'Can't you see?' he'd said, one day in March, sitting in the small, steamy café in Red Lion Street. 'It's a society getting its affairs in order, preparing for the end, drawing a bottom line under what it's done. That stuff and all the bomb literature . . . we're becoming a death-based society, in love with the past, seeing only annihilation ahead: annihilation we're fascinated by but powerless to do anything about. Vote Thatcher! Vote Reagan! Let's all die! Yip-fucking-pee!'

Graham took out a book on Marxist economics, opened it about a third of the way through, started reading. His eyes took in the words, but it was dry, hard, complicated stuff, and the meanings flowed over the surface of his mind and off again like water from a sun-creamed shoulder.

'Graham,' Sara said from the doorway. He turned round, heart thumping, to see her just leaning in from the hall, a white towel round her head like a turban, a thin blue dressing gown round her body. Her face looked white and painfully thin without its usual aura of black hair. 'I won't be long. Have a seat.' She went into the room across the hall, which he assumed must be the bedroom. He put the economics book back.

He sat down, looking around the room. After a while he rose to look at the record collection. It all seemed very dated; a lot of old Stones records, but much Led Zeppellin and Deep Purple: middle period Floyd and early Bob Seeger. Meatloaf was about the latest stuff. Funny. The collection must have belonged to the girl who actually owned the place, the one who was in America.

He inspected the bookshelf again.

At that moment, on St John Street, near the buildings of the City University and about a quarter of a mile south of the junction of Pentonville Road and Upper Street, a figure in black leathers, wearing a black full-face crash helmet with a smoked-glass visor, was crouched by the side of a BMW RS100 motorbike which was propped against the side of the kerb. The man in the black leathers sat back, looked up the road, north, in the direction he had been heading when the bike had suddenly started misfiring a quarter of an hour ago, while he was making his way, as arranged, to Half Moon Crescent. He cursed, leant forward again, quickly turning a small screwdriver as he fiddled with the settings on the carbs. STK 228T was the registration number of the bike.

Graham took out a book on ethics. It looked like the sort of book to be found reading, too. Slater, naturally, had his own views on ethics as on everything else. His philosophy of life, he said, was founded on Ethical Hedonism. This was the moral system virtually every decent, unblinkered, reasonably informed human able to scrape together a quorum of neurons lived by, but they didn't realise it. Ethical Hedonism recognised that one had to enjoy oneself where one got the chance these days, but that rather than immerse oneself totally in such diversions, one ought always to behave in a reasonable and reasonably responsible manner, never losing sight of the more general moral issues and their manifestations in society. 'Have fun, be nice, veer left, and never stop *thinking*, is what it boils down to,' Slater had said. Graham had nodded, and observed that it sounded like it was easier done than said.

He got bored with the book on ethics, which was even more obscure and difficult than the economics book, and replaced it in the bookcase. He went back to the couch and sat down, looking at his watch. It was four twenty-five. He took his portfolio up, set it on his knees. He thought about opening it up so that he would be looking at the drawings when Sara came in; perhaps even doing some last-minute alterations to them; he had a pen and pencil in the portfolio, too, in the bottom. He decided not to. He didn't have Slater's natural acting ability, that way of just adopting a persona. 'You should have been an actor,' he'd told Slater, late last year, sitting in Leslie's sandwich bar over a couple of cups of tea and two sweet, sticky pastries.

'I tried that,' Slater had replied huffily. 'They threw me out of drama school.'

'What for?'

'Over-acting!' Slater had said, dramatically.

Graham put the portfolio down again. He stood up, looking at his watch again, and walked back to the kitchen part of the room, to the window. A slight breeze blew the thin white curtains softly towards him. The view outside, round the corner of Maygood Street, was still. A couple of parked cars, closed doors, the usual grainy sunlight of the summer city.

A fly buzzed in through the window, and Graham watched it for a while as it flew around the kitchen area, hovering over the cooker, flying down underneath it, wavering in the air around the door of the fridge, floating over the black surface of the round table near the window, criss-crossing the air in front of the food cupboard. It settled on one of the thin plastic chairs pulled in around the table.

Graham watched as it stretched its two front legs over its head, cleaning itself. He picked a magazine up off the table and slowly rolled it up until it was tight, then he stepped slowly forward, towards the chair where the fly was. The fly stopped cleaning itself; its front legs went back down to the surface of the seat-back. Graham stopped. The fly stayed still. Graham moved into firing range.

He drew the clenched magazine upwards, tensing himself. The fly didn't move.

'Graham,' Sara said from the doorway, 'what are you doing?'

'Oh,' he said, putting the magazine down on the table.

'Hello.' He stood there, embarrassed. The fly flew off.

Sara wore baggy olive-green dungarees, a black T-shirt underneath. On her feet were a pair of pink trainers. Her hair was still swept back from her face, held at the rear of her skull by a pink ribbon. He hadn't seen her with her hair like that before; it made her look smaller, thinner than ever. Her white skin glowed in the light coming from the window. Her dark eyes, the heavy lids like hoods, regarded him from the far end of the room. She was putting her watch on; a black band round the thin cord of wrist.

'Are you early, or is my watch wrong?' she said, looking at it.

'I don't think I'm early,' Graham said, glancing at his own watch. Sara shrugged and came forward. He watched her face; he knew he could never draw it properly, never do it justice. It was flawless, precise, perfect, like something carved out of the finest marble and possessing an ultimate elegance and simplicity of line, but yet containing a promise of such softness, a tactile transparency . . . I'm staring again, he told himself. She stepped up on to the raised kitchen area, still fiddling with the strap on her watch, and went to the window, looking out of it for a moment. Then she turned to him.

She looked into his eyes, and he felt he was being assessed in some way; she took a deep breath, nodded at the table between them. 'Shall we sit?' she said. It sounded like an odd thing to say. Sara drew out one of the small plastic chairs, her back to the window, and sat down. She watched as Graham sat down too. She had her hands on the table; he put his there, spread out like fans, thumbs just touching, as hers were.

'When do the rest of the people for the séance turn up?' he asked, then wished he hadn't. Sara smiled at him in a strange, distant sort of way. Graham wondered if perhaps she was on something; she had something of the disengaged look people often have when they've been smoking dope.

'I didn't have time to get the salad together,' Sara said. 'Do you mind if we have a talk first?'

'No; on you go,' Graham said. There was something wrong; he felt bad. Sara wasn't the way she usually was. She kept looking at him with that odd, vacant, assessing gaze which made him uncomfortable, made him want to curl up and protect, not be himself and open out.

'I've wondered, Graham,' she said slowly, not looking at him but looking at her own hands where they lay on the black surface of the table, 'about how you . . . see the sort of relationship we've had.' She looked up at him briefly. He swallowed. What did she mean? What was she talking about? Why?

'Well, I . . .' he thought as hard as he could about it, but he had had no time to prepare, to think about the subject. With some warning he could have talked about it perfectly easily and naturally, but just to be asked outright like this . . . it made things very difficult. 'I've enjoyed it, to some extent,' he said. He watched her face, ready to alter the way he was expressing himself, even alter what he was saying, according to the reception of his words on the white surface of her face. Sara gave him no clues, however. She was still gazing at her pale, thin hands, the lidded eyes almost hidden from Graham's view. A small white section of the scar tissue round her neck showed from the square neck of the T-shirt, by the pale column of her neck.

'I mean, it's been great,' he said awkwardly, after a pause. 'I realise you've had . . . well, that you've been involved with . . . somebody else, but I . . .' He dried. He couldn't think what to say. Why was she doing this to him? Why did they have to talk about this sort of thing? What was the point? He felt cheated, abused; sensible people didn't talk about this sort of thing any more, did they? There had been so much rubbish talked and written and filmed over the years; all that romantic crap, then the idealistic, unrealistic naïvety of the sixties and the wide-eyed evangelism of the new morality of the seventies . . . all that had gone; people were less inclined to talk, more liable just to get on with it. He'd talked to Slater about this and they'd agreed. It wasn't so much a backlash, more a slack pausing for breath, so Graham believed. Slater thought it meant The End, but then to Slater little didn't.

'Do you think you love me, Graham?' Sara asked, still not looking at him. He frowned. At least the question was more direct.

'Yes, I do,' he said quietly. It felt wrong. This wasn't the way he had envisaged telling her. This afternoon setting, the lightness of the room, the distance of black-painted table between them; nothing suited what he had to say, what he wanted to tell her he felt.

'I thought you might say that,' she said, still staring at her long white fingers on the table top. Her voice chilled him.

'Why are you asking all this?' he said. He tried to sound a little more jocular than he felt.

'I wanted to know . . .' Sara began, '. . . how you feel.'

'Feel free,' Graham said, laughing. Sara looked at him, calm and white, and he stopped the laughter in his throat, killed the smile on his face. He cleared his throat. What was going on here? Sara sat for a moment, silent, while her fingers lay on the table, inspected and observed.

Perhaps he should show her the drawings he'd done of her, he thought. Perhaps she was upset about something, or just depressed in some general way. Maybe he ought to try and take her mind off whatever it was. Sara said, 'You see, Graham, I've deceived you. We have. Stock and I.'

Graham felt his stomach go cold inside him. At the mention of Stock's name something happened deep inside him, a gut reaction of ancient, evolved fear and distress.

'What do you mean?' he said.

Sara shrugged jerkily, the tendons on her neck standing out like taut ropes. 'You know what deception is, don't you, Graham?' Her voice sounded odd; not like hers at all. He formed the impression that she had thought this out, that like him she had thought in advance about the things she would say (but she, choosing the ground in advance, had the advantage), so that her spoken words were more like lines, something to be acted out on the tense stage of her body.

'Yes, I think so,' he said, because she was silent, and

it seemed they would go no further until her question was answered.

'Good,' she said, and sighed. 'I'm sorry you've been deceived, but there were reasons. Do you want me to explain them to you?' She looked up again, once more just for a second or so.

'I don't understand,' Graham said, shaking his head, trying, by the expression on his face, the tone of his voice, to make it clear that he wasn't taking all this as seriously as Sara was. 'How do you mean "deceived"? How have you been deceiving me? I've always known about Stock, I've known about your relationship, but I haven't . . . well, I might not have been ecstatically happy about it, but I didn't—'

'Do you remember that time when it was raining and you rang up from . . . a callbox, I think you said?' Sara interrupted.

Graham smiled. 'Of course, you were under the bedclothes with your Walkman turned up full blast to drown out the thunder.'

Sara shook her head quickly, briefly, so that the movement looked more like some nervous spasm than a sign. She kept looking down at her hands. 'No. No, I wasn't. What I was doing underneath the bedclothes was screwing Bob Stock. When you rang, and rang and rang, he took his . . . stroke from the pulses of the bell.' She looked up into his eyes, her face quite serious, even unpitying (while his aching guts turned inside him). A cold, uneven smile crossed her face. 'As a third party, you were quite a good screw. Rhythm and staying power.'

He felt he could not speak. It was not the fact of the tawdry revelation itself so much as the tone of its delivery which hurt; this clinical, deadpan expression, the flat voice, even if this outer calmness was belied by that tensioned neck, the jerkiness of her movements and gestures. She went on:

'That time I talked to you from the window, when you were down in the street, the day we went to Camden Lock . . . Stock was behind me; he put the window down on my back. All I had on was that shirt. He took me from behind, you know?' The corner of her lips jigged nervously twice, then twisted with a tiny dry hint of a smile. 'He'd always said he might do it, one of the times he was there when you called. I'd dared him to do it. It was very . . . exciting. You know?'

He shook his head. He felt he was going to be sick. This was absurd, insane. It was like all Slater had ever joked about, like all the most sexist caricatures of female deception. Why? Why was she telling him all this? What did she expect from him?

She sat on the far side of the circular black table, her hair severely gathered back, that thin, nearly translucent face brought to its own point, decks cleared for action. She was watching him now, he thought, the way scientists must watch a rat; some animal with its brain exposed, wires into it, hooked up to a machine with its tiny, electric, animal thoughts bleeped and phosphoresced, recorded by glowing green lines and the smoothly unrolled lengths of paper and the thin metallic scribbling of scratching pens. Why, though? Why? (And thought, does the rat ever know, could it ever comprehend, the reasons for the cruel uses it was put to?)

'You do remember,' she said, voice purring, 'don't you?'

'I . . . remember,' he said, feeling broken, unable to look at her, and stared at the table's surface and one or two small crumbs lying on it. 'But why?' he said, looking up at her. He could not keep his eyes on hers for very long. He looked down again.

'. . . even that first time,' Sara said, ignoring his question, 'when we met at the party. In the loo. Would you believe that Stock was in there? We had arranged it all in advance. He climbed up the drainpipe. I left that room we were in and went down there to meet him. That's what I was doing in the bathroom; fucking on the floor with Bob Stock.' She pronounced the words carefully.

'Really?' he said. He had forgotten it all, forgotten all he had ever felt for her. He would feel it again, he knew, and it would hurt, but for now he was putting it out of his mind. It didn't matter any more. She had changed all the rules, put the whole relationship that had existed between them into quite a different category. He stored the old self, the hurt young man for the moment, concentrated as best he could, while still reeling inside from the sheer force and extent of the change, on what was being said now, on this new set of rules, this role he was being forced into, for reasons he didn't yet understand. 'But why?' he said, trying not to sound hurt, trying to play it the way she was.

'Decoy,' she said, shrugging. She gazed at her fingers

again, spreading them out on the black paint surface. 'That divorce of mine . . . my husband was having me followed. Stock couldn't afford to be involved, but we didn't want . . . couldn't stop seeing each other. So we decided to use somebody else to seem to have an affair with me. You were seen to go upstairs with me at that party; we figured that whoever my husband had tailing me would be at the party, gate-crashing; following me. We thought that he would assume we'd been screwing. I really had, of course, but that was just a little extra. We've been stringing you along ever since. Sorry, Graham. Anyway, our man doesn't seem to be following you. Perhaps he's been called off the case or something. Maybe my other half just didn't want to spend any more money on me; don't ask me.'

'So,' Graham said, feeling faint, sitting back in the chair as though nothing was wrong, trying to stop his lips quivering, one hand on the top of the seat-back (where, he remembered for no good reason, the fly had been), his other hand still on the table, like some strange animal in a black and circular arena, on the far side of it from her pale fingers. His hand, trembling very slightly, scratched at a fleck of white paint on the black surface as he said, 'I'm not . . . of any use any more, is that it?'

'Sounds rather mean, doesn't it?' Sara said. She was still trying to sound calm, but her words sounded clipped. Graham laughed, shaking his head.

'Oh no; no, not a bit!' He felt tears starting to come to his eyes, and stopped them, determined not to show her what he was feeling. He shook his head, went on laughing, still watching his finger scratching at the white-paint fleck. 'Not at all, no.' He shrugged.

He was aware of a sort of tingling itch all over his body, as though the heightened awareness of his earlier anticipation was with him, in a single sense only, once again, and every nerve in his skin was receiving a maximum intensity, pouring into his brain a mass of static, average signals, a bodily white noise giving an impression of unattenuated, unsifted, exaggerated usualness; a paradigm of the pain of clearly felt normality.

'So it was all just an act, was it?' he said, after a while, when she had said nothing more. He still couldn't show what he felt. He kept thinking, wildly, that it might all be a cruel sort of joke, or even a test, a final examination before he was allowed closer knowledge of this woman. He couldn't, mustn't over-react.

'Sort of,' Sara conceded, voice deliberately lazy (he had the impression of her turning very slightly to the window, as though listening for something), 'but I haven't *hated* it. I quite like you, Graham, really I do. But having set out to use you, there wasn't a lot else I or . . . Stock could do but go on with it. Maybe I shouldn't even be telling you any of this now. Maybe I should just have told you not to come here, and then not have seen you again. But I wanted to tell you the truth.' She swallowed a couple of times, gazed at her hands on the table, clasped them.

Still there was that false coldness in her voice, he thought, as he scratched at the white fleck of paint; still she was not really telling the whole truth at all. She wanted to see what his reaction would be, how the words would

279

affect him. He sat there and wondered what he could do. What was there to do? Break down and cry? Become violent? Just get up and leave?

He glanced quickly at her, then away. She sat looking at him, still but somehow tensed. Looking again, he saw what might have been a tic, near the edge of her jaw, under her right ear. A pulse on her neck, over the white scar on her upper chest, beat rapidly. He looked away, eyes blinking.

He could not, he would not break down. She would not see him cry. A furious, vicious, angry part of him, some deep, buried kernel of animal hatred, wanted to attack her; slap and punch that cold white face; rape her, leave her wrecked and battered; reciprocate and outbid her in this awful, hurtful game she had suddenly chosen to play. The only part he trusted (but the part that had got him here, now in this situation, even if through no fault he could see) was equally revolted by the idea of either type of assault; to embrace either of the sexually conventional reactions, adopt either of those segregated responses was . . . insufficient. Pointless. Nor was there a way to stay in the game with (he searched for a word, inside himself) . . . *honour* (that was the only word he could think of, though it was too old and tainted, too historically misused to be quite what he wanted or meant. But in more sense than one, it was all he had).

'So this is the truth, is it?' he said, still with a sort of half-laugh in his voice as his finger picked at the table.

'Don't you believe me?' she said, clearing her throat awkwardly on the first word.

'I believe you. I suppose. Why shouldn't I? Why should you tell me any of this if it wasn't true?'

She didn't answer. He smiled emptily as he watched the finger, still trying to lift the stuck-down wisp of dried white paint from the black surface of the table.

Back at the bike, the black figure twisted the throttle, trying to gun the motor, but it stuttered, rasped then coughed, almost died. It ran more smoothly, but still not perfectly for a few seconds, then hesitated once more, missing beats. The man kicked the bike, then straddled it, revving the motor. He looked behind him for an opening in the traffic. He let the clutch in on first gear and the bike jerked forward, then the engine failed, dying again. The bike trickled forward as horns sounded from the cars and trucks behind; the bike revved, moved forward, but each time the engine tried to take the load it stuttered and the bike slowed.

'Fuck it!' the man shouted into his helmet. 'Oh, God.' He used his feet to trundle the bike back in to the kerb again. He got off quickly. Should he walk, or run, up to Half Moon Crescent?

'Well then, be there,' she had said. He'd laughed. They had been planning just how they would remove Graham from their private equation. 'I'll be there,' he'd assured her, 'no problem.' She'd said, kissing him: 'If you are not on time I might resort to Plan B.' He had asked her what that was. 'I give him what he wants,' she'd said, '*then* tell him to disappear . . .' Whereon he had laughed – he now thought – a little too heartily.

He got down quickly to his knees, took off his gloves and threw them to the pavement, opened one of the panniers at the back of the bike and snatched the toolkit out. 'Come on, Stock,' he said to himself, 'you can do it, son . . .' He took the small screwdriver out. Damn bike. Of all the times to let him down!

He had been concerned, mostly for her sake, that she wasn't too hard on Graham before he got there; she was only supposed to tell him she had decided to stay with Stock, not hurt the kid too much – dangerously much – with the truth about the way they'd used him. 'Let him down gently, won't you?' he'd said. She'd looked at him calmly for some time, then said evenly, 'I'll let him down.'

He looked over the top of the bike at a young man with fair hair walking up the far pavement. For one heart-thumping second he thought it was Graham Park, then saw it wasn't. As his gaze dropped to the bike again, he caught sight of something odd on the top of the black-polished petrol tank. He looked back again, more closely. There were fresh scratches on the paint round the chrome petrol filler cap, and clusters of small white grains. When he tried the cap it lifted easily, and would not lock. The small white grains felt sticky. 'Oh shit,' he breathed.

'Poor Graham,' Sara ffitch said, smiling jerkily at him, letting her head tip slightly to one side, as though she was trying to get him to look at her.

'Why me?' Graham said (and wanted to laugh in spite of it all, at the sheer absurdity of what he was saying, the falsity of the entire situation, the way that, because it was like a game and the sort of scene they had doubtless both seen portrayed in this popular culture a thousand times, there were only certain things he could say, certain viable responses he could make).

'Why not?' Sara said. 'I heard about you through . . . Slater. You sounded like the sort of guy I might be able to charm, you know?'

He nodded. 'I know,' he said. A small piece of white paint came away from the surface of the black table, lodging under his fingernail.

'I didn't think you would actually fall in love with me, but it did make things easier in a way, I suppose. I'm sorry for you, though. I mean, I don't think we can go on after this, do you?'

'No. No, I think you're right. Of course.' He nodded again, still not looking at her.

'You don't seem . . . very concerned.'

'No,' he shrugged, then shook his head. The last piece of paint stuck on the table's surface would not come off. He took his hand away, glanced at her, then sat forward in the seat, folding his arms, crossing his feet at the ankles, as though suddenly cold. 'You just acted it all, then?' he asked.

'Not really, Graham,' she said. He thought he could just make out, from the tops of his eyes, as he stared at the table, her shaking her head. 'I didn't act very much at all. I told a few lies, but I didn't promise very much, I didn't have to pretend very much. I did like you. I certainly didn't love you, but you're quite nice, quite . . . sweet.'

He laughed, briefly, quietly, at that last word, such faint praise indeed. And that 'certainly'; did she have to put that in, as though trying through every single word and nuance to find a way to hurt him? How much damage would she be content with? What sort of reaction was she trying to get from him?

'And I loved you, I thought you were so . . .' he could not finish. If he went on, he knew, he would break down and cry. He shook his head and angled his gaze so that she would not see his eyes glisten.

'Yes, I know,' Sara said, sighing artificially, 'it was pretty dirty, I know. Terribly unfair. But then who gets what they deserve, hmm?'

'You bitch,' he said to her, looking up and into her eyes through a film of tears, 'you fucking cow.'

Something changed in her face, as though the game had become more interesting at last; her eyebrows might have risen fractionally or her tiny smile, that twisted look at the side of her mouth, have reappeared, but whatever it was it struck him with almost physical force. He was not proud of the words, he knew what they sounded like, what the whole setting and implication of them was, but he could not help them; they were all he had to throw at her.

'Well,' she said slowly, 'this is a bit more like it . . .'

He stood up, his breath forced in and out of him in spasms, his eyes drying again but smarting, staring at her. She sat there and looked up at him, quizzically, some sudden quickness of interest, even fear illuminating the until then cool, quiet features. 'What the hell did I ever do to you?' he said, staring at her. 'What gave you the right to do this to me?' His heart pounded, he felt sick, he stood there quivering with rage, but still, still, remaining unaffected, a small part of him saw this unusual, unaccustomed anger within him, heard the words he spoke, with an amusement, a sort of critical appreciation, not unlike what he saw in her eyes and read on her face.

She shrugged, swallowed, still looking up at him. 'You did nothing to me,' she said slowly, 'or to . . . Stock. We had no right, of course. But what difference does that make? Does it really make you feel worse?' She looked at him as though she really was asking a serious question, something she could not find the answer to in herself, something she had to look to him or somebody like him to answer.

'What do you care?' he said, shaking his head, leaning towards her across the table. His eyes were bright, he could look at her now. She gazed back, something like fear quickening her, widening the hooded eyes. He saw the small pulse by the side of her neck again, he became aware of the shallow rising and falling of her T-shirt inside the olive dungarees. He could smell the oil she had put on herself after her bath, the clean fresh smell of her. She shrugged again, shoulders jerking.

'Just interested,' she said. 'You don't have to tell me. I just wondered how it felt.'

'What the hell are you doing?' He couldn't stop the words coming out in a gasp, couldn't stop the anger, the pain from being there. 'What are you trying to . . . Why did you have to do it this way?'

'Oh, Graham,' she sighed, breath ragged, shaking her head. 'I didn't set out to hurt you, but when I thought about what I had to tell you, *how* I had to tell you, I . . . saw it had to be done in a certain way. Can't you see?' She looked at him, intent, almost desperate; 'You were just too perfect. It had to go along certain lines once we'd set out. I can't really explain it to you. You . . . you asked for it.' She held up one hand, as though to catch something he had thrown at her, as he opened his mouth to speak. 'Yes, yes,' she said, 'I know, it does sound terrible, it's what . . . it's what rapists say, isn't it? But that's the way it was with you, Graham. That was all that gave me the right to do any of this to you, that's all you did; just be the way you were. All you were guilty of was being innocent.'

He stared at her, his mouth open. He walked round the side of the table. She stayed sitting as he approached her; the beat of her pulse quickened, her hands clasped quickly together on the black circle of the table. She stared away, at where he had been sitting. He went round the back of the seat she sat in, to the window, and stared out of it.

'So I just go now,' he said quietly.

'I want you to go, yes.' Her voice was thin and sharp.

'Do you, now?' he said, his voice still low.

I could, he thought, throw myself out of the window, but it isn't very far to the street, and why should I give her another little display of grief and petulance anyway? Or I could draw these curtains and turn on her, hand over mouth, throw her across the table, tear the clothes off her, pin her there . . . and act out another part, that's all. I could plead temporary jealous madness; depending on the judge, I could have a very good chance of getting away with it. I could say no violence was used (just that blunt instrument between the legs, just that even blunter instrument between the ears, just the age-old violence, the ancient cruelty, the ultimate obscenity of pleasure, *joy* twisted into pain and hatred. Yes, yes, that was it; what perfect torture; an archetype for all the cunningly designed machines us boys have played with. Shatter and destroy inside, leave no outward trace or bruise).

She led me on, Your Honour.

Yes, she led me on, and fuck *you*, Your Honour. I'll not do that, to her or myself. Always did think Pilate had the right idea; wash hands, let the mob have its grubby desire. *Slater, my brains are in the right place after all.* He turned round, half-expecting her to be holding a breadknife.

But she was still sitting there, in the seat, her back to him, hair gathered and bunched.

'I'd better go, then,' he said, and was hopelessly, emptily elated that his voice did not shake very much. He walked slowly past her, down to the carpeted section of the room, and took up his portfolio of drawings. He thought of leaving them for a moment, but he needed the plastic portfolio; it would be a pointless gesture to leave it, or even remove the drawings.

He walked out into the hall; from the corner of his eye, he saw she was not moving. She sat in the chair, unmoving, watching him. He let himself out by the thin, light, inner door, went down the stairs and out the front door. He walked across to the corner of Maygood Street, and straight up it. He almost expected to hear her call him, from the window, and had already decided not to turn if she did, but no sound came, and he just kept on walking.

When she heard the door close beneath, and the lock catch, and then the sound of his footsteps on the pavement outside, Sara slumped suddenly, puppet-slack, her head dropping as though in a faint to lie on the sweat-slicked surfaces of her forearms, near her still clasped hands. Her eyes stared over the smooth dark surface of the table. Her breathing slackened, and her pulse slowed.

He gunned the bike again, sending it out into the traffic, drawing a chorus of horns from behind as the bike's engine hesitated once more. He gritted his teeth, swore, felt sweat dribble inside the black helmet, and twisted the throttle again. The bike's stuttering engine caught and he surged forward, beside a flat-decked beer lorry with a few barrels at the rear of its long load platform. He gunned the engine, swept round the Watneys' truck, the aluminium barrels at its rear glinting in the sunlight. Then when he was level with the cab the engine failed again; he just got round in front of the lorry, then had to slow down. The truck's engine sounded, loud, right behind him. The dying engine would not restart; he would have to steer back in for the side of the road. He waited for a break in the traffic on his left which would let him get to the kerb, ignoring the pulsing horn of the Watneys' truck, which he was now holding up.

The engine spluttered, then suddenly caught and ran smoothly again. He hissed through his teeth, revved it. The bike shot forward. Some shouts came from behind, from the cab of the lorry at his back. They came to the lights at the junction of Pentonville Road and Upper Street; he would have to go over the junction and then cut down Liverpool Road, to get to Half Moon Crescent.

He waited at the lights. The beer lorry drew up along-side, the driver shouting at him, loudly asking him what he was up to. He said nothing. The lights changed, the truck moved off, the bike's engine died completely. He restarted it, roared off after the truck, caught it and started to pull in front. The lorry driver was keeping his foot on the floor, the truck's engine screaming. The bike stuttered once again. The engine caught, failed, caught again; together the bike and lorry roared up the wide stretch of Upper Street, the beer lorry stopping the bike from pulling in towards Liverpool Road.

He saw a hole in the tarmac in front of him (and was vaguely aware of people on the pavement, waiting for buses, as their faces flashed by on the far side of the truck's flat deck). The long hole in the road surface ahead of him wasn't too large; he could avoid it and the long dark plume of disintegrating tarmac strewn out on its far side; he swerved the bike neatly.

At first it looked as though the lorry with the beer barrels would miss the hole, too, but it swerved suddenly towards the hole and bike – as though avoiding somebody stepping out into the road from the bus-stop – and its wheels went thumping, crashing into the ragged trench in the roadway with a huge hollow-sounding noise, and from the truck's lightly laden, suddenly bouncing rear, something flew into the air . . .

Graham walked up the street, through the hard sunlight of the late afternoon, over Penton Street and into an area where most of the buildings had been demolished. Around him were some echoes of buildings; rows and corridors of corrugated iron, new and zinc-bright in the sunlight, standing on end around empty, dusty sites where weeds grew; in the distance were old buildings, tall crumbling places, leaning and twisted, worn old slates with many missing, roofs bowed under the ancient weight, old windows, glaucomaed with age, eaten timbers making up ramshackle additions to the top storeys. New kerbs, un-made-up pavements, dust and sand. He caught glimpses of the empty sites through spaces in the corrugated iron. Most were flat, filled with swirled patterns of rubbish and growing weeds. Some were being worked on; he saw the naked bricks and ragged lengths of concrete-bottomed trenches which would become foundations; lengths of string marked lines and levels for bricks.

He walked through this summit of iron and dust, seeing it but numb to it, through the slightly humid air and the sounds of the traffic and sirens, through the smells of cement dust and rotting rubbish, down to Liverpool Road and over towards Upper Street.

He could only think of what had just happened to him as something he had watched, not actually taken part in. He could not appreciate it directly, he could not cope with it in any personal way, on a level which related to what he regarded as his real self. It was something too important to be assimilated quickly; it was as though some vast besieging army had finally smashed the main gate into a great city, and swept in to overwhelm its ruined defences but could do so only through that one point, so that, while the forces spread throughout the streets and houses and the city's fall was assured, already underway, for a long time in many places within it there was nothing immediately wrong or affected, and life could go on almost as normal.

When he got down to Upper Street there was a traffic jam, and the flashing blue light of an ambulance waiting somewhere at the bus-stops; people were looking in that direction, trying to see over the tops of the other people's heads, edging closer, trying to find out what happened. He could not go near, did not want to see other people.

He crossed the lanes of stationary traffic, waited for a break in the still moving south-bound streams, crossed to the far side, walked past another huge building site where tall cranes stuck into the sky and dust moved in the wind, then went down through smaller streets, ignoring people, clutching the black portfolio to him, heading towards some trees he could see.

Richard Slater lay in bed with his elder sister, the woman

Graham knew as Mrs Sara ffitch, but whose real name was Mrs Sarah Simpson-Wallace (née Slater).

The shared, mingled sweat dried on their naked bodies. Sarah took another Kleenex from the box under the bed, dabbed at herself, then put the soggy tissues in the small split-cane bin at the foot of the bed. She got up, stretching her arms and shaking her black, tangled hair.

Slater watched her. He had bruised her again. Dark blue marks were forming on the tops of her arms, and under her buttocks, at the top and rear of her thighs. He had bitten her, too, on the white scar (where she didn't feel it so much). She had whimpered at the time; cried out, but – perhaps because she was relieved she had received no physical retaliation from Graham – she did not seem to be in a mood to complain today. Still, Slater felt guilty anyway. He was too rough, and despised himself – and maybe even her – for it. He had never been like that with anybody else, never even felt like being that way. With her, he couldn't help it. He wanted to be like that, he wanted to grip her, squeeze her, to impale and imprison her, to shake and pummel her; mark her. It was that or it was nothing; cold, without feeling, almost masturbatory.

Why? he asked himself for the thousandth time. *Why do I do that to her? Why do I need to?* He knew he wasn't like that really. It went against everything he believed in. So why?

Sarah took a plain, blue silk dressing gown from the bottom of the bed and tied it around her. She still wore the pink training shoes she had put on after her bath.

Slater sighed. He said, 'None of which alters the fact

that you shouldn't have done it, not without me here.'

Sarah shrugged, without turning round. 'I'm going to have some orange juice,' she said. 'Want some?'

'*Sarah.*'

'What?' She turned to look at him. Slater looked at her accusingly. She grinned back at him. 'I handled it,' she said. 'Nothing went wrong, did it?'

'He's bigger than you are. He might have got violent. He is a man, after all, dear. We chaps are all the same, didn't you know?' He could not resist smiling as he said it.

'Luckily, you aren't all the same at all,' Sarah said, and went through the doorway, across the hall to the sitting-room and kitchen. 'Not at all,' she said from the other room as she walked. 'Not even slightly.'

Slater lay on the bed, shivering once as his flesh dried. He got up and took a piece of paper from the small dressing table by the side of the bed. It was an old Labour election leaflet, blank on one side. He took a pen from the inside pocket of his biker leathers – strewn on the floor with her dungarees and T-shirt – then sat up in bed and started to write, quickly and in a small, scratchy, precise hand. He wrote:

Dear Graham,

I know what Sarah has told you. It was not the whole truth, I'm afraid. The fact is that *I* am Stock (and so, once, was Sarah, as I'll explain). There is no Bob Stock, there's only me.

Sarah is my sister and we've had (horror of horrors!) an incestuous relationship for the past six years or so (blame single-sex public schools, I say). Sarah *is* married and her husband *was* having her followed. I couldn't risk being seen with her, so I invented Stock; I keep the bike in a car park at the back of the Air Gallery; I know somebody who works there and they keep the leathers and crash helmet. I dress there and visit Sarah using the bike, looking terribly butch and incognito.

So far so good, you might think, but we needed more; it wasn't all that important that Sarah was known to be committing adultery, but it was important, at least until very recently, that it wasn't known who with. Quite apart from the fact that what we're doing is reasonably *illegal*, it would have done terrible things to our parents. Dear dad, you see, was Conservative MP for Salop West. Even *you* might have heard of him; very strong line on family life, morality and that sort of thing; supported the Festival of Light, the National Viewers and Listeners Association (Mary White-house's mob), and SPUNK, or whatever they call it; the Society for the Prevention of Unborn Conservatives (sick!). Pro-hanging, of course.

The old bugger having made his reputation peddling this sort of reactionary moralist nonsense, the revela-tion that his two children were humping each other would have finished him; that applied at the start of all this, but became even more important when Mag the Hag announced the election. Anyway, going back to where you came in, I think you'll appreciate that the situation was such that we needed another safeguard to stop me being identified. We needed somebody else, to draw the heat, to distract the chap we knew was trailing Sarah. We chose you. All right; *I* chose you.

Why couldn't we just have stopped seeing each other? I hear you ask. Tried that. Just not poss. Sarah got married trying to get out of this whole thing, and I moved down here, but neither of us could stop thinking about the other; just couldn't forget. I suppose we must be doomed for each other.

I think you fell for Sarah a bit (though being you you made it impossible to tell; you could have been cranium-over-Achilles for the girl and still have given nothing away; acting Joe Cool as usual) and if my fucking bike hadn't conked out on me (I think some bastard put sugar in the petrol tank) we were going to let you down easier; I was to appear in the street outside while Sarah was explaining to you in the flat that she liked you too much to start anything because she was basically a bad 'un and she and Stock deserved each other . . . well, it seemed like a good idea at the time; you hustled out the back door as Sarah panicked; unrequited but *smug*, knowing You Were Too Good For Her, and her, worthless bitch, back with the bad guy. Oh well.

Anyway, the election's over, as you might have noticed, and our father was one of the only two Tories to lose their seats in a Conservative landslide (to a Liberal; ha ha), and he's retiring from politics. Sarah isn't being followed any more, as far as I can tell, so

the need for most, if not all, of the subterfuge is gone
. . . sorry.

Why protect the old fascist in the first place?

What can I say? That blood is thicker than water
maybe, but also that if anything had come out about
Sarah and me it might not only have ruined our father
but it would certainly have killed our mum, who really
isn't a bad sort. (Fuck it; we both still love her. There.)

Family loyalty, in other words. I don't know.

Well, you must admit we were thorough; we even
arranged for you to see 'Stock' when I was there (you
remember; in the pub?); that was Sarah, padded out
with jeans and jumpers and walking on tip-toe with
several dozen of my socks stuffed into the bottoms of
my boots.

I don't know how to—

Sarah came back then, with two glasses of orange juice
and a large plate with small pieces of bread topped with
pâté, various cheeses and honey. 'Here,' she said, putting
the plate and one glass down by the side of the bed, on
the small dressing table. 'What are you writing?'

'A letter to Graham, telling him the whole truth. All
of it. Nothing but,' Slater said. Sarah looked at him without saying anything, took a drink from the slim glass she
held.

Slater looked at the letter, reading his own scrawled
lines with a frown on his face. 'You know,' he said to his
sister, 'I really wish I could send this to him.'

'If you've told the whole truth, you certainly can not.'

'Hmm. I know. But I need to write it anyway. For me.'
He looked at her. 'I guess I'm still tense.'

She moved closer to the bed, looked down at him, 'You
still worried about that crash?' she said.

Slater put the pen and the paper down on the dressing table. He rolled his eyes, then put his hands over his
face. 'Yes, yes!' he said, and pushed his fingers through
his dark hair, staring at the ceiling while she watched him
calmly. 'Oh God, oh Doom! I just hope they didn't get
the number!'

'What, of the bike?' she said, drinking her orange juice.

'Yes, of course!' He shook his head at the ceiling, then
levered himself back up on one elbow, and read over the
letter Graham would never read. What to say next? How
to finish it off? Sarah watched for a while, then turned
away and combed her hair. She heard a rustle of paper,
the clatter of the pen on the dressing table, after a while.
She turned to look at him.

'Better?' she asked, putting the comb down. Slater lay
on the bed, the paper crumpled in one outstretched hand.
He shook his head, still staring at the ceiling, then let the
crumpled ball of paper roll out of his hand. At the same
time he croaked, 'Rosebud!' The paper ball rolled along
the floor. She smiled, kicked the paper with one pink-
shoed foot towards the bin.

She turned and studied herself in the mirror, calmly
stroking her bruises.

'Have you ever,' Slater said, 'entertained the idea that
we might be evil? I mean that despite the fact you're
beautiful and I'm *right* . . . that nevertheless, for some

horrible, maybe genetic reason, maybe class, even, we—'

'I have never even considered any other explanation,' Sarah said, smiling, still looking at herself. Slater laughed.

He did love her. It was all that a brother-sister relationship was supposed to be, all that people meant when they talked of loving someone like a brother or a sister . . . it was just that, but not only that. He *wanted* her. At least sometimes, at least when he did not hate himself for wanting her in the way he did.

Perhaps it was possible, though. Perhaps he could just love her solely and conventionally as a sister. She was worth all that alone, after all. She could not mean less to him. Sex was only that, surely, and indeed with her only more intense . . . more *dangerous* in its feel than with others; not better. Worse, in fact, in its penumbra of guilt and self-disgust. He should, he really ought to make an effort; let what had happened to Graham, what they had done to him be a tragic landmark, a reason almost . . . at least not let it go to waste . . .

Sarah went to the old mono record player which stood on a small table on the far side of the bedroom. She took her current favourite Bowie album, his latest, and put it on at the start of her favourite track, the song which was a single and still in the charts; *Let's Dance*, the title track. The stylus scraped into the groove, neatly between tracks. The old speaker crackled slightly and hissed; she turned the volume up, put the arm mechanism on to repeat.

Slater lay on the bed, turned sideways, watching her. He forgot about the accident he had helped cause, about Graham and the hurt he had contributed towards, as he watched his sister sway and move in front of the record player. The music punched out, filling the small room; she nodded her head, her body moved inside the thin blue silk, in time to the first few lyrical bars of the song. He felt his desire grow for her again.

She knew the song well. Just before Bowie's voice started, just before the words 'Let's dance,' she turned, smiling to her brother, put her slender fingers to her shoulders, opening the blue silk gown and letting it fall from her, collecting in soft folds about the pink trainers as she nodded twice in time to the music and over the first phrase mouthed the words 'Let's *fuck . . .*'

And for a moment, behind his eyes, where he felt he really lived, he felt complete despair, and the absolute necessity of keeping what he felt away from her, of stopping it from showing on his face.

He seemed to halt then, in some frozen moment, an expression of feigned delight and surprise impacted on his face, as behind it, inside him, a pain he could not name, like his wanting, with his wanting, arose and overwhelmed him.

From the notebook of Detective Sergeant Nichols; interview with Thomas Edward PRITCHARD, Islington Police Station, 28/6/83.

Q: What about the bike then did you get its no?
A: O yes I got that bastards no. alright. It was STK 228 something. Either I or T. T, I think.

Dr Shawcross

Mr Williams – Mike, as he liked to be called – was Steven's friend in the hospital. He called Doctor Shawcross 'Doctor Shock' because he said if you were bad and didn't do what they told you to do, they gave you electric shocks. Mr Williams was funny. He made Steven laugh lots and lots. He could be cruel sometimes, too, like when he had dropped the spiders into the lap of Harry-the-guy who-hated-spiders the other day (Mr Williams had used a long word instead of 'the-guy-who-hated-spiders', but Steven couldn't remember what it was). That had been cruel, especially as they had been at dinner at the time, but it had been funny too.

Steven had been blamed for that, and they had punished

him for it, but he couldn't recall what the punishment had been.

The crows called his name.

Dr Shawcross sat in his office, staring out of the window at the unleaved trees of the Kent countryside, watching a few crows flap lazily from tall branches, out over the bare brown fields. In front of him, spread out on his desk, was the file on Steven Grout. Dr Shawcross had to write a report on Steven, for the insurers of one of the vehicles involved in the accident which had resulted in Grout ending up here, in the Dargate Sheltered Unit.

It was February 16th, 1984 (Dr Shawcross had already noted the date on the sheet of paper he was going to draft the report on). It was cold. The car had been very slow to start that morning. Dr Shawcross hummed tunelessly to himself and reached down to the floor where his brief-case was. He glanced over the previous reports on Grout as his right hand fumbled in the case for his pipe and tobacco. He found them, put the pipe on his desk and started to stuff the tobacco into the bowl.

His mind wandered when he saw the date of Grout's accident; June 28th last year. He sighed. Summer seemed such a long way away, but at the same time there was that paper he had to write for the conference in Scarborough in June; that would come around soon enough; he'd be pushed for time on that, he'd bet.

Steven Grout (no middle name) had been involved in a road traffic accident on June 28th, 1983. A beer barrel struck him on the head after bouncing off the back of a lorry. Grout had fallen into the stream of traffic and been run over by a car. His scalp was lacerated, skull fractured, both clavicles and the left scapula sustained fractures, and he had multiple rib fractures as well.

Dr Shawcross experienced an odd sensation of *déjà vu*, then suddenly recalled that he'd read something about the trial of the case which resulted from this accident in the paper just the other day (was it yesterday?). Hadn't somebody famous been involved, or somebody connected with somebody famous? Some public figure, anyway, and some sort of scandal. He couldn't remember. Maybe the paper was still in the house. He'd check when he got back in the evening, if he remembered, and Liz hadn't thrown the paper out.

Dr Shawcross read through the previous reports, packing the tobacco into the bowl, putting the pipe in his mouth, then patting his pockets one by one as he searched for his matches. His eyes flitted over the typed sheets as he refreshed his memory, only certain important words and phrases really registering: cyanosed . . . flail chest . . . intubation . . . raised intracranial blood-pressure . . . Dexamethasone and Mannitol . . . pulse slowing . . . blood pressure increase . . . very slow response to deep painful stimulus . . . eyes deviated dysconjugately . . . possible frontal lobe contusion . . . neck angle a tracheostomy was performed . . .

Dr Shawcross tutted to himself, pulled open a drawer, rummaged briefly, found a box of matches. He lit his pipe.

The latest of the reports concerned Grout when he was physically more or less recovered, and in the rehabilitation ward of a hospital in North London. Grout had been totally disorientated in time and space, the report said. He had been capable of holding a conversation but unable to remember any fact for longer than a few minutes; no recollection from day to day of the nursing staff who tended him.

Dr Shawcross puffed away on his pipe, once waving a lock of blue smoke away from his eyes as he read (he was supposed to have given up for the new year. Well, at least he didn't smoke in the house nowadays. Well, hardly ever).

The patient improved only slowly; conscious and alert but still disorientated; marked impairment of reading ability and memory; vague recollections of the distant past (now knew he had been brought up in a children's home), but thought the date was June 28th, 1976.

One phrase kept cropping up time after time in the report, as various follow-up and check-up examinations were recorded, and Grout's post-traumatic amnesia lengthened: little insight into his disability . . . no insight into his disability . . . lack of insight into his condition . . . still no insight into his disability . . .

Grout was usually quite euphoric, always smiling and nodding and giving the thumbs-up sign; he cooperated fully with physical examinations and seemed anxious to help and cooperate in the memory tests and other examinations of his mental faculties he was asked to undergo. But while he felt quite sure he was capable of living by himself, and of undertaking any job or career, his poor short-term memory and total lack of drive and initiative made him totally unfit for anything but the sheltered environment he now lived in. To that extent, he was permanently disabled, with little, if any, chance of any further improvement in his condition.

Dr Shawcross nodded to himself. That was it, all right. He'd examined Steven that morning, and the man, while quite happy and content, had no prospect of leaving the Unit in the forseeable future. He was still euphoric, though when pressed did admit that his memory wasn't all it had been. Dr Shawcross had asked him if he recalled ever having been on any day trips with the other patients in the Unit. Steven had looked exaggeratedly thoughtful and said that he thought he had been to Bournemouth, hadn't he? Dr Shawcross knew from the file that Steven had been on one day trip, but that was only as far as Canterbury.

He told Steven a little story which he asked him to try and remember: a man in a green coat, with bright red hair, went for a walk with his dog, a terrier, in Nottingham. Then he talked to Steven about how he had settled into the Unit since his arrival in January.

After about five minutes he had asked Steven if he could remember the little story he'd told him. Steven had frowned, looked very thoughtful for a while. Was there something about a bald man? he had asked. Dr Shawcross had asked him if he could recall any colours involved in the story. Steven had creased his brows again. Was the man wearing a brown jacket? he had said. Dr Shawcross had said that sounded like a guess, and Steven had smiled sheepishly and admitted it was.

Dr Shawcross's mouth made small papping noises as he drew on the pipe. He sat back a little in his seat, looking out of the window again. The sky was full of low grey clouds.

He wondered if it would snow, or rain.

Steven was in his favourite place.

It was a sort of little tunnel under the raised bank of the railway line which passed along one side of the hospital grounds. Strictly speaking it was out of bounds, but only just. The tunnel was only about fifty or sixty feet long, but it was nice and dark and secluded because both ends were overgrown with bushes and small trees. In the direction that Grout sat facing, over the naked earth fields and the distant lines of trees, over low rolling hills, towards the unseen sea, the end of the tunnel was barred by a lop-sided wooden gate, twined round with brambles and long grass.

Steven sat on an iron seat; a saddle-shaped iron seat which itself sat on a rusty old grass-roller with a broken towing bar. The broken grass-roller was one of many interesting things in the dark, damp, soft-earthed tunnel. There was an old, pale pink plastic bucket with a split bottom, four woodwormed fenceposts with three staple nails in each, an old car battery with the top bit missing, a torn plastic Woolworth carrier bag, two crushed, empty Skol lager cans, an uncrushed Pepsi can, various sweet wrappers, an old damp matchbox with three dead matches inside, a yellowing sheet of paper from the *Daily Express* dated Tuesday, March 18th, 1980, and several dozen cigarette ends in various stages of decomposition.

The grass-roller was the best thing, though, because you could sit on it, nice and dry and quite comfortable, and you could look out over the mass of undergrowth at the end of the tunnel, and see the sky and the trees and the fields. Crows flew around the trees, over the naked-earth fields. The crows called out, calling his name.

Steven was happy. It was cold (he wore two T-shirts and two pullovers and a parka), and he could feel the cold of the iron seat under his bum seeping through to his skin; his breath glowed in the dark tunnel and he had to keep his hands in his pockets because he'd lost his gloves again, but he was happy. It was nice to get away now and again, even though he quite liked the hospital. Mr Williams made him laugh, the tricks he played and the funny things he said.

They went on day trips, sometimes, though Steven couldn't quite remember where. He read a lot. Important books, though their names escaped him just for the moment.

He used to be happy, then unhappy (he seemed to recall) and looking for things, but now he was happy again. He had mentioned all this to Mr Williams, about how he'd been unhappy and looking for things, and Mr Williams had given him an old big rusty key and a plastic sign which said 'Way Out'. Steven kept them in his locker, and took them out and looked at them sometimes.

He had other things in his locker; things from before, when he had been unhappy. They had given him these things . . . he couldn't remember when, not at the moment

. . . but it would come to him . . . anyway, they had given him a radio and an atlas, some books and a metal sort of sculpture thing of a lion or a tiger or something. He kept them because you weren't supposed to throw away things people had given you, but he didn't really want them.

Then there were some bits and pieces from games which Mr Williams had given to him. There was a chess piece which looked like a little castle, and another which looked like a little horse, also some bits of plastic with letters on them and little numbers, and other bits of plastic which had spots on one side.

In the old country house around which the hospital had grown and spread since its foundation after the First World War there was the Sheltered Unit's library. An old man and an old woman sat in there, playing games over an old coffee table. Mr Williams took pieces from their games when they weren't looking, just for a laugh. He would give them the bits back later on, of course, so it wasn't really stealing, but oh, it was funny, watching them get all upset!

Steven thought Mr Williams was naughty, but he did make him laugh, and Steven liked to feel trusted, and liked being in on Mr Williams's jokes and secrets. It was good.

The crows called his name again, wheeling above the turned-over fields, scraps of black against the greyly shining clouds. Steven smiled and looked round the littered surface of the tunnel floor. He leaned down and picked up the matchbox with the three dead matches inside it and turned it over in his hands. He heard a train hooter in the distance.

Soon a train would go noisily overhead, on the rails on the top of the banking the tunnel ran through. Steven liked the busy, steely noise the trains made over his head. It wasn't frightening at all. He squinted at the words on the faded cover of the little matchbox:

McGuffin's
¡ZEN BRAND!
matches
average contents: $\sqrt{2}$

Steven didn't understand. He turned the matchbox over and read a riddle printed on the back. He didn't understand that, either. He read the words out slowly to himself. '*Q*: What happens when an unstoppable force meets an immovable object? *A*: The unstoppable force stops, the immovable object moves.'

Steven shook his head and put the matchbox back down on the ground. He shivered. It would be time for tea soon.

Dr Shawcross scratched behind his left ear with one finger, brow furrowed like the ploughed Kentish fields. He couldn't think of any other way to put it, so he wrote, finishing the sentence and also the report, apart from the summing-up: . . . *euphoric, but still totally lacking insight into his disability.*

Steven stared at the bright inverted U of light, as the train clattered and whined overhead and the little iron seat on top of the grass-roller vibrated slightly. The crows called his name, their hoarse voices not quite drowned by the passing train: 'Ger-out! Ger-out! Ger-out!'

He was happy.

Tunnel

Quiss stood on the parapet of the balcony, staring down at the white plain beneath. His mouth was dry, his heart beat quickly; he was trembling, and a nervous tic jigged at one corner of his mouth as he stood, swaying slightly, getting ready to jump.

He was going to kill himself, because now he knew the secret of the castle. He knew what it was founded on, what underlay it; he even knew where it was and when. The red crow had shown him.

They had played a game called Tunnel, which was based on a game called Bridge. They played two hands each, using blank cards, trying to make things called tricks. The idea was that Tunnel was like Bridge played underneath the table, or in the dark. As in Spotless Dominoes, they had to go through the motions of playing the game, hoping that eventually they would play one game in such a way that the blank cards – which the little games table had ascribed values to, new ones for each game – would end up displayed on the table in a logical sequence, the 'tricks' correctly composed of similar-suit cards.

The game was over; after a thousand days they had done it, but they were still undecided what to give as an answer to the riddle. They couldn't think of anything they both agreed was a reasonable response. Quiss didn't care any more. It wouldn't make any difference, anyway. There was only death here, death or what the red crow had shown him. He looked down at the snow. It lay over the jumbled crags of slate far below, at the base of the castle. It was about a hundred metre drop. There would be a lot of wind noise, he would feel cold for a while, weightless for an instant, then . . . nothing. He should do it now, but he had to prepare himself. Still, Ajayi might not be away for very long (she had gone looking for books as usual), and he didn't want her seeing him there. He leaned forward, over the drop, biting his lip.

No machine-gun this time, he thought.

He had been down in the guts of the place.

More locked doors. The same ancient corridors, dimly lit. His scullions would not help him find keys for the doors; they said they had no influence with the key-keepers, they didn't know any of them and if they started

311

to make any inquiries they would be under suspicion immediately; they thought the seneschal already knew of their allegiance to Quiss, and merely tolerated it.

Quiss tried to engage the attendants he met down here, deep under the castle, in conversation, on the odd occasions when he encountered them; but they were taciturn, unhelpful. He thought about knocking one over the head sometime, seeing if it had a key which he could steal and use, but as soon as he had even hinted he might try this his own scullions had started weeping and begging him not to. He and they would be terribly punished if he tried to open the castle's doors like that. The black minions, they said, in quivering voices; the black minions . . . Quiss assumed they were talking about the attendants he had seen only once, with the seneschal that one time he had found an open door and the seneschal and the black-robed minions arrived in the creaking elevator. He reluctantly shelved the idea of taking a key by force.

He walked along the corridor. He was in the general area of the door he had found open, many many days ago. He thought he could just make out a sort of half-felt, half-heard thumping noise, and suspected he was somewhere near the number-crunching room; *dee pee* as the snooty attendant had called it.

The corridor opened out to about twice the cross-section which he regarded as the castle's standard. A slate bench on one wall faced a row of twelve large, stout, metal-strapped doors.

He was weary, so he sat down on the bench, looking through the gloom at the tall, dark doors.

'Tired, old man?' a voice said, from above him. He turned and saw the red crow, perched on a peg stuck into the wall high above the slate bench, near the vaulted ceiling.

'What are you doing way down here?' he asked the creature, surprised to find it so deep in the castle's structure.

'Following you,' the crow said.

'To what do I owe such an honour?'

'Your stupidity,' the red crow said, stretching its wings as though stiff. One of its small eyes glinted in the dim light from the glowing, transparent tubes at the apex of the ceiling.

'Really,' he said. If the red crow was just insulting him, let it. If it wanted to talk it would have to start things off. He suspected it did want to talk. It was here for a good reason.

'Yes, really,' the red crow said testily. It flapped off the perch on the wall and landed in the middle of the floor, facing him. It folded its wings. A little dust swirled around it. 'You won't listen to reason, so I'm going to have to rub your nose in things.'

'Are you indeed?' Quiss said coldly. He didn't like its tone. 'What "things"?'

'Call it *truth*,' the red crow said, spitting the word out like a lump of gristle.

'What would you know about that?' Quiss scoffed.

'Oh, quite a lot, as you'll discover, man.' The red crow's voice was calm, measured and mocking. 'If you want to, that is.'

'That depends,' Quiss said, frowning at the bird. 'What exactly are we talking about?'

The red crow jerked its head, indicating the wall and the doors behind it. 'I can get you in there. I can show you what you have been looking for all this time.'

'Can you really?' Quiss said, stalling. He wondered if the crow was telling the truth. If it was, *why* was it telling him?

The bird, its bright plumage dulled to burgundy by the gloom, nodded. 'I can. Do you want to see behind the doors?'

'Yes,' Quiss said. There was little point in denying it. 'What's the catch?'

'Ah,' the red crow said, and Quiss thought that if the bird could have smiled, it would. 'I must have your word.'

'On what?'

'That I show you what I show you of your own free will, that you go willingly on the understanding that without any outside influence from me or anything else you may not desire to come back, or may desire to kill yourself. You may not, of course, but if you stay, or if you kill yourself, you must give me your word you will say that I warned you of this first.'

Quiss narrowed his eyes, leaned forward on the slate seat, putting one elbow on his knees, one hand to his lips. His chin was rough with stubble. 'You are saying that what you will show me may make me wish to stay behind those doors, or may make me desire death.'

'In a word: more-or-less,' the red crow cackled.

'But you won't use any dirty tricks to influence me.'

'No need.'

'Then I give my word.'

'Good,' the red crow said with some satisfaction. It flapped once and rose into the air, and Quiss had the impression that it was done too easily, that the wings had not powered the bird at all, that it flapped them merely for show. The bird turned and flew off down the corridor, in the direction Quiss had been heading. It disappeared round a corner in the dim distance.

Quiss got to his feet, wondering if he was supposed to follow the creature. He scratched his chin, looking at the dozen doors. His heart started to beat a little faster; what was behind the doors? The red crow wanted him and Ajayi dead; it wanted them to admit defeat and give up their struggle with the riddle. That was simply part of its job, though it claimed it really did want rid of them anyway, because they were boring. It knew that Quiss knew this, so it must be very confident that whatever was behind the doors would have a considerable effect on Quiss; enough to break him, perhaps. Quiss was nervous, keyed up, but determined. He could take whatever the red crow was going to throw at him, whatever it had to show him. Anything which might help him find the way out of this thing, even just give a new angle on his and Ajayi's plight, would be useful. Besides, he suspected the red crow did not know that he had been behind one of those doors once, even if only briefly. If the revelation beyond that heavy wood and metal strapping had something to do with the ceiling-holes and the place called 'Dirt', then Quiss was already prepared.

The door nearest Quiss clicked. He heard a tapping noise, and went forward. There was a metal-lined slit in the door which he took to be a handle. He pulled on it; the door opened slowly, smoothly, and revealed the red crow hovering in a long corridor lit by small glowing globes fixed to the wall.

'Welcome,' the crow said. It turned, flew slowly down the long corridor. 'Close the door; follow me,' it said. Quiss did as he was told.

The bird flew, and he walked, for about ten minutes. The tunnel led down and to the left, curving gradually. It was quite warm. The red crow flew, silently, about five metres in front of him. Finally they came to another door, similar to the one through which they had entered the tunnel. The red crow stopped at it.

'Excuse me,' it said, and disappeared through the door. Quiss was startled. He touched the door, to make sure it was not a projection; it was solid, warm. It clicked. The red crow reappeared over Quiss's head. 'Well, open it,' it said. Quiss pulled the door towards him.

He walked, with the red crow behind him and over him, into a strange place.

His head swam; he felt himself stagger momentarily. He blinked his eyes and shook his head. He felt at once that he had walked *into* a place, but also out into the open air.

It was as though he stood on a flat desert floor, or the dulled bed of a salt lake. But the sky was within touching distance, as if some flat layer of clouds had lowered to within a couple of metres of that salt or sandy surface.

Behind him (as he turned, dizzy, looking for a point

of reference in the confusing, pillared infinity before him) was the door they had just come through. It was set in a black wall which at first sight seemed straight, but which he soon realised was curved; part of a gigantic circle. The red crow flapped lazily just overhead, watching with amused malevolence as Quiss turned again to the space in front of them.

The floor was smooth slate, the ceiling composed of the glass and ironwork and water common to the castle's upper storeys. Slate and iron columns supported the roof, which was at the same height it had been in the room Quiss had found his way into such a long time ago, when he discovered the hole in the glass with the creature over and around it. All that was missing, in three out of the four directions, was a wall.

It was not bright, with only a few of the luminous fish waving lazily over his head and nearby, but it was light enough to see that the space he was now in seemed endless. Quiss peered into the distance, but all he could see were pillars and columns, growing smaller and smaller in the squeezed, twisted depths before him. Pillars and columns and . . . people. Human figures stood on small stools, or sat in high chairs, arms in iron hoops, shoulders hard up against the undersurface of the endless glass ceiling. Some of the things he had thought were pillars or columns at first, stunned sight were not; they were people with their heads stuck in the ceiling, dark shadowy forms above them in the glass, surrounding holes in the ceiling like the one he had stuck his own head into, briefly, in that small room long ago.

He shook his head again, peered again into the distance. The narrow space between floor and ceiling vanished, all around, into a thin line, hazed by distance. The line looked very slightly curved, like a horizon of empty water seen from a ship on a planetary ocean. He felt dizzy again. His eyes could not accept it; his brain took in the short space between floor and ceiling and so expected walls, expected a room-space. But if he was in a room (and if this was not some sort of projection, or even some unsubtle trick with mirrors) then its walls appeared to be somewhere over the horizon.

He turned again, carefully, trying to recall his early training for the Wars, which had included balance and disorientation exercises that had left him feeling a bit like he did now, and looked again at the black wall just behind him, with the metal-strapped door in it. He looked along the very slightly curved wall, trying to estimate the diameter of the circle it implied. It must be several kilometres; sufficient to encompass the castle, mines and quarries. This wall was the castle's root, its foundation. This endless space some sort of vast basement.

'What is this place?' he said, and felt as though he was whispering; his brain expected echoes, but none came. It was like speaking in the open air. He looked round at the people stood on stools and slumped in tall chairs as the red crow said, 'Let's take a walk. Follow me and I'll tell you.' It flapped slowly past him, and he walked slowly after it. He passed near one of the standing figures: a man, dressed in furs similar to his own, but older-looking. The man looked skinny. A pipe led from the furs round the man's crotch to a stone jug on the floor. They passed him by.

Some movement, far in the hazy distance, attracted Quiss's eyes. It looked like a small train; a narrow-gauge railway with a small locomotive on it, hauling hopper-like carriages. It was difficult to estimate the distance, but he guessed it was at least four hundred metres away, moving out from the castle, away into the thin space of standing people and supporting columns. He remembered the train he had seen, long ago, in the kitchens.

He looked round, trying to estimate the density of people in the place. There seemed to be about one person per ten metres square. Fascinated, he stared at them, seeing hundreds, thousands of them. If the density was the same throughout the space he could make out in the dim haze of distance before floor and ceiling seemed to meet, then there must be . . .

'It has no name,' the red crow said, flapping in front of him, facing away from him, its voice far away. 'Technically I believe this is part of the castle. It may even be thought of as the basement.' Its voice became a chuckle for a moment. 'I have no idea how large this place is. I have flown for ten thousand wingbeats in many direc-tions and not even seen a wall. It is all very, very uniform. Apart from a greater concentration of railway lines in the floor, what you see here is what you would see anywhere, in any part of it. There must be many tens of millions of people here, with their heads stuck inside the ceiling, in these reverse goldfish-bowls.'

Quiss didn't know what a goldfish-bowl was, but he

thought it best to feign ignorance of what these people were doing with their heads stuck in the ceiling. He asked the crow about this.

'There is a type of animal which sits over the hollow glass semi-sphere the people have their heads inside,' the red crow said. 'The animal translates thoughts through time. Each of these people is inside the head of a human being from the past.'

'I see,' Quiss said, hoping he sounded more blasé than the red crow expected. 'The past, you say?' He scratched his chin. He still could not believe what his eyes told him; he was walking forward, not bumping into anything, but some part of him still expected to hit a projection screen or wall.

The red crow turned easily in the air in front of him, so that it was now flying backwards, something it appeared to do with the same facility with which it flew forwards, or smoked a cigar. 'You haven't guessed, have you?' it said to him. There was a smirk in its voice, if not on its expressionless face. Iron reinforcing bands in the ceiling cast bands of shadow over the slowly flapping red wings.

'Guessed what?'

'Where this is. Where you are. The name of this place.'

'Where? Tell me, then,' Quiss said, and stopped walking. The small train had disappeared in the distance. He thought he could just hear it, though; rails singing. A whisper of that noise seemed to fill this place, like low voices.

'Hmm,' the crow said, 'well, you may not have heard

of it; even at the times of the Therapeutic Wars the memory was being lost . . . well, anyway. This is, as you might have guessed, a planet. Its name is *Earth*.'

Quiss nodded. Yes, that made more sense that what the small attendant had told him in the room he had found his way into. 'Dirt', indeed!

'That is the name of this place; that is where the castle is; on Earth, towards the end of the planet's life. In a few hundred million more years the sun will become a red giant, engulfing the inner planets of its system. In the meantime, with no moon any more, and having stopped wobbling and spinning, with only the castle, as far as I know, on the surface and all trace of previous civilisations and the species of humankind just weathered away or ground beneath continental plates a billion years ago, this is your inheritance.'

'Mine?' Quiss said. He looked about. Some distance behind him, the gentle curvature of the castle's base-wall was more evident than it had been closer to.

'This,' the red crow said 'is one of two fates that wait you. If you want, you can join these people; become one of them, dreaming of a past time, within the body of whoever they choose, billions upon billions of years ago.'

'Why should I want, or not want that?'

'You might want it because you do not wish to die now. You may not want it because you have what they sometimes call a civilised consciousness. You see, each of these people has tried and failed to do what you and your lady-friend are trying – and will fail – to do; escape. Every one of them, all these millions of individuals, is a failure.

Each one has given up trying to answer the riddle they were set, and while others have chosen oblivion, these have chosen to live out what time they have left as parasites, in the minds of others in forgotten times. They experience what others have experienced, they even have the illusion of altering the past, so that they seem to exercise free will, and apparently influence what their hosts do. It is to delay death, to turn to something like a drug, to turn away from reality, to refuse to face one's own defeat. I have heard it said that this is better than nothing, but . . .' the creature's voice trailed off. Its beady eyes stayed fixed on Quiss.

'I see,' he said. 'Well, I must say I don't find it all all *that* depressing.'

'Perhaps you will, though, later.'

'Perhaps,' Quiss said, and did his best to assume a nonchalant air. 'Do I take it that these people have to be fed, and that the castle kitchens are as large and as busy as they are because they must cater for them?'

'Oh well done,' the red crow said, only a little sarcastically. 'Yes, they run little trains from the kitchens, full of soups and gruels, to the furthest points of the place, wherever those may be; some trains get lost for years, others never return. Luckily these failed unfortunates need little in the way of nourishment, so the castle kitchens can just about cope, though even so they couldn't do it if they didn't mess around with subjective time . . . For all I know, this universal basement extends right round the planet, and the castle supplies all those people; or perhaps there are other castles; one does hear rumours.

Well, the castle feeds all the people you see, at any rate. They're eased out of the head-hole and given a bowl to sup from; they sit there with empty eyes, as though asleep, drink or sup, then like zombies go back to their own little world again. Their wastes are taken away in the same trains.' The red crow cocked its head, and its voice sounded almost puzzled: 'But don't you find this all rather . . . sapping? This is what awaits you, man. This is where almost all of them end up, and a lot of them were a lot brighter than you. Ask the seneschal, if you like. He will confirm what I say. *Very* few escape. Virtually none.'

'All the same, though, like you say,' Quiss said, 'it's better than nothing.'

'To be a parasite? To end up with your head stuck inside some cheap biological time machine? I don't believe it. I thought more, even of you. I haven't lied to you, you know. The truth is quite awful enough. It's not as though these zombies really do influence the people whose brains they inhabit. The seneschal might like to pretend that they do, that free will increases with time and these people account for the sudden impulses in the primitives they haunt, but that's all nonsense. The creatures around the holes may make them think that, but experiments I have carried out myself indicate quite definitely that only the illusion of this effect exists . . . and anyway, which is the more likely explanation?

'I tell you: these people are as good as dead. Theirs is a dreaming death.'

'Still better than nothing,' Quiss insisted. 'Definitely.'

The red crow was silent for some time, flapping lazily

in front of him, hovering there, black eyes staring, expressionless. Eventually it said, 'Then, warrior, you have no soul.'

It flew in a semi-circle around him, heading back for the black wall which was the castle's base. 'We'd better get back,' it said. 'Ask the seneschal about this place, if you like. He will be angry, but he will not punish you and he cannot punish me. Ask him,' the red crow said as it beat back to the curved wall of the roots of the Castle Doors, the Castle of Bequest, 'anything at all. He will confirm that almost none escape, that most end up here, or – the brave ones, the really *civilised* ones – kill themselves.'

They arrived back at the door; it was still ajar. The red crow flapped at its side as Quiss, following it back, walked past the pillars and columns and dreaming people. At the same man, in furs, on a stool, he had looked at earlier, he stopped and turned to the red crow saying. 'Let me ask you something.'

'Yes, of course you can have a preview,' the red crow said, and started to fly towards him. 'There's an empty—'

'Oh no,' Quiss said, shaking his head, looking at the bird as it stopped near him. Quiss nodded at the skinny man in the furs with his head stuck in the glass ceiling. 'I was just wondering if you knew anything about him, say. What's his name? How long's he been here?'

'What?' the red crow said, sounding a little confused, even upset (Quiss concealed the thrill of triumph which shivered through him). 'Him?' The red crow fluttered a little closer. 'Oh, he's been here for ages,' it said, its voice recovering its usual composure. 'Name's . . . Godot? Goriot? Gerrut; something like that. The records aren't perfect, you know. An odd case . . . listen, are you sure you don't want to see what it's like? I can show you where—'

'No,' Quiss said firmly, and walked smartly to the door leading back to the castle. 'I'm not interested. Let's go back now.'

And he had gone to the seneschal, who in the kitchens' clamour had confirmed most of what the red crow had said.

'So?' the seneschal had said, obviously annoyed. 'You have seen your most likely fate; what of it? What am I supposed to do about it? Just think yourself lucky you didn't take the red crow up on its offer; once you're in one of those things properly you don't come out of your own free will; too beguiling. If somebody doesn't come to get you out you stay there, tapping every form of human excitement. By the time your belly rumbles you're hooked. You come out for food and it's just a grey dream compared to what you have just left.

'That's what the bird was up to. It would have shown you the free ceiling-port down there, then just have left you. And don't trust it on free will, either. The ceiling-ports allow full control of the primitives' minds. Everything can be altered. Every mind contains its own universe. We can be sure of *nothing*. That is all I have to say. If you want to enter officially that place which you have already seen informally, file a notice of surrender with me through the proper channels. Now go away, please.' The seneschal had scowled, and gone back up the rickety wooden steps to his office, away from the continuing chaos of the kitchens.

Quiss had gone back to the games room, his old legs quite exhausted by the time he got back.

He said nothing to Ajayi.

He stood on the parapet of the balcony.

Yes, the red crow had been right. It did not know it, it could never have been sure, it had probably only dwelled on the awfulness of the dreamers' fate to bluff him into trying the experience out, so that it could leave him there, but it had been right, nevertheless, about the eventual effect of its revelation.

The thought of that low, limitless space beneath the castle had filled Quiss's thoughts – and, more importantly, his dreams – for almost a hundred days and nights since. A deep, dark depression had settled on him, weighing him down like some heavy suit of armour. He felt like some warrior, chain-mailed, stumbling into quicksand . . .

He could not keep his mind from dwelling on what he had seen, on the sheer extent of the place beneath them, that impression of claustrophobic infinity. So many people, so many failed hopes, lost games, surrendered dreams; and the castle, a single island of warped chance in a frozen ocean of missed opportunities.

That bright, beguiling image he had held on to all these days, of those brown arms, that blue sky, the single shining line of contrail; it returned only to hurt him now, taunt him in his dreams. In that deep, dark, echoless and echo-filled space far beneath him, his mind was already lost; sideless, wall-less the place, bottomless his despair.

His hope, his determination – once so fierce, so furious and powerful and energetic – had ground to a halt, rusted up; seized.

The castle's doing. That was its effect, on those within it as well as on itself. To grind down, to slowly, slowly abrade and at the same time fuse, wearing away and seizing up at once, like sandladen water in some huge engine. He felt like that now. He felt like some grain of sand inside the place, no more important.

He stared down at the crags and snow far below him, rocked once back and forward on his feet, felt himself tremble. His jaw wanted to shake, but he clenched his teeth. The wind gusted, swaying him. *Cold as a glacier*, he thought, smiling grimly. A slow-flowing glacier. A fit image to take to his death, he thought, and remembered the room of flowed glass, the final straw which had eventually followed the red crow's revelation. That had been the real trigger, that was why he really stood here.

It was a room he had discovered, just that day, on one of his now infrequent walks. He had wandered, lost as usual, then he had come to a room inside the thick walls where the wind blew in and snow heaped on the glass floor under the windows.

In the window spaces there were the remains of metal frames; he noticed this as he went to the aperture to look out and so get his bearings from the landscape beyond (he should see the slate mines if his sense of direction was right, but it had been failing him with increasing frequency lately).

Something like clear tar had flowed from the almost empty frames, where only a thin edge of glass lay in the bottom of each hexagon of the metal frames. The glass under his feet was dark. He looked out of the windows, eyes narrowed against the cold, funnelled wind moaning quietly through the deep slit. The floor sloped slightly, up to the windows. Clear stuff, like ice, stuck to the walls under the windows. He stooped, grunting with effort, to examine it, finally got down stiffly to his knees, scraping at the floor (there was a slate floor just underneath the thin covering of glass). He tapped at the clear stuff still in the window frames above, then ran one finger down from the glass still in the frames, over the sill, down over the clear flow on the walls until finally his finger slid all the way down without a flaw, crack or join registering under his fingertip, to the floor.

The glass in the bottom of the frames, on the narrow sill, on the walls under the windows and on the floor of the room was joined. It was all one. He stayed kneeling and let his hands rest in his sloped lap. He stared ahead.

He recalled, from when he could not remember, that glass – ordinary glass, made from sand – was theoretically a liquid, that in old buildings very sensitive measuring equipment could detect a significant thinning at the top of the pane, and a corresponding thickening at the bottom of the sheet as the glass gradually gave in to the incessant pull of gravity. In the Castle of Bequest, in places at least, the process had simply had time to go further. The glass had flowed – was still flowing – from the frame, over the sill, down the wall, to the floor.

He knelt, realised this, and after a little while, to his own astonishment, he started to cry.

The mines, anyway, had not been visible from the windows; he had wandered again, mind blank, until he found himself back where he had started, in the empty games room.

He had made for the balcony almost automatically, then stopped to think; vaguely, almost innocently surprised at the ease with which he was suddenly able to accept his own death, even desire it.

And, thinking, there was nothing.

So he had climbed up on to the cold stone parapet.

Now he knew what the red crow had meant by soul, and that a-religious quality of irreducible character, that selfness, would now articulate its most profound self-statement, in its own destruction.

Quiss closed his eyes, leaned forward into space.

Arms closed around his waist; he was pulled back. He opened his eyes to see the sky tipping, the wall of the castle above the balcony slanting over him as he fell. Ajayi gasped as they thumped together on to the slate of the balcony floor. Quiss rolled over, into the warmth of the games room, banging his head on the glass floor.

He looked up, dazed, to see Ajayi lying on the floor of the balcony itself, her chest heaving, her eyes wide and staring at him. She was picking herself up. 'Quiss—'

He scrambled to his feet, drew back his hand and hit her hard across the face, knocking her to the ground again. 'Leave me alone!' he shouted. 'Why can't you leave me alone?' he screamed. He bent down and picked her up. Her mouth was bleeding, her face was white. She cried out, and put her hands up in front of her face to protect herself; he threw her into the games room and she staggered across the floor, tripped on some fallen books and went sprawling. He went after her. 'You just can't leave me alone, can you?' he sobbed. His eyes were filling with tears, his hands and arms shook. He bent and picked the woman off the floor again; she brought her hands up, her eyes tightly screwed up, face grimacing; he slapped her and she cried out again, falling to the floor as he let her go. He drew back his foot to kick her, as she lay, curled up on the glass floor, hands over her head, crying.

He saw the games table, not far away, with the pack of cards lying on it. He didn't kick the woman, but stamped over to the small table, got hold of it by two of its legs, took it over to the woman, then as she looked up, eyes wide with fear, he raised the table over his head (she cringed, cowered, hands over her head again; the cards fluttered down), he swung the table down, into the glass floor near her head, shattering the table and smashing a network of cracks a jagged metre in diameter on the floor's transparent surface.

The table disintegrated; the small red jewel at its centre broke into a thousand pieces, a tracery of shining filaments burst from the table's intricate surface, sparking and spitting for a second, then smoking and going dull, and the solid legs of the table sprang open, cracking and revealing tightly compressed pages with print on them. Quiss kicked the debris, then turned away, covering his eyes with his hands and sobbing.

He stumbled off, into the back of the room, away from the balcony.

Ajayi looked up, over the remains of the shattered table, and saw Quiss bump into the wall by the winding-stair. He staggered down the first few steps and disappeared. She breathed again, dabbed at her split lip with the hem of her furs.

She sat up properly on the glass surface, moving away from where a thin pool of warm salty water was spreading from the cracks where the table had hit. She was trembling.

She looked at what was left of the table.

Well, they had played their last game; they had been left in no doubt about that. No table, no valid games. So they had just their one, unused answer left.

She tried to think calmly, wondering what had made Quiss want to kill himself. She didn't know. He had been increasingly morose recently, but would not talk about the reasons, if there were any. She had hoped he would come out of it; he had been depressed before, as had she, but for the last hundred days there had been a special sort of despair about him, and he had just kept on going down-hill, unwilling to talk about it or be cheered up. Perhaps she shouldn't have left him alone just now, but what could she do? If he was determined to kill himself there was nothing she could really do about it. It was his life, it was his right. Maybe she was just being selfish.

She stood up shakily. She was a little dazed, and she hurt in a variety of places. Well, nothing was broken; that was something to be thankful for.

She noticed that the legs of the small table had been made out of books. A couple of them had torn covers and pages; bits of them were still stuck to the veneer of wood which had covered them when they were still part of the table. There had been one or two books making up each of the three legs. The books were written in English.

'*Titus Groan*,' she read, talking softly to herself. '*The Castle, Labyrinths, The Trial* . . .' And another book, which had the title page missing. She glanced over the torn remains of the first page instead, and frowned.

She looked at the other books she held. This was interesting. She had been looking for a couple of them, having read about them in some of the literary guides and commentaries which she was using to select which books she ought to read. They hadn't been in the places in the castle where she had expected to find them. Perhaps it was significant that they had turned up instead inside the games table. She looked again at the book with no title page.

She decided she would read this nameless book first. Anyway, it might help calm her down, take her mind off things . . .

Yes, she thought, as she walked over to her stool, she would read this one first, then the others. She would just

have to hope Quiss would be all right. They still had that
last answer to come up with.

She sat down.

She started reading.

After all, what else was there to do?

The story began:

He walked through the white corridors . . .

SIX

Truth and Consequences

The trees stood around the canal where it appeared out of the tunnel under the hill he had just walked over. Graham went through a small gate and down a path to the old towpath, through grass and flowers. Some distant part of his mind seemed to whisper to him that he had followed the line of the tunnel over the hill, that he had walked from the house in Half Moon Crescent, which was over the tunnel, to here, its mouth.

A sudden, quite physical pain made his guts constrict as he remembered the day he had stood in the street, talking up to her about secret passages down to the tunnel . . . he shook his head to dislodge the thought.

He found that he had to breathe deeply, more deeply

than he had been, to clear his head and quell his stomach. He stood on one bank of the canal, looking over to the far side and the bank of grass there, over the calm, still water. He listened to the distant noises of the traffic; another wailing siren, perhaps the ambulance he had seen. He looked around for a place to sit, and walked along the path a little way, until he came to a place where some tarmac had been scattered and there were black drops of what looked like dried blood lying on the dusty surface of the towpath; flies buzzed.

In the grass he saw a magazine lying, torn. He looked more closely at it, saw a woman's buttocks, over a pair of hairy knees. The woman's bottom was reddened slightly; there was a hand poised, too obviously posed, not in motion, over her. A small breeze ruffled the pages of the magazine for him as he looked, as obligingly as any Hollywood wind-machine stripping a calendar between scenes. The pictures in the rest of the magazine were almost all identical.

He turned away, disgusted with something other than the pathetic but relatively harmless fetish of the magazine, and saw a flurry of flies swirl into the air from something dark in the grass; it looked like an animal's leg.

He closed his eyes, willing tears to come, some final part of him giving in only now, wanting the surrender to animal emotion which until now he had fought against, but as he stood there he could feel no tears coming, only a sort of resigned, ugly bitterness, a comprehensive revulsion for everything around him, for all the people and their artifacts and thoughts, all their stupid ways and pointless aims. He opened his smarting eyes, blinking angrily.

Here it was; this was what it all really meant; here was your civilisation, your billion years of evolution, right here; a soiled and tattered wanking-mag and chopped domestic animal. Sex and violence, writ small like all our standard fantasies.

The pain in his belly which had afflicted him earlier returned, sharp and fierce as a rusty blade.

It swelled in him then, like some wildfire cancer; a rapid disgust, a total allergy syndrome directed at every-thing around him; at the filthy, eviscerated mundanity of it all, the sheer crawling awfulness of existence; all the lies and the pain, the legalized murder, the privileged theft, the genocides and the hatreds and the stupefying human cruelties, all the starveling beauty of the burgeoning poor and the crippled in body and brain, all the life-defying squalor of the cities and the camps, all the sweltering frenetics of the creeds and the faiths, all the torturingly ingenious, carefully civilised savagery of the technology of pain and the economies of greed; all the hollow, ring-ing, bullshitting words used to justify and explain the utter howling grief of our own cruelty and stupidity; it piled on him, in him, like a weight of atmosphere, that awful mass of air above for those moments no longer balanced by a pressure within, so that he felt at once crushed, smashed inside, but swollen too; bursting with the sickening burden of a cheap and tumid revelation.

He turned towards the canal, his belly like a lump of lead inside him. His tongue felt swollen; there was a thickness in his throat, and his tongue, that instrument of articulation, felt like a great poisoned sac, some gland caught full of all the body's wastes and debris, tight with putrid volume, ripe as any bloated carcase. He fought the urge to heave, tried to ignore his trembling guts. He took his portfolio, and by the side of the canal he opened it and drew out the large sheets of paper inside.

They were drawings of her face, done in hundreds of small lines to make a maze within them, all carefully penned in thin black India ink. He thought, still, even now, that they were the best work he had ever done.

He looked at them, swaying as he stood, feeling sick, sick to the stomach, sick to the brain, then one by one he dropped the drawings into the slack, limp waters of the dark canal. They slipped and side-slipped through the air, some falling together, some landing all by themselves, some landing face up and some face down, some obscured by others, some gazing up at the clear sky or down into the cloudy water. He watched as the water penetrated them, making the ink run blackly over the many versions of her face, while the slow current of the canal gradually took them, moved them, swept them away from him, towards the mouth of the tunnel, back under the hill and the houses and the distant traffic.

He watched them go, standing there, less sick now, the pain in his guts still there, his eyes unable to cry, then he zipped the portfolio up again. He was about to go, then he changed his mind; he went back to the grass bank, picked the spanking magazine up, threw it into the canal too, then waved the flies away from the bloody stump of black and white furred leg, picked it up by one still protruding claw, and slung it in the water as well.

He watched it all float towards the tunnel mouth; the great flat rectangles of paper like black-stained leaves from some strange winter tree; the magazine, like some dead bird, its spine sunk, pages like limp wings; the barely floating stump of leg, a couple of determined flies still hovering over it.

Then he kicked the blood-spotted dust off the towpath, sending it into the canal, stones sinking, dust coating the water. And as the dust floated in the air and on the water, and settled slowly on the path again, he walked off; away down the canalside, back up towards the little gate, towards the city again.